Call Down
the Hawk

~

Critical Praise for *Beyond Confusion*
by Sheila Simonson, Willa Cather Award–Winner

~

"Taut… Simonson's ambitious plot casts a wide net—from treating themes of racism and religious intolerance to thwarted love and good old-fashioned greed—but she pulls it off with a sure hand."

—Publishers Weekly

"*Beyond Confusion* grabs the reader's attention almost from the very first page and never lets go until the final, satisfying one…. The outcome is a surprise that I didn't see coming. Good book and well worth the read."

—Bookloons

"As usual, Simonson's plot moves briskly along, highlighted by the beautiful Northwest scenery."

—Mystery Scene

"The book was written for all of us who love libraries. It made me want to cheer, and left me with such a good feeling that now I want to read the other books in the series."

—Bristol, VA Library Reference Dept.

"It all comes together beautifully in this charming cozy. Simonson creates characters worth booing and cheering for, many of whose first impressions may be intriguingly misleading to readers. Best of all, Simonson is able to tie up all the loose ends of the ongoing mystery in a very satisfying finish, while casting a wide net in terms of the themes she takes on while telling her story."

—Reviewing the Evidence

MYSTERIES BY SHEILA SIMONSON

The Latouche County Series

Buffalo Bill's Defunct
An Old Chaos
Beyond Confusion
Call Down the Hawk

The Lark Dodge Series

Larkspur
Skylark
Mudlark
Meadowlark
Malarkey

Call Down the Hawk

A LATOUCHE COUNTY
MYSTERY

~

Sheila Simonson

Perseverance Press/John Daniel & Co.
Palo Alto/McKinleyville California 2017

A Perseverance Press Book
Published by John Daniel & Company
A division of Daniel & Daniel, Publishers, Inc.
Post Office Box 2790
McKinleyville, California 95519
www.danielpublishing.com/perseverance

Distributed by SCB Distributors (800) 729-6423

Book design by Eric Larson, Studio E Books, Santa Barbara,
www.studio-e-books.com

Cover image: picmax/iStock

10 9 8 7 6 5 4 3 2 1

LIBRARY OF CONGRESS CATALOGING-IN-PUBLICATION DATA
Names: Simonson, Sheila, (date), author.
Title: Call down the hawk : a Latouche County mystery / by Sheila Simonson.
Description: McKinleyville, California : John Daniel & Co, [2017]

Identifiers: LCCN 2017000088 | ISBN 9781564745972 (pbk. : alk. paper)
Subjects: LCSH: Sheriffs—Fiction. | Columbia River Gorge (Or. and Wash.)—Fiction. |
GSAFD: Mystery fiction.
Classification: LCC PS3569.I48766 C35 2017 | DDC 813/.54—dc23
LC record available at https://lccn.loc.gov/2017000088

To my Mickey

Cast of Characters

at Hawk Farm:

Bill Hough (recently deceased); a hero
Alice Hough, his widow; a member of the Klalo tribe
Russell Hough, their son
Judith Hough, their daughter; also a hero

in the August household:

Frank August, a retired banker
Libby August, his current wife; a wind surfer
Francis August, Jr., his son; a banker (*aka* Gus)
Jane August, his daughter; an artist
Gerd Koeppel, his wine maker
Tom Dahl, his vineyard manager
Irma Castro, his housekeeper/chef

of the Klalo Nation:

Madeline Thomas, principal chief
Jack Redfern, her husband; Alice Hough's half brother
Leon Redfern, Jack's brother

Latouche County functionaries:

Beth McCormick, county sheriff
Rob Neill, undersheriff and head of investigations
Meg McLean, his wife; head librarian
Linda Ramos, sergeant, county detective
Todd Welch, deputy, county detective; member of the Klalo tribe
Catherine (Kitty) Grant, deputy, uniform branch

Call Down
the Hawk

~

1.

ROB NEILL went for a swim. His wife was preparing for a Friends of the Library fund-raiser the next day, an outdoor luncheon because it was August and the weather was cooperating. That meant he'd spent a couple of hours after work hauling stuff in and out of the big Victorian house he had inherited from his grandmother, the legendary head of the Latouche Regional Library of which Meg was now the chief librarian.

Though they had lived together quite a while, he and Meg McLean had been married less than a year. A happy year. And they had moved to the Victorian house only a few months ago. Meg was still trying out house and yard as venues for entertaining. One of her foibles involved feeding as many people as possible as often as possible, and Rob was inclined to indulge her. Hence the bash. Hence the heavy lifting. Hence the heavy baking. He smiled to himself. There were worse faults than compulsive cookery.

It was a little after nine, not quite dark yet, and the Klalo municipal pool would close at ten. He drove there, though he would have preferred to walk. Still, he had been assaulted twice walking home from the pool at night, and Meg had extracted a solemn promise that he wouldn't run that risk again. It was a small risk. There were no cases pending that involved violence. However, a promise was a promise.

The parking lot was empty except for the attendant's clapped-out Subaru and a dusty Blazer, perhaps abandoned.

The last pool hour was set aside for cops of any description—town, county, even staties if there were any in the area. Rob had pried that concession from Mack McCormick, the previous sheriff, when Mack refused to fund membership for his deputies in the health club of choice, along with day care and other wishes.

The present sheriff, Mack's widow Beth, was also a shark when it came to negotiating benefits, but she was a strong proponent of fitness. Under her aegis, the old gym got new mats, and she did sponsor a day-care center. The center went down when the economy tanked, but the new mats and the old pool hour survived. Unfortunately, Rob's deputies didn't get the point. They preferred the gym. He was sure of a solitary swim Tuesdays and Thursdays, and the pool was never crowded on the other days. Today was Friday.

He drew into the lot and parked virtuously beneath a light. The attendant, nose in a textbook, waved in his direction as he signed in. Rob wore swim trunks under his jeans, so he shed shoes and outer clothes in one of the cubicles, ducked through the shower, and took the towel he had brought with him to the edge of the pool. There he discovered he was not alone. Someone, a man, he thought, was churning down the far lane, doing laps.

Rob called a vague greeting and set his towel on a bench near the deep-end ladder. He slid into the water, let the coolness embrace him, and turned over to swim. Or to wallow. He never used swimming for anything other than undoing the kinks. That was what it was for. Counting laps did not appeal because he was not competitive by nature, not even with himself. More like hedonistic. He swam because he liked to, and right now his muscles appreciated his choice.

He crawled a while and did the butterfly for fun, then flipped over and watched his toes as he chugged along on his back. He was thinking about the fraud case Ellen Koop had decided to prosecute, two sweet-talkers with a van scamming seniors over aluminum gutters. The scammers had been operating in Oregon. When they crossed the bridge from Hood River and began to prey on Latouche County residents, Rob's team of deputies had been ready for them. He ticked over the evidence in his mind and visualized the indignant victims, eager to testify. Slam dunk, or maybe scam dunk.

A blur of motion brought his mind back to the pool. The other guy was leaving. *Good.* He flipped his hand in farewell and wondered who the man was. *One of the uniforms?* Rob had a hard time remembering all their faces when they weren't dressed in brown and tan. He squinted at the other swimmer but couldn't see his features. Straight dark hair, light build, ropy muscles.

The man swam to the shallow-end ladder, grabbed the guard rails high, and heaved himself up. He hopped to the top step, reached down for a metal crutch, and slid it onto his left arm. Rob squinted.

The other swimmer had only one leg. Rather, he had one-and-a-half legs. The left was gone below the knee. He bent for his towel, blotted his head and chest, then swung into smooth motion and disappeared into the dressing room. He didn't look back.

Who the hell was he? Not a new cop, unless Beth was being over-conscientious about recruiting the differently abled. Rob would have known. She consulted him on all new hires. And the department was not hiring.

The swimmer wasn't one of the few amputees Rob knew in town—two women with diabetes and a Vietnam vet. If the guy wasn't a cop, why had the attendant let him swim? Rob wallowed another quarter hour before curiosity got the better of him—curiosity and cold. He was pretty sure the water heater had been turned down early. Half an hour before the pool closed was fine. The water cooled slowly. The temperature drop was noticeable within an hour, however. He decided he had issues with the attendant. What was his name? Ken. A student who commuted to WSU in Vancouver.

The amputee was long gone, and if the textbook was an indicator, Ken was still deep in History of the Pacific Northwest, a course required of all education majors. It was August. School wasn't even in session. Maybe he was making up an incomplete. Rob puzzled over the sign-in sheet while he waited for Ken to surface from the thrill of the Whitman massacre or whatever he was reading about.

"Hey, Rob," Ken said at last, bookmarking his page with his finger.

"Hey. Who was the one-legged swimmer?"

Ken stared, blank.

"The man who was in the pool when I came."

"Uh, whatshisname, some kind of bird. Crow? Uh, Hawk. That was it."

Rob stared at the signature. R. HOUGH. The family pronounced the surname *Hawk*, though Rob would have guessed *Huff*, as in tough, from the spelling. Bill Hough's son, had to be.

"I know he's not a cop, but there wasn't anybody in the pool, so I let him in."

"It's all right. I was just curious. Did you really not notice?"

"Notice what?"

"He has an artificial leg, and he must have been using a crutch when he came in."

"He wasn't using the crutch. He carried it. Didn't limp or anything. You sure about the leg? Did I do something wrong?"

Rob sighed. "If you don't know somebody, you ought to ask for I.D."

"It's, like, embarrassing. I challenged a couple of guys who came in Wednesday. They showed their badges, said they'd been in before with a bunch of deputies. They razzed me."

"It's okay." It wasn't as if someone was going to dive into the pool and drown a cop who had pulled his car over for expired plates. Still, Ken was on the dim end of the lighting spectrum.

Imagine turning the heat off early. When Rob mentioned that, Ken looked guilty and resentful.

Rob drove home, thinking. William Hough—a farmer, a local hero of both the football and military varieties, and a true local pain in the butt—had killed himself late in July. Rob and Meg had been off at Tyee Lake for two weeks.

As undersheriff and head of investigations, Rob responded to all cases of unattended death, of which there were not a great many. However, Linda Ramos, the detective who took the call, had told him over the phone that it was clearly suicide—single shot to the head, powder burns, weapon on the floor. Hough's wife would not collect on his life insurance policy because it had a suicide clause.

Sgt. Ramos and the technical crew had examined the scene meticulously. Photos bore out her judgment. Hough had been depressed and drinking. The wife and daughter had heard the shot. The daughter found the body immediately. Neither woman showed signs of having fired a gun, Linda said, and GPR tests bore her out. Hough died intestate, so everything would be left to the wife—community property. The son lived somewhere in eastern Washington, around the Tri-Cities or Walla Walla, and hadn't been home in years. The death was sad but not suspicious.

Rob had attended Bill Hough's funeral—in uniform, which he hated—but the son had not showed up for it. There was a good turnout of creaky Boomers, the VFW, and such elected officials as had been in town. The sheriff, Beth McCormick, had come more because she had taught Hough's kids language arts in high school than because she was now a public servant paying her respects to a hero.

Still. Here was the son swimming during the hour set aside for cops, so he was back in town. What was with the leg? Bill Hough—Purple Heart, Bronze Star—had been a vocal super-patriot. If his son had served in either Iraq or Afghanistan, everybody would have heard about it. *Wait a minute. The daughter served in Afghanistan. Two tours.* Rob could not remember the old blowhard trumpeting about that. *Why not?*

What else did he know about the Houghs? Hawk Farm lay on the east side of Two Falls between the Columbia River and the basalt cliff that paralleled the river. Highway 14, which also ran east–west, divided the farm along its length. Most of the arable land lay on the south side of the road in the flood plain of the Columbia. The soil was rich, and the fields seldom flooded these days because of the dams. The farmhouse with its garage and a half-dead cherry orchard lay on the slope that ran up to the bluff on the north side. The house abutted the western property line; the orchard lay to the east.

Three years before, a banker from California had bought the vineyard west of Hawk Farm and built a palatial house atop the bluff with a view of the river and Mount Hood. The small vineyard below the house produced pinot noir and merlot grapes. The previous owner had sold them to whichever wineries wanted them. The new owner, Frank August, meant to open his own boutique winery. He even had a label. *Château Joyeux.* The House of Mirth. To that William Hough had objected loudly and persistently.

He pointed out that the new *cave* or tasting room would draw traffic to a place that was already congested owing to the trucks that hauled his own produce to market. True. Mr. August submitted plans for a turn lane and access ramp, neither of which Hough had supplied for his trucks. Hough protested that the new winery would violate the restrictions on building in a National Scenic Area. August pointed out that his vineyard was grandfathered in. It had been in operation well before Hough's great-grandfather set up shop and certainly before the Gorge was designated a Scenic Area. August got approval from the Gorge Commission for modest signage and a structure that would blend into the hillside as if sprung from the earth.

He knew what he was doing. His House of Mirth would probably turn out to be an asset to the community—if putative tasters weren't put off by Hough's billboard next door. It announced, for the world to see, that all the country needed was GOD, GUNS, AND GUTS. Hough was still complaining to the county about the construction going on next door when he killed himself. In fact, that was the sole suspicious thing about his suicide. How depressed could he have been if he was still complaining?

On the whole, Rob was predisposed to approve of Frank August, if only because of the contrast with Bill Hough.

~

AS she did every night now, Judith Hough watched the big house up the hill. Tonight she sat concealed, door closed, light off, at the window of her workroom. They couldn't see her, not even with night-vision oculars, as long as she sat back and didn't move. Her own night goggles gave everything a ghastly green glow.

The wide two-story window of the mansion's great room was dark, as usual. The Augusts didn't use the room much, and even with goggles all Judith saw was the vague bulk of furniture. The room was a puzzle. Why build such a generous space if you weren't going to use it?

To the left, at the level of the second story, three of the rooms—bedrooms, she supposed, or workrooms—showed lights but no sign of action, so those people, the ones who lived there and their guests, must be somewhere in the wing that ran south to north on the right of the great room, the wing she couldn't see into from her concealment. To the far right, though, beyond that wing, the swimming pool enclosure and the guest house glared bright as a box-store parking lot on Christmas Eve. The pool must be in use. It was a hot night. Still, she saw no motion. She would have to make a reconnaissance after all.

She scanned the darkness below the big house. Nothing. Her brother hadn't turned the electric fence off then. He'd threatened to. If he had, there would have been deer, or worse, maybe. Maybe intruders.

She cocked her head, listening. She heard her mother's light soprano and a baritone rumble, her so-called brother, ghost brother. Still downstairs. Well, she could wait. She backed very slowly away from the window to the closet. She saw the rifle aslant against the back wall of the closet, her father's souvenir, or so he had said. He was such a liar.

She allowed herself to make no betraying sounds as she lifted the comfortable weight of the AK-47. So far neither her mother nor her brother had missed it. Kalashnikovs were common as blackberries in Afghanistan, taken, as like as not, from dead Russians decades ago. But this one wasn't hers. It was her father's, whether he had taken it in Nam, as he claimed, or bought it at one of the gun shows he frequented. She had no souvenirs, didn't want any. Still, she liked the old rifle. It comforted her.

She sat again and waited.

~

NEXT day, forty people, two-thirds of them women, buzzed around the big yard, wineglasses and plates of hors d'oeuvres in hand, watching as Meg and her staff of librarians set out the salads and breads. Meg would trot out the main course of the luncheon in half an hour. Rob had suggested hiring trumpeters when he saw the salmon in aspic gleaming on its outsize platter. She'd given a perfunctory smile, but her mind was on the other three entrées. She had risen at five to bake the whole fish.

Rob liked the Friends of the Library. They included most of the more distinguished members of the community, many of the wealthiest, and a lot of people who just liked books. He preferred the last group. They had interesting things to say.

He was drinking a glass of local pinot grigio and talking with Helmi Wirkkala about a diary she'd acquired for the Historical Society. It dealt with the early days of farming in the uplands east of Klalo, the county seat. Some of her Finnish forebears had been neighbors of the woman who kept the diary. Helmi was telling about a man who had survived four wives and three of his eleven children, and Rob listened with interest. The children's descendents popped up all over the county, prosperous and not, law-abiding and not, always full of energy.

"Oh, how nice," Helmi said, interrupting herself. "Here's Jane August. Have you met her? Let me introduce you." She waved at a tall woman, who approached trailing an older man some inches shorter than she was. He looked sulky. She looked stylish in a vague, arty way.

Jane August shook hands with Rob. "You're the undersheriff, aren't you?"

"That's right. More to the point, I'm Meg's husband." He liked saying that.

"She's a wonder." Jane spoke lightly, but he thought she was sincere. "Let me introduce both of you to my father, Frank August. Dad is here under duress."

August mumbled something and shook hands with Rob. He nodded at Helmi. "Historical Society. That's in the old Carnegie library, right?" He was short and grizzled, and looked as tough as old gristle.

"That's the place." Helmi loved the handsome brick structure. She beamed.

"Pity to waste a building like that."

"Waste?"

"It would make an outstanding microbrewery—like that one in the old poorhouse east of Portland."

Rob took a hasty sip of wine. *Was the man crazy?* Beside him, Helmi spluttered.

"Or a high-class restaurant. The town needs one, God knows."

The silence deepened. Rob looked at father and daughter. Frank August kept a poker face. Jane's eyes narrowed, her mouth set.

Rob cleared his throat. "Wouldn't a microbrewery compete with your *cave*, Mr. August?"

"Can't have too much free enterprise." August roared with laughter. His daughter didn't crack a smile.

Helmi Wirkkala gave Rob her glass, turned, and walked away. Rob watched her go.

August tossed off his wine and handed the glass to a passing library aide. "No comment, Mr. Neill?"

"You have a talent for making enemies."

Jane August snorted.

Rob disposed of his two wineglasses on one of the small tables he'd set up the evening before.

"Enemies? Her?" August smirked. He meant Helmi.

Rob nodded. "And me. I don't like bullies." He smiled at August's daughter. "I understand you're a painter." He had Googled William Hough that morning. And Francis August, as an afterthought. The daughter was mentioned, and a son in California, also Francis.

She nodded. "Mixed media. I'm going to teach at the community college branches in Hood River and The Dalles."

"You'll enjoy commuting across the bridge this winter."

"I have the feeling I'll be living in Hood River by then." Her tone was dry.

"That will be our loss. If you'll excuse me, I see my wife beckoning."

"Pussy-whipped?" Frank August's eyes glinted. *Was he drunk or high?*

"I suppose you were an *arbitrageur* in another life, and you're aiming at *provocateur* in this one. Good luck."

Rob found Helmi inside, crying quietly in the shadowy living room. He gave her shoulders a hug. She was seventy-five and a firecracker, but her bones felt fragile.

She sniffed and blew her nose. "I always cry when I lose my temper."

"Thanks for not decking the bastard in my backyard."

"Believe me, it took restraint." She gave a choke of laughter. "He's right, you know."

"How's that?"

"It would make a great microbrewery."

Rob smiled. "Just what we need, more booze. What do you know about the family?"

"The Augusts? Not much. They're in-comers. His current wife is three years younger than poor Jane. She isn't here today, the wife. He retired from an investment bank in California fairly recently, handed the reins to his son a couple of years ago."

"Mob connections?"

"Could be." She sounded doubtful. "There's the casino…"

Madeline Thomas, the principal chief of the Klalos, had been making casino noises lately. She did that whenever she wanted something from the county commissioners. So far no ground had been broken.

"What about the Houghs?" Rob asked. "Bill Hough tangled with August."

"Easy to do." She sighed and sat on his grandmother's beige sofa. "So sad about Bill. Poor Alice."

"Alice? Ah, Bill's widow." He sat beside her.

"She's Jack Redfern's half sister, you know."

"I didn't." He let out a low whistle. Jack's sister and Madeline Thomas's sister-in-law.

Helmi was telling him about the high school romance between the great football hero and the first Klalo homecoming queen all those years ago. "Alice was so pretty. They went off to college, a first for both families, and of course Bill had a football scholarship."

"What happened?"

"He flunked out—too much partying, I guess. He was drafted. They got married before he shipped off to Vietnam. He came back another kind of hero. The war changed him. Everybody noticed. They cut him a lot of slack, Rob, but he managed to alienate most people."

"What about Alice?"

Helmi frowned. "It's hard to describe what happened to her. She got her teaching certificate. She taught for a while, several years anyway. Then Russell came along, and she stopped working full-time. I guess Alice just faded—from a combination of isolation and Bill."

Faded was a good word for Alice Hough. He remembered the dim figure at the funeral.

"They lived in Two Falls at first, then out there on the farm," Helmi went on. "His father made the place over to him, moved down to Arizona, and married again when Bill's mother died.

The old man passed away five years ago. Bill was an only child. I always thought that was part of his problem. But that's a cliché. He liked the sound of his own voice."

"They had two kids?"

"Russell and Judith. Judy was an afterthought. She's a good ten years younger than her brother."

"She joined the army?"

"Yes. I don't understand the dynamics. Bill was a hero. Medals. A big noise with the NRA and the VFW. You'd think his son would try to imitate him, not his daughter. But that's what happened. She had two tours in Afghanistan, got caught in one of those roadside explosions. She was injured, but she saved several of the wounded under fire from snipers. She's the one with medals from this war. I understand Daddy was speechless, for once, when he heard. Alice cried."

"What about the son?"

"Russ and his father were at each other's throats until Russ left home. The day he graduated from high school."

Rob had also left home right out of high school but without hostility. He'd loved the grandparents who raised him—and been unable to hang on their coattails one day longer than necessary. Neither he nor his grandmother had understood that at the time. It just happened. He left. Now he thought his grandfather had understood and approved of his independence. At the time, Rob had felt guilty and gleeful in about equal measure. He'd come back from Silicon Valley to visit often, and he'd come home for good when his grandmother began to fail. That was more than fifteen years ago. Sometimes it felt as if he'd never left Latouche County.

"So Bill and his son fought. Did they get physical?"

Helmi shifted on the sofa. "I don't know that Bill beat him. There were rumors, but there would be. Bill was an angry man, and strong, at least until the booze got to him. He bad-mouthed the boy. Russell could never please him. By the time Russ reached high school, he'd stopped trying. If Dad wanted him to play football, he turned out for baseball. That kind of thing. It was almost as if he was taunting his father. And then he just went away. Bill wrote him off."

"How so?"

"Wouldn't file a missing person report. Refused to allow Alice to search for her son. At the funeral, she told me Russ was coming home. She didn't have time to tell me where he'd been."

"He's home now."

"Where was he all those years?"

"I don't know, Helmi." He meant to check. He started to tell her about the missing leg but hesitated. It seemed an unnecessary intrusion on the man's privacy.

She frowned and leaned toward him. "Are you sure Bill killed himself? He was Catholic, you know."

He drew a long breath. "Linda Ramos did the investigation, and I trust Linda to be thorough. There's no room for doubt." He explained about the suicide clause in the insurance policy. "A Catholic family would surely have pushed for a verdict of accidental death if there'd been any justification for it." He didn't mention murder.

"I suppose so." Helmi sounded doubtful, despite the fact that there had still been a heavy judgment attached to suicide in her generation.

"Rob! I need you." Meg, from the kitchen.

He gave Helmi another pat and responded to his wife's call.

~

JANE August took her father home after they'd both tried the salmon. It was probably exquisite, but Jane was so angry she tasted nothing but bile. She stood over her father while he wrote the library a large check. The librarian was gracious. Then Jane drove Frank home in his big white SUV.

He had collected enough speeding tickets to place his driver's license in jeopardy in the three years he'd lived in Washington. Next time he'd lose it, so she had spent a good part of the summer chauffeuring him here and there. At first she didn't mind. It gave her a chance to get to know him. Now she wasn't sure she wanted to.

She was the child of his first marriage. Her mother lived happily in San Francisco with her second husband, Daniel Sylvester, and Jane had grown up there, thinking of Dan as Dad, though she knew he wasn't her father. She had two half brothers, one from her mother's remarriage and one, Francis, Jr., from her father's third marriage. Frankie was six years younger than she was, which made him twenty-seven. He'd earned an MBA from Wharton, but he'd had no experience when their father had handed him the reins of the family's private investment bank three years earlier. That was right before banks started collapsing all over the place. Mortgages.

Frank, Sr. must have foreseen what was coming. The bank was still in deep trouble, and she thought her little brother was on the verge of his own personal meltdown, but her father had made a clean getaway. He had quietly sold out when Frankie took the bank public. Just in time.

Frank had celebrated by divorcing his fourth wife, brandished her pre-nup in the judge's face, and made out like the bandit he was when it came time to settle up. Had Jane's stepmother been a pleasanter woman, Jane might have felt sorry for her. Shortly afterward, Frank married Libby.

Little Libby, or Witto Wibby, as Jane thought of her, was thirty years old going on eighteen. She had a high little-girl voice, perpetually waxed limbs, and a tendency to adopt fashion trends two years late. She was small but tough—athletic, an alpine skier who actually left the lodge—and she had taken to wind surfing since moving to the Gorge. She chose to spend Saturday afternoon on the river rather than with the library folks, though the evening breeze was only now beginning to blow. Jane thought Libby liked life in the Gorge better than Frank did. He had probably not counted on that. Or on other things. There were tensions in the marriage Jane did not understand.

As Jane paused at the one traffic light in downtown Klalo, she glanced at her silent parent. He was hard to fight, because he enjoyed fighting. She decided to deny him the pleasure. "So what do you want for dinner?"

"Who gives a shit?"

"'Gey few, and they're a' deid.'"

"Smart-ass. I dunno. Mexican?"

Mexican was a safe bet. "Irma wants me to get some things from Safeway." Irma Castro was the chef/housekeeper. Her food was a little predictable.

Jane chugged past the courthouse, admiring its Art Nouveau extravagance. There was always something amazing to look at in the Gorge, either natural or man-made. It was a pity the architect who designed the county seat hadn't survived to build the main branch of the library, the building that had succeeded the small, outmoded Carnegie library, but he would have had to live a hundred years to do it.

Safeway lay on the edge of town. So far there were no box stores outside Klalo to kill the Victorian downtown, though fast-food chains had sprung outlets like tumors along Highway 14. Jane tried to imagine an Art Nouveau McDonald's and failed. She pulled into the grocery store lot and left her father listening to the financial news on NPR with the windows down. It was pushing ninety out but not humid. Jane missed San Francisco fogs.

Half an hour later, she wheeled three bags full of produce to the car, stowed them in the hatch, and returned the shopping cart like a good citizen. She decided to drive home on the scenic route, though her father groaned when she turned onto the unnumbered road that bypassed Two Falls over the Choteau River. The road flooded every spring, but it was high and dry in August.

She was admiring a stand of Douglas fir with its attendant vine maples when Frank said, "What do you want, Janey?"

"Want?"

"Yeah. I can't figure you out."

Heavy stuff. "Hmm. I want to paint the Missoula Floods." The Missoula Floods, so-called, had formed the Columbia Gorge at the end of the last Ice Age. When it came to subjects for her paintings, Jane inclined toward magical realism. "What do *you* want?"

He snorted.

"I can't figure you out either. I thought you wanted to settle in here, establish your reputation as a wine maker like Francis Ford Coppola, and make a big splash on the Washington wine scene."

"I do."

"Then why go out of your way to insult local people at the library bean feast? Mrs. Wirkkala's a woman with a lot of clout in the county, and Robert Neill is the sheriff's fair-haired boy. Both of them know everybody who is anybody and most who aren't."

He squirmed on his seat. "It was such a girly scene."

"Girly? Aha, the old testosterone defense."

"What are you talking about?"

"Look, Dad, like it or not, women do a lot of things, especially at the local level."

"They think they do."

"And elsewhere, Daddy dear." She was allowing her anger to push the accelerator. She eased back to the speed limit as a laden logging truck wheeled into sight. She edged past it.

Frank muttered something.

"What's that?"

"I said 'women drivers.'"

"I'm not the one with a hatful of speeding tickets."

"Shit." His voice was fretful now rather than angry, almost plaintive. "So answer my question. What do you want?"

She negotiated the narrow bridge over the Choteau. "Right now, I want to find an apartment in Hood River and move out."

"Tell me what you want."

She gripped the wheel and organized her defenses. "I thought it was about time I got acquainted with you. That's what I had in mind when I came north in June, and it's all I had in mind."

"If it's money—"

"Money! Look, when she divorced you, Mom insisted on a cash settlement instead of child support, as you should well remember. She supported me perfectly adequately. So do you think she blew the settlement in Vegas? Her financial advisors invested it for me. I went to college in the Bay Area, lived at home, and stopped well short of a doctorate, so I have enough left to give me an income for life if I don't touch the capital. I own a little house in San Francisco, also an investment, and I rented it out before I came north. There's another hunk of cash. I also have a job, starting in September." Never mind that it was only a part-time job. Adjunct professor they called it. "I do not need money, Dad. I'll pay rent for my room if *you* need it."

"I don't!" His indignation was comic.

Jane laughed.

After a moment he did, too. "What's going on with Libby?"

"How should I know?" Libby did not confide, not at all. Jane said, carefully, "I kind of like her, you know, but we don't have much in common. She doesn't know gouache from goulash."

"Neither do I."

"I just mean she's illiterate about art." Maybe illiterate in general. Jane had once seen her stepmother flipping through *People* magazine, but she'd never seen Libby with a book, though the house had a small library. Maybe Stepmama listened to books.

What do the two of them talk about, Jane wondered. *Their friends?* She thought Libby's friends and her father's had even less in common than Frank and her young stepmother. He had half a dozen local cronies his own age. They talked sports and business and played poker, and twice they had brought their wives over for barbecue around the pool. Jane had been the odd person out. Jane, and Libby.

Libby hung with the surfers who were surprisingly varied in age and background. They appreciated the swimming pool when they came to the house, but they didn't come often, because Frank was only marginally courteous to them. Maybe the social dynamics were better in winter. Jane thought her father skied.

She turned onto the meandering drive. The house sat on three acres of prairie that the landscape architect had had the sense to leave in its natural state. Libby had assured her she'd see a spectacular array of wildflowers right through the spring months with a second burst of glory coming after the autumn monsoon. Jane had not yet experienced a full season of wildflowers.

The land sloped south enough to encourage grapevines. An acre east of the house was planted in the syrah grapes Frank was fond of. The vines wouldn't bear for several years and looked spindly.

Jane didn't much like the house. Too many ledges and turret-like excrescences. A côte for buzzards? She had to admit it was comfortable—as comfortable as a spread with eight bed-rooms, a media theater, a library, a great room, and a formal dining room could be, not to mention the kitchen, three "studies," and enough bathrooms to cope with a plague of dys-entery—one for each bedroom and two for emergencies. The swimming pool lay out of sight of the drive on the south side along with the guest house where Frank's wine maker was living (one-and-a-half baths).

When she had hauled the groceries in for Irma's inspection, Jane changed into her bikini and a robe. Time for a swim. Frank, Jr. had called, Irma said. He was coming tonight. What did that mean?

2.

FRANK HAD disappeared into his study with Gerhard Koeppel, his wine maker, and the vineyard manager, Tom Dahl. Gerd lived in the guest house, and Dahl's office was in the *cave*. Frank could meet with both men at a snap of his fingers.

A colorless man in his forties with a toothbrush mustache, Dahl deferred to Frank too much. Jane liked Gerd. He was a native of the Moselle region of Germany with enough degrees to call himself Herr Doktor Professor back home. Here he was just Gerd, an easygoing but by no means spineless man, and a genius at blending wines. Frank had hired him the previous January from a group of eight candidates, because Gerd didn't hesitate to speak his mind.

He was a devoted skier, so Libby said, schussing the slopes of Mount Hood when he was in the mood for steepness or taking the cross-country trails on the Washington side when the spirit moved him. Skiing had been one of the plums that drew him away from his job with a winery near Prosser, even though coming downriver had meant giving up his part-time position at WSU–Richland. Frank paid him an enormous salary just to buy grapes, because so far the *cave* didn't require much supervision. Dahl had seen to it that the vats and the elaborate temperature-control system were ready, so the wine maker could start making wine all right, but this year would be a trial run.

Gerd had returned from a month-long buying trip that took him from his old stomping grounds near Yakima in a loop that touched southern Oregon before curving north again through the many Willamette Valley vineyards. Jane was glad to see him. She had missed his European viewpoint and lively sense of humor. He was a few years older than she was and no more than five or six inches shorter, a round man with a balding head of blond hair dyed cerise.

She slipped into the pool. The water was glorious, warmed by the afternoon sun but not too hot. She swam laps hard to wash away her irritation with her father, then rolled over and floated on her back until she started to turn into a prune.

She rinsed the chlorine off at the outdoor shower, slipped into her robe and flip-flops, and strolled over to the low wall that kept acrophobes from feeling dizzy at the top of the cliff. Below lay the decrepit Hawk Farm house with Frank's established vineyard to the right. The vineyard looked rich and ripe in the lowering sun, and from this angle the unfinished *cave* wasn't visible. A decaying garage loomed in the foreground. To the left of the Hough garage, slanting rays of sunlight picked out trees in the cherry orchard.

Friday a crew had harvested the last of the cherries while distant voices called back and forth in Spanish. By this morning, someone had removed William Hough's contentious billboard, a sign of progress. Jane had noticed the giant absence when she and Frank drove down to Highway 14 on the way to the library gathering.

Now the farm was quiet, the silence unnatural, house and garage deserted. They ought to have a dog, she reflected, but the silence made sense. Hawk Farm was a place of mourning. And it was Saturday—maybe the family had gone out to dinner. Suddenly ravenous, she picked up her towel, tossed it into the bin, and trotted to the house.

Around seven, Frankie drove up in a Lexus he'd rented at

the Portland airport. They were finishing Irma's torte, and Libby was wittering about a friend she'd bumped into at the Hood River marina. Jane jumped up to give her brother a bear hug. He looked as if he needed it.

He squeezed her arm and let go. "Dad?"

Frank stared at him without expression. "Well?"

Frankie just shook his head like a horse with a pesky fly. "We have to talk."

~

MADELINE Thomas, principal chief of the Klalos, spotted the Houghs as soon as she and her husband, Jack Redfern, entered the Klalo Pizza and Fry-bread Emporium, but she only had time to give her sister-in-law Alice a wave of the hand before the tide of greeting swamped her. KP, as everybody called it, was a popular hangout for local people as well as tourists. Of the locals, about half were tribe members who felt free to tell the chief what was happening. The restaurant was a Klalo tribal enterprise, and Maddie was never able to convince the young proprietors that she hadn't come on a tour of inspection, that she just liked their pizza. Tonight, having eaten abundantly at the library luncheon, she wasn't even hungry.

Jack was. He'd called in their order, and it was almost ready to pick up, according to the chef, who bustled out to greet her. But Jack saw the Houghs and walked straight to the last booth where they sat, half-hidden. Russell stood and turned to greet him. Jack bent to kiss Alice, who was facing the room with her back to the wall, and reached to give his niece Judith a gentle pat. Then he stood, his back to Maddie's constituents, in silent communion with the nephew who had caused him so much grief.

They did not embrace. Klalo men rarely did. She thought Russell was saying something. As Madeline listened with half an ear to the complaints of an elderly fisherman, she watched her husband's shoulders ease. Then the four of them sat down together, Jack beside his sister, and Maddie could breathe again.

She doled out a pat to the fisherman and smiles to everyone else and let the talk sweep over her. She injected a word here and a touch there, and gave the Houghs time with Jack, because she knew, in a rare moment of humility, it was Jack they needed.

~

JANE slept and woke and slept again. She thought she heard voices raised in anger. Thunder rolled sometime in the night. Lightning flashed. She had a vague thought about wildfires, but it faded. A while later the rain started, not the heavy deadly rain of the high desert but a soft Pacific patter borne on a southwest wind. The sound eased her deep into a dream of wildflowers. When she woke at last, the clock said nine, the Sunday sun shone, and she supposed the life-giving rain had been a dream, but when she went to the window she saw that the dust had been washed away. The world was new. Except for a single cloud at the summit, Mount Hood hung like the charcoal sketch of a mountain, gray and white against pure cerulean blue.

To ignore such a sight was more than she could bear. She made a bathroom run and dressed, then grabbed her sketchpad and a pen. What in the foreground? Nothing. For now, it was enough to capture the mountain. It came and went. When conditions were right, people said "the mountain is out," meaning they could see it. They often couldn't. Jane thought they might also mean that the mountain had gone away and sneaked back when no one was looking. The idea enchanted her.

The pool area provided the best views of the mountain and the river below it. She must have sketched for an hour, capturing both the scene before her and the perceptions that flitted through her mind. She drew. She took notes. As she recorded what she saw, she was vaguely aware of life going on around her—and down at the farm. Voices, a car door slamming, other doors, the splutter of an old engine. She heard low voices from her father's house, too. She saw Gerd cross from the guest house and gave him a wave. She heard a car leave. At some point, Irma brought her a cup of coffee and went off when Jane mumbled that she didn't want breakfast. Another car left, probably Gerd's. The vacuum cleaner started, unusual on Sunday, but Irma wanted Monday and Tuesday off.

Jane flipped another page of the sketchbook as the light shifted. Clouds coming from the west. She wondered how long it would take to drive to the other side of Mount Hood. If her mountain was going to advance and retreat, she ought to have a look at its backside. And where would it go? She visualized a map of Oregon and Washington with the other peaks laid out in a rough south-to-north line, as she had seen them poking up through a layer of thick cloud when she flew in to Portland. Mount McLoughlin, Mount Jefferson, Mount Bachelor, Three Fingered Jack and the Sisters to the south. To the north, Mount Adams, the stub of Mount Saint Helens, and Mount Rainier. There were others.

A sharp crack startled her out of her internal vision. Annoyed, she stepped forward and peered over the wall that divided her father's property from Hawk Farm. At first she spotted nothing wrong. Then she saw that a large bough had fallen from one of the cherry trees. It looked as if something lay beyond the heap of foliage—metal and a blur of light blue. She looked around for the mini-telescope her father used for bird-spotting, but someone had tidied it away—Irma anticipating rain? For a brief moment, Jane considered calling 911. She patted her pockets as if her cell would materialize, but she only carried the phone when she was on the road or expecting a call.

She walked to the end of the wall and looked down. From this angle it was clear there was something beneath or behind the fallen branch, but she couldn't see what, and there was no sign of movement. Someone had probably left the ladder stuck in the tree yesterday. The storm last night had then weakened the bough, and when it had fallen, it had knocked the ladder down. Simple. Nevertheless, she had to be sure. With a sigh, she laid her sketchbook on the flat of the wall and jumped down the three feet or so to the surface of the vineyard.

She trudged along the barbed-wire fence that marked the property line until she came to the three-barred wooden gate that was supposed to provide the Houghs with access to their orchard through Frank's syrah vineyard. Bill Hough had never used it. Instead, he had laid his own single-wire of electric fence atop the other. It had quite a charge. She looked around for a stick she could use to lift the bail that held the gate closed, but she didn't see one. She cocked her head, listening, but heard no hum. Emboldened, she touched the electric fence. It was dead.

Must have turned it off after they removed that asinine bill-board. "God, guns, and guts." If you just have enough guts and guns, you'll find God? Unlikely, but was it more likely that God would supply guns? Guts maybe. She yanked the gate open and left it that way, in case she had to beat a hasty retreat. Nothing happened. Her sneakers sank into a mast of leaves and fallen cherries. The ground looked as if the harvesters had churned it with their boots. Yellow jackets zipped around her. *Ugh.*

She brushed one away from her face. "Hello? Are you all right?"

No response.

She had a better view now. She saw a fallen ladder, the tele-scoping kind, and fabric that looked like a blue work shirt. She ran to the large branch that had come down and gave it a heave. A moan rewarded her. "Hello?"

Silence.

The branch was heavy. Fearful that she would drop it on the dark-haired man who lay beneath it, tangled in his ladder, she jumped backwards, yanking away, and fell on her tush with an armful of tree in her lap. Not a graceful move, but she had cleared the victim's head and torso. He lay on his back.

She scrambled to her feet. Shoving the branch aside, she knelt at his head. "Hey, are you okay?" *Manifestly not.* She touched his cheek, which was cold and sweaty. "Hey!" *I've got to stop saying that.* She ran her hand over the top of his head and felt a lump. Her fingers came away sticky. "Oops. Head injury. Listen, I'm going to run up to the house, the August house, I mean, and call 911." She wiped her hand on her jeans.

Another groan. He frowned and licked his lips. "Don't."

"What? You're concussed."

"'m all right."

"I don't think so."

"Don' wan' ambulance." He cogitated, still frowning, eyes still closed. "Gerd back from Oregon?"

"What?"

"Gerhard. Li'l ol' wine maker. Drive me to 'mergency."

What! At least he was willing to go to the hospital. *But Gerd?* "Gerhard just left for town. I heard his car drive off."

"Shit." His mouth set in a tight, hard line. She fought an impulse to kiss it. *What!*

"I'll drive you," she announced. "You must be Russell Hough."

"Mus' be." He didn't sound enthusiastic.

"I'm Jane August."

"Hey."

"I'll bring the SUV down the access lane. Wait a minute. What about your mother and sister? Can't they drive you?"

"Hood River. Shopping. Walmart."

Jane remembered hearing the old pickup leave. She heaved a sigh. "Okay. Let's get the ladder off your legs first. Then I'll drive down here, and you can hop in." She glanced at his face.

"I don' think so. Take a look." He grimaced and reached with his left hand to jerk the leg of his cargo pants up. "Ladder smacked it when I fell."

Jane stared at what had to be the latest thing in artificial legs. It gleamed titanium-bright; it flowed like the arch of a WPA bridge; it twanged with such power her fingers itched to sketch it. And it wore a sneaker fastened with Velcro over an athletic sock. *Magic.*

"My God, that's a beautiful object," she heard herself say. "I bet it has everything but GPS."

He choked. "Video c-cam."

"You're pulling my leg."

They looked at each other. His mouth twitched in a grin.

Jane sat beside him and laughed until she gasped. "I'm not usually so suave." She wiped her eyes on her sleeve. "So tell me what I should do here."

He took his time answering. At last he said, "Don' make me laugh again. Head hurts."

Jane nodded.

"I think I broke the good leg."

"Oh, no!"

His eyes clenched shut. "Yeah."

"You'll have to have an ambulance."

"No. Can you move the ladder?" He was talking more clearly. He meant, move the ladder from his legs.

"I think so, but it's going to hurt."

"No shit."

It did. At one point he let out a yelp. She took the rest of the bough away, twig by twig, and then looked at the ladder. Moving it meant moving both legs. The artificial limb came off in her hands.

"Lay it here," he said through clenched teeth. "Where I can reach it. I'll put it back on."

"You can't. It's bleeding."

"What is?"

"Your, er…"

"Stump," he said flatly. "Bleeding but not a lot. I told you the ladder hit the prosthesis."

"Should you replace it?"

"I'll have to if I'm going to stand up. No way will I stand on the other leg, not before they take an X ray." He drew an uneven breath. It came to her that he was afraid of losing the use of his good leg. "You'll have to help me get up. My balance will be off."

Jane thought about that. Then she slid the heavy ladder off, inch by inch, until the other leg, the whole one, was clear. He passed out. She had plenty of time to think about liability suits. She would just have to trust him. He would just have to trust her. *Wonderful.*

When he had blinked his way back to consciousness, she said, "I'm going for the SUV."

"Water."

"Yes, I'll bring you water." *And a blanket and pillows to prop the broken leg.*

She stood and dashed up through the dying orchard to the

gate. In her father's house the vacuum cleaner hummed away. She folded pillows and a duvet from her bed and grabbed her purse with all its accessories, including the house keys, the car keys, and the cell phone. She didn't turn the phone on.

Jane left Irma a note on the kitchen table and remembered to take a bottle of water from the fridge. She drove the SUV, wobbling and slewing all the way, down through the open gate and the orchard.

Hough was sitting, slumped, and had reattached his artificial leg. She maneuvered the SUV until she thought it was close enough for him to grab the door handle. She bailed out and ran to his side, passed him the water bottle, and waited for him to drink.

He drained it and threw the empty over his shoulder. "Thanks."

"Litterbug!"

He didn't smile. He scrunched back on his rump and reached up for the door handle with both hands. Only the right reached it. "Okay, I need you here at my elbow. Left elbow. When I say 'now,' shove up." He positioned the fake foot as close to his body as he could, knee to chest, and straightened the other leg. "Okay. Now."

Jane levered his rigid elbow up. To her surprise, he jumped upright in a single shove. He swayed, but the false leg held. Then he leaned against the car, eyes closed, and embraced it for several long breaths. "Can you open the door?"

"Er, no. You'll have to, er, move left about six inches."

"Hell." His left hand cramped on the roof, and he did an awkward, one-footed heel-and-toe to the left. "Far enough?"

"Two more inches. That's it. Good." She eased the door open a crack. "Watch out."

He held the edge of the open door in his right hand and moved it wider. "Now comes the fun part." He faced forward. "All right. Open it wide for me, please."

Jane complied, narrowly missing his nose.

He leaned in and grabbed the Hail Mary handle inside with his right hand and the roof with his left. Without so much as a deep breath, he executed something like a leaping pirouette that slung the whole left side of his body onto the seat. She thought he grazed his head going in.

At any rate, he passed out again. He was sliding, about to fall out. She jumped to his side and shoved him into the car. His right leg dangled. She lifted it in and straightened it. Then she found the correct lever and inched the back of the seat down until he was reclining. She ought to prop his good foot. The stump of the other leg had bled through his khaki cargo pants. Pants and blue shirt were speckled with plant debris. She brushed him off.

Her father kept a box in the back that held tire chains, hardly necessary in August. She found it, stuck it beneath the foot, and inserted one of the pillows atop the box. *That should do the trick.* She put the other pillow under his head which was no longer bleeding. Then she tucked the duvet around him. He was probably suffering from shock. *Whiskey? No. Sugar.* She ran to the driver's side and scrabbled in her purse until she found a foil-wrapped power bar. Then she threw the purse in the backseat and climbed into the car.

He was looking at her.

She ripped the foil open and handed him the bar. "Eat that."

"What?"

"Sugar, for shock."

"Uh, I will when I don't feel like throwing up."

She started the engine and strapped herself in. She wished she could strap him in. "I'm going to drive down past your garage and house and go out onto the highway that direction. Too much jolting the other way."

He closed his eyes. "Okay."

The distance to the house seemed interminable. The SUV wobbled and bumped. After she hit the graveled driveway things went easier. "Do you have your insurance card?"

"Wallet. Back pants pocket."

"Good. Then we're off." She pulled onto Highway 14 behind a truck with a semi-trailer. She was grateful to the driver for keeping to the fifty-five-mile-an-hour speed limit, because the cars tailgating her could blame the truck for the slow pace. Any faster and the SUV would have swayed too much for her unbelted passenger. The drive to the county hospital in Klalo took almost an hour, though she usually made it to town in forty minutes. Fortunately there was a stretch with a passing lane, and the impatient tourists streamed past her. Some of them got stuck behind the truck. They deserved it.

Hough didn't say anything. As Jane turned off for the hospital lot, she said, "May I ask you a personal question?"

He cleared his throat. "If you insist."

"What the hell were you doing up in that tree?"

3.

JACK REDFERN showed up on Sunday afternoon while Rob was out in the yard with a trash bag collecting the last of the debris from Meg's garden party. The new bookmobile, there on exhibit, had been moved back to the library.

Rob dropped the bag on the grass to shake hands. They went through the ritual questions. *How's Maddie? Good, and Meg? Fine. Your brother?* Rob knew and liked Leon Redfern. *Oh, that's good, very good. And Bitsy?* Bitsy Thomas was Maddie's cousin. Jack asked after the daughters, Meg's and Rob's. They were fine.

At long last, Jack came to the point. "Got to talk to you, Rob. It's my sister, Alice Hough. She has a problem."

"With the law?"

"No."

"Let's go in and have a sit-down. Get you something to drink?"

Jack shook his head. "Don't have the time. I'm on my way to pick my nephew up from the hospital."

The hospital? "Would that be Russell Hough? I hope he's not sick."

"Fell out of a cherry tree." Jack gave a "go figure" shrug.

"I heard that George Washington chopped down a cherry tree."

"More like Russ *pulled* it down." Jack chuckled. "Neighbor lady brought him in, but that was this morning. He told his ride it would take a while, that she should go home. Alice don't drive and Judy won't, least she won't drive Russ, so that leaves me." He cocked his head. "Not that I mind. Good to have Russ back home."

Rob nodded. "I understand he was gone a long time."

"Seventeen years. Couldn't come back while his dad was around." Jack considered. "They fought."

"I heard that."

"Who from?"

"Helmi Wirkkala."

"Thought maybe it was the sheriff. She taught Russ and Judy in high school."

They drifted across the yard toward Jack's little pickup. There were two wheelchairs in the back, one a scooter, both secured with bungees.

At last Jack said, "It's Judy. Alice is afraid the kid's losing her marbles. Sometimes she hides in her room for days. Other times she's all loud and angry like her dad."

"She doesn't work?"

"No. She tried a couple of office jobs after she got her discharge from the army, but she ended up quarreling with the people she was working with and quit in a huff. Then she tried college and quit, said it was nonsense. After that, she just stayed home, worked at her quilts."

"Quilts?"

"She does quilts, makes hangings. She's pretty good, I guess, but she doesn't try to sell them. Bill nagged at her, and they quarreled. Easy to do with Bill."

Rob was sorry to hear about all that family strife but didn't know what he was supposed to do about it.

When they reached the pickup, Jack turned to him. "Alice is afraid that Judy will kill somebody—the neighbors, her brother, herself."

"Has Judy threatened to do that?"

"Not exactly. She rants. Like Bill." Jack met Rob's eyes. By Klalo standards, the gesture was either hostile or desperately earnest. "She needs to get herself cleansed."

"Go on a spirit quest?" Rob had been trying to study Klalo customs, but a lot of them were unwritten.

Jack's eyes cut away. "That, too." He heaved a sigh. "See, Judy don't trust the VA doctors, and I gotta sympathize with her, but that girl is not right in her head. She needs help."

Rob was seldom at a loss for words. This was one of the times.

"Trouble is, Maddie says there's no ceremony for a woman warrior. A man, now, that's different."

"What does Maddie think?"

"She says that Judy wasn't raised in the traditions, that the ceremonies wouldn't work for her even if she was willing, and she isn't."

"No, I can see that. Would it help defuse the situation if Russell left the house? He could stay here. We have lots of room." *Meg is going to kill me.*

Jack sighed. "I dunno. I don't think so, but thanks. I'll tell him you offered. He's working the farm, you know. Has to be there." A long pause. "Russ doesn't quarrel with Judy. But he keeps making changes, like taking that billboard down."

"He did that? I'm damned." Rob was diverted. Bill's contentious billboard had been a blot on the landscape for years.

Jack rubbed the back of his neck. "Stupid sign."

It was indeed. Rob took in the implications of Russell Hough's action. "G, G, and G" was an NRA slogan. Bill had amassed guns. Rifles, pistols, antique revolvers—you name it, Bill had it. As far as Rob knew, he hadn't collected grenades, but Rob would not have put it past him. "Getting rid of Bill's arsenal would be an even better idea."

Jack said, "Prob'ly can't do that till the estate's settled."

"Probably not. Russell could bury them."

Jack laughed. "I'll suggest it." He sobered. "But that's just what Judy doesn't want. Changes. She grew up with the guns in place. Not that she got along with her dad. Nobody did. But he's dead now."

"And that makes his wishes sacred?"

"Not exactly. Changes throw her off her stride." Another pause. "Russ is going to take out the orchard. It's dying, and he says the land can be put to better use, but Judy won't hear of it."

"And Russell ignores her objections?"

"Ah, now, he listens to her, but he has to do what he thinks he ought to. If Bill hadn't committed suicide—I mean, if his death had been an accident—Alice could afford to hire a manager. But there's no money. Russ only has a year to put things right at the farm, so he can't wait around for Judy to come to her senses."

"A year?"

"He has a year's leave of absence from his job, that's what he told me. He works for Eismann upriver."

Eismann was a major wine producer in the southeastern part of the state, a name notable, among other things, for ice wine. The private corporation owned dozens of vineyards and had two major labels. "What does he do?"

"Manages one of the big vineyards. Near the Tri-Cities."

Rob whistled through his teeth. *Not bad for a kid who took off at eighteen with no money and a high school education.*

"It's a good job," Jack was saying. "Pay's good. He likes it."

"So why bother with the farm?"

"It's Alice's livelihood. She can't draw Social Security yet."

"Why doesn't Alice manage Hawk Farm? Or Judy?"

Jack scowled. "D'you think Bill Hough allowed Alice out of the kitchen? My sister can't even drive a car."

"I see your point. But Judy left the farm. Two tours in Afghanistan?"

"I told you how it is with Judy. Some days she don't get out of bed." Jack opened the driver's door. "I gotta go. Will you think about Judy, see if you can suggest something?"

"I could ask around. Maybe Beth…"

Jack hesitated a long moment. He was a deeply private man,

which made his successful marriage to a politician strange. He was private, but by no means stupid. "Yeah, maybe the sheriff could talk to her." He slid behind the wheel. "Judy might even listen." And he was off, heading for the hospital.

Rob retrieved the trash bag, went into the house, and called Beth McCormick about her former pupil. He had a bad feeling about Judith Hough.

~

"WHERE the devil have you been?" Frank demanded. He was sitting by himself at the dining table. It was set for five.

"In the shower." Jane flipped her ornately folded napkin open and laid it on her lap to protect the silk tunic she'd put on. Irma had made chicken *mole*.

Jane was ravenous. Between sketching the mountain and running an amateur ambulance service, she'd skipped breakfast. Irma didn't fix lunch on Sundays, so Jane had eaten the rejected power bar. She could have lunched at the hospital but didn't. Fortunately, Sunday dinner was served at four.

Frank regarded his only daughter with no hint of amusement. "Where have you been since ten o'clock this morning? I needed you to drive me."

"You still have your license, Dad. Try for a light foot on the pedal."

"You took the fucking car."

"I took the SUV. You could have driven my Prius." Or Libby's Jeep, with or without Libby as chauffeur. When Jane had found herself driving almost everywhere in the SUV, she posted keys for her car on the board in the utility room where the extra house keys were kept.

Frank made a face. He despised the little hybrid. "So where were you?"

"Klalo."

Irma entered with a tray and began to serve the starter, half an avocado enlivened with a dollop of freshly chopped *pico de gallo*. Jane swallowed saliva at the sight, and never mind that the salsa would clash with the *mole* sauce. The chef was experimenting. At least she hadn't tried sauerkraut on the avocado.

Frank was still growling as Gerd and Libby bounced in, dressed for the marina. Jane's stepmother was determined to teach Gerd to surf as soon as the wind picked up, and he had no objection. Indeed not.

"Sorry we're late, Frank darling," Libby fluted. Both of them seated themselves without ceremony. Frankie slunk in, looking hung-over. Frank glowered at all three of them. Jane thought they didn't notice the cook. Irma slapped the other three starters down and huffed off to the kitchen.

Frank poured himself a glass of wine and passed the decanter. Jane poured, passed, and tasted. Nice. Her palate wasn't precise. She thought the wine was a riesling. *Probably the wrong wine for Mexican food, but who cared?*

"Did you have a good day, Jane?" Gerd at least had excellent manners.

"I met a friend of yours." She took a pensive spoonful of avocado.

"A friend here?"

"Russell Hough."

His eyes widened. "Ah, excellent news, but how does Russ come to be here? He is at odds with his father, the estimable William."

"Bill Hough is dead," Frank growled. "Forgot to tell you. Killed himself while you were gone."

"How peculiar." Gerhard frowned, noticed the decanter at his elbow, and poured a glass. "I should have said he was a man who enjoyed causing trouble, and surely he was causing enough to be in a state of bliss. Well, well, an e-mail will not suffice. I must call Russ at once to condole." He took a healthy swallow of wine and made to stand.

Jane said, "I think he's still in the hospital."

"Hospital!" Gerd sat with a thump.

She ventured another bite, this time with more of the *pico de gallo*. She took a sip of wine to cool her tongue. "He doesn't have his cell phone with him."

Everybody stared at her, even Frankie, so she set her spoon down and gave them a condensed narrative of her day, much of it

spent waiting in the lobby of the Emergency Room while technicians did things to Russell Hough in the depths of the hospital.
"Mr. Hough wasn't really up in the tree," she concluded, "he
was under it, trying to remove the ladder. It slipped from his
hand and knocked against a weak branch. That fell on him, and
he tangled his legs in the ladder as *it* fell."

Gerd sucked in a sharp breath. He had to know about the
artificial leg, but he didn't say anything.

"I think he has a mild concussion," Jane offered. "He was
more concerned that he may have broken a leg. They were still
doing X rays when I left."

"What I don't see is why you involved yourself," Frank
grated. "Mark my words, he'll sue."

"I don't think so." Jane dug at her avocado. Everyone else
had finished with the starter. The moment she set her spoon
down, Irma materialized, scowling, to remove the small plates.
She returned with the piping-hot *mole*.

Everyone ate in silence for perhaps ten minutes. The chicken
was tasty and served with a flavorful variation of "Spanish" rice
Jane had never eaten before. She determined to ask for the
recipe. She could make it when she had her own kitchen and eat
it for a week with different accompaniments. Cooking for one
was a pain.

"…and I'm leaving early in the morning, so I'll say good-bye
now." Frankie's voice was a flat monotone. He seemed to be
speaking to her. Gerd and Libby nattered on about the river.

"But you just got here."

"I won't be back."

Frank had listened to his son with cold attention. At that, he
gave a sardonic laugh. "You'll be back, hat in hand."

Jane stared at her father. Was his escalating rudeness the
sign of ill health, maybe a mini-stroke? She had been in his company a good six weeks now. He was gruff, but he could laugh
and knew how to relax. Sometimes he was almost charming.
Had he got worse before the library luncheon, and she hadn't
noticed?

She looked from father to son. They were not much alike.

Her brother was taller and slim, almost reedy, a runner rather than a weight lifter, and his manner was usually diffident. Just now, though, both men wore identical bulldog expressions. "What's the matter, gentlemen?"

Frankie said, "The bank has gone into receivership. It pleases our father to blame me, though I wasn't the one who approved all those sub-prime mortgages."

After a cold moment, Jane remembered that, thanks to her mother's financial wizards, her own investments were independent of the August bank. Then she heard Libby shrieking and saw Gerd's bewildered face. Did he know what "receivership" meant? Probably. He kept up with the news.

"Oh, shut up, Libby," Frank snarled. "I took my money out three years ago."

His wife rushed from the table, sobbing. Gerhard had gone pale.

Irma stood in the doorway to the kitchen, hands on hips. "Can I clear now?"

"I'm sorry, Irma. Your *mole* is delicious. We've had disturbing news, that's all. Please do clear away." Jane got to her feet. "I'll help you, shall I?" She didn't wait for an answer.

When Jane and Irma had taken all the plates and serving dishes to the kitchen, the chef burst into tears and offered to quit immediately if her cooking was not satisfactory, so it took Jane a while to soothe her and send her off. Jane promised to serve the *flan* herself. *Of course they loved Irma's cooking. They loved Irma. They would love her lovely* flan. *Of course she should go off to Portland, just as she'd planned. Good-bye, good-bye.* Hasta luego.

When Jane brought the tray of desserts in, the three men were snarling like a cageful of alpha dogs. "Pudding?"

Frankie leapt to his feet and stalked out the hall door.

Frank pushed himself up. "None for me." He walked from the room looking about a hundred years old. Jane felt no sympathy.

Gerhard remained seated. An unaccustomed frown drew his blond eyebrows together. *He ought to dye them to match his hair.*

Jane laid the tray in the middle of the table, sat down beside him, and handed him a dish of custard. She took one herself. "Try it. It's soothing." They ate.

A car engine started, and they cocked their heads. Frankie's rental. Jane hoped he wouldn't drive it into an overpass or another vehicle. The sound of the engine faded.

When Jane felt she had done Irma's *flan* justice, she said, "Tell me about Russell Hough. How did you meet him?"

Gerd laid his spoon in the bowl with a clatter. He looked at her. "What's this about a broken leg?"

She told him what little she knew and repeated her question.

"Then it is not so serious, the accident." He gave a brief smile that looked genuine. "You asked how we met. He was the one who told me about this job. Did you know that?"

"No."

"When I first came to the Land of Lost Opportunities, Russ was my boss. He was kind and amusing. He showed me the rope. Do you say that?"

"Ropes." Jane watched him slot the corrected idiom into his mental lexicon. "He was your employer?"

"My overseer. Ah, supervisor, I should say. He manages the vineyard I first worked at." Gerd spooned pudding. "I like him. We e-mail each other. When he heard the job here was open, he let me know. I haven't seen much of him since I moved to Prosser, but I look forward to renewing the friendship. I took him to Germany once—to see the vineyards on the Rhine."

"And?"

He grinned, and this time there was no doubt of his amusement. "I was between jobs. It was Oktoberfest. We had a good time."

"With beer."

"Of course with beer. Russ learned the schottische. My sister Hilde is in love."

Jane could imagine that, and she could also imagine him dancing to an oom-pah band. "What happened to his leg? The war…?"

"No, no. Just a motorcycle accident, no heroics. He says only one hero is allowed to a family, and his father is already a hero. But now of course there is his sister."

"What?"

"She is a hero, too. That doesn't sound right. Heroine? That doesn't either. English is an appalling language. No order, no simplicity."

"It's a mongrel," Jane agreed. "Russell's sister is a hero?"

He nodded. "In Afghanistan. She was wounded. She saved lives. She has medals like Russ's father, the horrible William."

"Good heavens," Jane said faintly. "The poor thing."

"Ha! Sexist!"

"Gerd!"

"If I had said of Russ that he was wounded, saved lives, and had medals, you would not have said 'the poor thing.' Am I right?"

"Yes, oh dear, I suppose you are. Isn't that strange?"

"Strange that you should be sexist?"

"Just strange," Jane muttered. And it was. Nevertheless, it was true. Far from being praised and paraded, the moment Judith Hough was acclaimed a hero, men like her despicable father would call her sexuality into question. Because a heroine is not a hero.

After an awkward pause, Jane asked Gerhard whether he had invested money in the ill-fated bank, and he admitted he had lost perhaps ten thousand euros. Not, you understand, his entire savings, just the signing bonus Frank had given him and a few thousand more. Frank had not known of the investment. Of that Gerd was certain. Frank had not warned him off, however.

The wine maker was more philosophical about his probable losses than Jane would have been, so she murmured encouraging phrases about FDIC insurance and government bailouts, but she had the feeling it would be a long time before Gerd saw his money.

She put the food away and shoved the dishes into the dishwasher. She could have used help, speaking of sexism.

When she reached her room, she turned on her cell phone and found half a dozen messages, including one from Russell Hough. Though he sounded resigned, like any man used to telephone tag, his news was good. Both legs were bruised, but the right ankle was not broken, and his uncle had driven him home from the hospital. He thanked her for her help. She jotted his phone number down. Then she dealt with the other calls, one from the Hood River campus of the community college to remind her of an obligatory faculty orientation the second week of September.

Galvanized by the message, and by her urgent desire to leave her father's house before the press siege began, she booted her computer and logged onto one of the real estate sites that listed apartments and small houses available across the river.

She had not yet explored the area. Most of her colleagues and students would live in town, but one of her classes would meet in Hood River and the other in The Dalles, at the main campus to the east. She could live in either town or halfway between. Her first goal was to find a place with good northern light for her own work, and a view of the river. The river was a mile wide and changed color by the minute. Alternatively, she thought one of the small communities south of Hood River might provide her with a close view of the mountain, though living there would involve a winter commute to both campuses.

She created a list with addresses and e-mail contacts and sent out a message to the real estate offices outlining her needs and the price range she thought reasonable. As she worked, she heard Libby's voice rising and falling and her father's answering rumble. A door slammed.

When she tired of house hunting, Jane took out her sketchbook and looked at her views of Mount Hood. Beautiful as it was, the mountain was something of a cliché, like Mount Fuji. Hundreds of landscape painters had "done" Mount Hood sherbet pink at sunset. A nineteenth-century artist had painted the north face imbedded in scenes from the southern slopes, a juicy concept for a magical realist. Her fingers itched for pen and paints and paints and pastels and chalk and camera.

Someone in the house turned a television on briefly, breaking her concentration. A train whistled down by the river. It was getting late, so she set the sketches aside for the time being. She thought about watching the tube herself but activated her Kindle instead and began to reread a comedy of manners she'd enjoyed ten years before. It was even funnier the second time around and distracted her from her uneasiness.

Libby and Gerd had not gone off to the marina after all. She wondered what Gerd had done with the time. Phoned all his friends upriver? Called home? No, it was early to telephone Germany, given the nine-hour time difference. She thought she heard him rummaging in the kitchen, or it might have been Libby. She heard voices.

Jane read on, laughing from time to time. Around ten-thirty she heard a car come in, probably Frankie if he meant to leave for the airport at the crack of dawn. Male voices rumbled but she couldn't make out what they were saying. She yawned, decided to call it a day, and went to bed with the wired comedy. She hoped Russell Hough was not in too much pain and decided to check up on him in the morning. She could walk down to the farmhouse through the cherry orchard. Perhaps Gerd would like to come, too. She fell asleep with the Kindle on. Fortunately it turned itself off.

JUDITH was later than she should be. A mild fog hung in the air. She liked fog, it was so different from raw desert air. But fog hid. Fog distorted. It condensed on her goggles, so she took them off, let them hang around her neck, and stood still while her eyes adjusted. Black-clad with a scum of dirt to camouflage her face and hands, she was standing behind the garage, holding the old rifle. She stared into the pool of darkness until she could make out the shapes of things.

The house on the hill bulked dark to the northwest. The single security light on the southeast side cast a pallid glow over the pool area. Wisps of fog flowed through the cone of brightness. The guest house was dark.

At first she thought they'd all retired for the night. It was past midnight, after all. The old man stayed home and went to bed early. However, Mrs. August came in at all hours and so did the wine maker, and the daughter sometimes did, so the air of sleepy calm might be an illusion. She thought someone else was there now, too, another guest.

Her family had always turned in early. It surprised her that, after seventeen years away from home, her brother did, too. He could have broken the habit. He'd rejected everything else their father had insisted on.

A noise off to the right startled her. The butt of her rifle hit the wall of the garage with a soft thud, and she froze in place.

Something white drifted downhill from the August vineyard. Heart pounding, she squinted through the fog. Russ must have turned the electric fence off after all, damn him. Or *they* cut the fence. The gate gaped open. A white vehicle, an SUV, rolled to a stop inside the orchard. No engine sound, no lights.

She crept along the back wall of the garage. From the west corner, she could make out the fallen ladder and the bough that had brought it down on her brother. The tree masked the SUV from view, but she caught sound, a dull click, and movement, a white blur as the hatch rose in back. Something rustled. When another white blur and a thump suggested that the hatch had been closed, she took her chance and ran, cat-footed, to the fallen branch of the cherry tree.

But the fog had thickened. She squinted past the trunk of the tree. Somebody was moving around on the other side of the SUV. She listened to sounds she could not interpret, soft sounds, shuffles, more rustling, faint thuds. What was happening? Sweat dried on her face and arms, and she began to shiver.

After interminable minutes, she heard the SUV's engine cough and rumble to life. The lights did not come on, but the vehicle inched up the incline backwards. It reached the open gate, reversed, and drove off out of sight. She glanced at her watch. The incursion had lasted less than fifteen minutes. What did it mean?

She checked around her, but nothing stirred, neither up on the hill nor back at the farmhouse. Cross and edgy, she made her quiet way up the slope to the open gate. She stumbled a little on the loose soil and made out the pattern of the SUV's tread marks, but the driver hadn't dumped anything she could see. She'd have to look again in broad daylight. At least she could secure the gate, for all the good that would do. It wouldn't keep the deer out, let alone human intruders. She made her way back down the slope.

She was brooding so hard about the trespass she didn't notice the train approaching across the highway, coming from Two Falls. Freight trains and two passenger trains ran along the river, one every couple of hours. Living at the farmhouse, you learned to adjust to the noise. Unless you were jumpy. She was. At the first rising hoot, her hand clenched. The rifle discharged.

Oh no fuck it. She thought she shouted, but the train whistle, on its second bleat, drowned her out.

Shaking, she flicked the safety on, clutched the rifle to her chest, and ran zig-zag to the porch. When she reached the door to the kitchen—the porch wrapped the house on two sides— she stopped dead. Had they heard? *Surely not.* She hadn't been that close to the farmhouse. Her mother had been asleep for hours, and Russ had retired to the couch in the living room that would serve as his bed until his foot healed. Though he'd said he was going to read, his light had gone off before she slipped downstairs to go out on patrol. He'd had a long day, and he was probably doped up.

She paused in the kitchen while her eyes adjusted to the interior darkness, but she saw nothing and heard nothing other than her own breathing.

When her pulse slowed and her breathing evened out, she set the rifle on the kitchen tablecloth and the night goggles on the folded napkin at her place. She lifted her chair and turned it so it faced sideways to the table, easing it down with exquisite care. Then she sat and began to remove her left sneaker.

She didn't hear him at all, so absorbed was she in edging the Velcro tab open without making a sound.

"Jude." He spoke quietly but might as well have shouted.

She jumped and muffled a scream, hands to her mouth.

Russ sat in his manual wheelchair, blocking the doorway to the hall and watching her. He could not have been there when she entered or she would have seen him, and he could not have just come from the living room or she must have heard him.

"You've been waiting in the hall," she said dully. "With the lights off."

"I didn't want to wake Mother. I still don't." He drew a breath. "Bring Dad's little souvenir to the living room."

She bit back a protest and picked up the rifle. She would have to talk to Russ. She didn't want to.

4.

WHEN JANE got up the next morning, a mild fog hung in the air. It made her homesick for San Francisco. The mountain had gone away.

She dawdled around the kitchen, hoping for company. If he had kept to his plan, Frankie was probably already on his flight south. She made coffee and emptied the dishwasher. As she was pouring herself a lonely bowl of Cheerios, Libby drifted in. Eight o'clock was early for her. Jane said so.

Libby stretched luxuriously and said *mmm*. For a woman who had fled the dining room shrieking the night before, she looked almost pleased with herself and somehow keyed up. Jane wondered whether Frank had reconciled his wife by means of inventive loveplay but decided that was improbable. Gerd came in, also sleek and rosy, from the direction of the guest house. He poured two mugs of black coffee and handed one to Jane's stepmother. Libby gazed into his eyes.

Three lemons clicked into place in the slot-machine of Jane's mind.

She did not feel sorry for her father. Frank probably deserved a little betrayal. But who was the shtupper here and who the shtuppee? She spooned cereal and chewed. *Nominative or accusative. Does it matter? Not to me.*

As she arrived at that comfortable conclusion, Gerd said, "I had a message on my cell from Russell. I mean to call on him this morning. Shall you come with me, Jane?"

"Sure. Why not?"

"Libby?"

"Bill Hough's son?" Libby made a face. "I don't think so. I'm going to the marina, Gerd. You could join me." She gulped coffee and set the half-full mug in the sink. "Me for a shower."

"See you later, *Schatzi*." Gerd stuck his head in the refrigerator and pulled out a loaf of Tillamook extra-sharp white cheddar. He cut a thick slice and a slice of wheat bread, made a sandwich, and washed his breakfast down with coffee. The sight made Jane queasy. She went to her room.

There was no sign of Frank by the time Jane was ready to rejoin Gerd, so she left a note for her father on the kitchen table. *"Off to Hawk Farm. Back soon. J. 9:00."* She thought about warning Libby that the media might show up. Local radio news had mentioned the bank failure. She visualized Libby holding a press conference and said nothing to alert her stepmother.

Gerd was ready to drive down to the farm, but Jane made him walk. She led the wine maker through the orchard. Something had changed, but she couldn't think what. Someone had closed the gate; perhaps that was it. She showed Gerd the wilting foliage of the fallen bough. The ladder lay where she and Russell had abandoned it. Gerd clucked his tongue and shook his head. She wished she didn't like him.

The farmhouse was as still as a tomb. Gerd rang the bell, and when that produced no result he rapped sharply on the blistered wood of the door. They heard a scuffing noise, and the door creaked open.

"We don't want any." A middle-aged Klalo woman regarded them without expression.

"May we speak to Russell Hough? I am Gerhard Koeppel, a friend of his."

The woman looked at Jane.

"I'm Jane August. We're concerned about Russell's leg."

The woman's smile transformed her. Jane saw that she had once been pretty. "Please come in. I'm sure my son will want to speak to you, Miss August. I want to thank you, too. He might have lain there for hours if you hadn't seen him fall." Her eyes flicked to Gerd. "And you, too, Mr. Er."

"Koeppel," Gerd repeated. "I'm Herr August's wine maker."

"Come in, come in." She ushered them into a cluttered hallway and led them down it to the kitchen. "I've just brewed a fresh pot of coffee. Russ should be back soon. He was checking on the new crew."

Jane was horrified. "I hope he didn't walk to the fields!"

"No." Mrs. Hough went to an automatic coffeemaker. It was still burbling.

"That's a relief."

She turned back to Jane. "The doctor told him not to stand on the good leg for a week or so. And he can't attach the artificial leg to the stump until the cuts heal, so he can't use crutches."

"I didn't think so. You know, he could use Dad's golf cart. I wish I'd thought of that. How did Russell—"

"He asked my brother Jack to bring one of those electric scooters for him, the kind old ladies use to ride around town. Bill, that's my husband, was my husband—" She gave her head a shake as if disoriented. "Did you notice the ramp? Bill put it in when my mother came for a long visit. He never got around to removing it after she died, so Russ can get the scooter in and out of the house. I hope he isn't run over by a produce truck when he crosses Fourteen." Fourteen was what locals called the highway. "The drivers never look where they're going. Have a chair, Miss August."

"Please call me Jane."

She smiled. "I'm Alice. Coffee?"

"Yes, thank you."

"Mr. Koeppel?"

"Yes indeed, Mrs. Hough. And I'm Gerd."

"You must be the one Russ went to Europe with. I'm pleased to meet you. He told me you showed him a very good time."

"I'm glad he enjoyed himself."

Jane and Gerhard exchanged glances and seated themselves at a round oak table. The kitchen was not only bright with crisp curtains and new paint, it was sparkling clean and smelled of fresh-baked bread. Jane decided to spend the rest of her life there.

Alice poured three mugs of coffee. "Cream and sugar?"

They shook their heads *no.*

"Would you like a slice of bread? It's warm from the oven."

"Yes, please," they said in chorus and laughed at themselves.

They were on second slices of bread with melting butter and huckleberry jam when banging noises at the front door announced Russell's return. Alice went on telling them about her family's hereditary berry patch.

"Ma!" The kitchen door crashed open. A motorized wheelchair zoomed in and stopped short. Russell gaped at them. He was sweaty and dusty, his extended right foot covered with a plastic bag. He was not wearing the artificial limb. "I didn't see a car. You two must've walked down. Gerd, *wie geht's?*"

Gerd jumped to his feet, bread in hand. Jane rose less abruptly.

Russ smiled at her, teeth very white in all that dust. "Miss August." He shook hands with Gerd, who said something in what sounded like Spanish and took another bite of bread.

"*De seguro.* Excuse me, while I go sluice off the dirt." And he backed the scooter out the swinging door and disappeared.

Alice shook her head. "Always in a rush. More coffee?"

Gerd said, "Russ is the only Yank farmer I know who bothers to speak to his work crews in their own language. He said he learned to speak Spanish when he was a boy, working on the farm. And of course he studied it in school."

Of course. Jane wondered what Bill Hough had thought of that. He'd been hostile to Hispanics.

Russell took his time getting clean. Alice's huckleberry reminiscences dried up, so Jane talked about her upcoming classes across the river. Gerd finished her second slice of bread. He seemed to find the flavor of huckleberries fascinating.

At last, Russell entered the kitchen in an ordinary wheelchair, closely followed by a young woman wearing jeans and a red T-shirt with a faded screaming eagle across the front. The eagle bulged at breast level.

Russell's hair was damp. He'd removed the plastic bag from his injured foot, he was cleaner than he had been, and he wore an unironed work shirt over the dusty cargo pants. He was not smiling, and Jane saw that he had not slept well. He looked at his mother, then turned to Jane and Gerd. "My sister, Judith. Jude, my friend, Gerhard."

The girl inclined her head. She didn't smile either. Gerd was staring at her as if the Virgin Mary had appeared on the refrigerator door.

"And Jane August, who drove me to the hospital yesterday."

Jane murmured something polite. So did Judith.

Jane looked from sister to brother. Judith's skin was ivory lightly sprinkled with freckles, her eyes were gray, and her hair light brown. Otherwise she was an exact duplicate of her mother, as her mother must have been thirty-some years earlier. Russell had his mother's dominant coloring, but otherwise bore no resemblance to either. He was good to look at because of his vitality, but his features were bony and irregular. Judith, on the other hand, was beautiful. They might have been unrelated.

She was beautiful but blank. She did not want to be there.

Everyone sat. Russell moved his wheelchair closer to the table. Alice was saying something about Judith working upstairs on her quilts as she poured her daughter a cup of coffee.

"You make quilts?" Jane asked, to have something to say.

"Hangings."

"Ah, another artist."

"If I were just a quilter, I wouldn't be an artist?"

Jane's mouth formed a smile. "Some quilters follow standard patterns. Others are artists, certainly. Do you do your own designs?"

"I make crazy quilts." She gave a short laugh. "Some would say because I'm crazy."

Jane let that one pass. "Do you work by hand or with a sewing machine?"

"Both. I use my great-grandmother's treadle."

Jane sat up straight. "A treadle sewing machine? Can I have a look at it?" She had seen treadle machines in museums.

There was a silence. Jane thought Russell and Alice were holding their breath. At last, Judith said, "If you like." She shoved her chair back. "I warn you, it's a mess up there."

"Then you must be an artist."

At that Judith did smile. Jane heard Gerd catch his breath at the sight.

Jane and Russell's sister went up the steep uncarpeted stairway, leaving the men in the kitchen with Alice. Judith had chosen a bedroom on the north side of the house as her workroom, and it had good light. It also had a view across an edge of the vineyard to the August house at the top of the bluff. The window of the great room glinted in the sun.

A big quilt frame almost buried in heaps of cloth stood on end in one corner of the workroom, and the treadle sewing machine sat beside the window looking out. Judith had been piecing a stretch of fabric. Jane could discern no pattern. Crazy indeed. She didn't like the color combinations.

Judith removed what she had been working on and cut the thread from the bobbin. Then she inserted a scrap of faded denim and gestured for Jane to sit. It didn't take Jane more than a few minutes to master the machine. It went forward and backward on the cloth—that was all. No zigzag, no buttonholer, no fancy embroidery stitches—but it was smooth and elegant in its motions. Judith said it would punch through leather with the right needle. Something about nineteenth-century engineering made it very human. Jane tried to express what she felt about the rhythm of the treadle. Judith listened in polite silence.

Jane stood up. "Thank you. It's a wonderful instrument."

"My mother showed me how to quilt with it when I was

twelve. I used to work on my quilts after school. Dad didn't want me to bring kids home, so I needed something to do inside when the weather was bad." Judith's mouth quirked in a grin that was like her brother's. "I worked in here all day during an ice storm once. There was no power—and just the light from the window—but I didn't need power. It was great."

Jane tried to imagine that and failed. "Will you show me your work?"

The smile faded. "Not all of it. You can see Mom's quilt. I made it when I was in high school."

～

"IT was good, yes?" Gerd stopped beneath an ailing cherry tree and fixed Jane with his sharp blue eyes. His cerise crest ruffled in the breeze. "The quilt, a work of art, right?"

They were trudging back through the orchard, sloshing with coffee and stuffed full of bread and huckleberry jam. Jane was still puzzling over the change in the orchard, whatever it was.

Thanks to Jane's diversion upstairs, the visit had extended well beyond politeness. Russell had taken a call—he needed to go back to work. Alice had started another batch of bread. When the visitors rose to go, Russ and Gerd agreed to meet the next day, and Jane invited Judith to speak to her classes about fabric art. Though Judith declined, she seemed pleased to be asked.

Jane turned Gerd's question over in her mind, then shook her head. "No. It was a cheerful patchwork quilt but no more. She was still learning the craft when she made it. However, I spotted a hanging at the end of the hall that was something else." She walked on and Gerd followed. Both plodded, because the way was soft underfoot, and the slope, though not steep, slanted uphill through a break in the bluff.

"Something else?"

"Different, other, something else. Idiom. Something remarkable. Unfortunately, it was also disturbing. Like a crazy-quilt explosion, you might say." In all the colors of blood. A work of art that nobody would ever want to hang on the living room wall. Jane would not have hung it at all.

She was not a pretty-pretty painter, and her independent income, though modest by her father's standards, meant that she didn't have to sell her work to interior decorators on the prowl for soothing landscapes. All the same, she would never have displayed something she couldn't live with. What she felt for Judith Hough was a strange mélange of respect and pity. And fear. Jane was afraid of Judith and for her.

Gerd nattered on about Judith's beauty. The breeze had picked up.

When they reached the August house, a tear-slubbered Libby told them Frank was missing.

FRANK was missing, and so was the SUV.

"He still has his license," Jane said in her most soothing voice.

"We quarreled," Libby sobbed. "When I woke up, I thought he'd slept in another bedroom. I'll never forgive myself. I drove him away."

"So where did you drive him?"

Libby glared at her over a sodden tissue. "You're so funny, Jane. Not."

They stood facing each other in the utility room/laundry where stacks of fresh linens awaited the many bedrooms, not to mention towels for both bath and swimming pool, and piles of clean dinner napkins. Above the folding table hung the cork board with hooks for the keys to the August kingdom. One set of keys to the SUV had vanished.

Jane had already checked the garage. Gerd went off to telephone Frank's cronies and the airport. He would try to find out if Frank, Jr. had made his flight. Libby continued to wring her hands.

Probably because drones of the sort used in combat were still being tested in the Gorge, not to mention the training of foreign drone operators, satellite coverage of the area was now excellent. Jane wondered whether the state police or county deputies were using drones to find missing cars. She hoped not. So far the press had not found Frank's Washington residence. No doubt they were looking for him in the District of Columbia. Or they had found the state but couldn't find the house. *What am I thinking? They have GPS, not to mention Google Earth.*

It was not even noon, way too early to call in the police. She refused to allow Libby's operatic hysteria to infect her consciousness. Frank had driven himself to Klalo and would collect his ultimate speeding ticket coming or going.

"Have you checked the studies and the media room?" she asked when her stepmother's sobs dwindled to sniffles.

"I checked every room in the house including the bathrooms. The bookroom is locked, but he never uses it anyway."

Jane shivered. She thought of Bill Hough's suicide. Maybe Frank had locked himself into the library. It lay in one of the architect's whimsical towers, beyond the guest bedrooms on the second floor. Her father had seemed depressed. Would a gunshot in the bookroom be heard at the other end of the house? She took the master key from the board and ran upstairs. But if the SUV was gone, Frank was surely the driver. Gerd's BMW, Libby's Jeep, and her own Prius still sat in the garage beneath the east wing. Frankie's rental had gone, as promised.

Jane was panting by the time she reached the library door. She rattled the handle and called, then called louder. No response. She took a steadying breath, used the key, and opened the door wide.

Nothing. The room was dusty. Irma must have locked it to hide her negligence. It looked as if no one had used it since the last time it was dusted. Jane resisted the temptation to inscribe a *J* on the nearest flat surface with her finger. No need to hurt Irma's feelings. She closed the door neatly behind her but did not lock it.

She drifted back down the hall to the study in the south wing that Frank had appropriated as his own. It was not locked, nor was he there. She stuck her head in the connubial bedchamber next door with its dressing room and bath suite. *No joy.* There was evidence, obvious even from the hall, of Libby's presence—clothes draped here and there, an iPod lying on one of the bedside tables, the odd potion or lotion strayed from the dressing room. The unmade bed looked as if only one person had slept in it.

So where had Frank slept? Or had he? A chill went down Jane's spine. It was conceivable that Frank had gone off in the SUV the night before with no one the wiser. He had quarreled with both Frankie and Libby, or at least spoken in a voice audible several rooms away. Libby had found consolation in the guest house. She must have gone to the master suite at some point.

Jane had not sought her father out to say good night. He would have questioned her sanity if she had. And Frankie, if it was Frankie who had driven in around ten-thirty, would not have reconciled with his father. She didn't know that as a fact, just as a conviction. Frank had taunted him. Her brother could be diffident, but he was capable of sustained resentment. She thought of the bank. If he believed Frank had set him up, he had to be furious. Would there be legal complications, questions Frank would have to answer? She reentered the study/office and went to the computer.

When she touched the mouse, the screen activated. The machine was on. The screen saver showed a view of the Columbia from the great room. She counted at least a dozen icons besides the ones that accessed technical programs. She clicked on the toolbar and brought up Yahoo. She tried to get into Frank's mail there but couldn't. When she typed in his e-mail address, access was password-protected, and she had no idea what the password was.

~

MADELINE Thomas rose earlier than she usually did in order to catch Jack before he left to fish. The steelhead were running. Things were beginning to look up. The count of chinook salmon that came up the Bonneville fish ladder had risen for the first time in years. The steelhead numbers looked good, too.

Jack Redfern made a decent living because he was the canniest fisherman on both rivers he fished, the Columbia and the

Choteau, but maybe he could take things easier now. Today he was making for his family's small platform on the Choteau.

He blinked up at her over his last cup of coffee. "Hey, Chief." He teased her sometimes.

She let it ride. "Hey yourself. How's young Russell?"

"Not so young. Russ was thirty-five this spring." He turned her question over in his mind. Jack was a careful thinker. "He'll be all right. He didn't break the good leg."

She said a quick Klalo blessing. "But he needed Wally's scooter and the wheelchair?"

"Right. Russ has to keep working. Bill left a mess at the farm."

"More ways than one."

"That's the truth. I talked to Rob Neill."

Maddie waited.

He took a long swallow of coffee and rose to go. "He thought maybe the sheriff could help Judith." He stood looking at her. "You had something else on your mind."

She nodded. "The Augusts, that family who live on the bluff above Hawk Farm, what do you know about them?"

He shook his head. "Nothing. Never met 'em. Russ told me the daughter saw him fall and drove him to the hospital. Nice of her."

"Yes. She's an artist. She seemed okay. I met her and her father at Meg's library lunch. *He* said hello and walked away without looking at me. I don't like being invisible."

Jack grinned.

"And last night on the news I heard about his bank. It failed. It was one of those we had trouble with when we went looking for mortgages." By "we" she meant herself, the council of elders, and the two sub-chiefs.

Her aim was to secure decent housing for tribe members who chose to live in Latouche County. Many were single mothers, underemployed or unemployed, and the elders had agreed to co-sign some loans when they thought the people looking to buy houses were reliable. Tribal enterprises brought in funds that could be used for the good of all the Klalos, and keeping a strong presence in the area was one way of doing that. The northern and eastern parts of the county were traditional territory, and though there was no reservation as such, the BIA recognized the tribe. They had trust lands from the time the dams were built and had acquired other property. Maddie wanted to make the county a place of refuge for the whole tribe, a place to raise children.

"There have been two foreclosures," she went on when she saw Jack glance at the door.

"That's not good." He frowned and named the ousted families, right the first time. Jack knew what went on. He never talked much, but he listened. People confided in him.

Maddie grimaced. "Both of the foreclosures were justified, unfortunately, but that's money down a rathole. I hate those bankers. They don't care what they do—tempting people to take loans they can't pay, raising the interest rate, rigging balloon payments, foreclosing when they could renegotiate." She drew a breath. "I want to know whether this man August is involved."

"And if he is?"

"If he is, I want to freeze him out of Latouche County. I want to strangle him, too, but I probably won't do that."

"Better not." Jack gave her a quick kiss and took himself off.

~

THE first call regarding the missing banker came in as Rob Neill was about to go to the sheriff's office to talk over the puzzle that was Judith Hough. It was not yet two in the afternoon. August had not been missing—or, at any rate, missed—for anything like forty-eight hours, so he couldn't be considered a missing person. Rob took the call only because Miss August asked for him by name. Ordinarily MisPers cases went through the uniform branch first before landing on his desk.

Jane sounded apologetic. "My stepmother is convinced he's missing. They quarreled last evening." She paused as if editing her remarks. "He also had words with my brother. Frankie left this morning for San Francisco, and I guess he made his flight, but I haven't heard from him yet. Dad isn't answering his cell phone, and his car, his SUV, is gone."

"I see." Soothing noise. Rob didn't see.

"Two things. He was depressed about the failure of his bank. Well, strictly speaking, it's not his bank now. Frankie took it public three years ago, and Dad sold his shares. Still, Dad's decisions when he was CEO will be called into question, and I'm sure he's not looking forward to that."

"You said two things."

"The other is the missing SUV. Dad hasn't been driving because of speeding tickets. He could. He's still legal, but it's almost as if he's superstitious about getting behind the wheel. I've been his chauffeur most of the summer. I took the SUV yesterday and left him stranded, as he saw it, so he may just be asserting ownership, but it doesn't feel right."

"Is he ordinarily considerate?"

That startled a laugh from her. "He doesn't go out of his way to inconvenience the rest of us. He also likes to eat at home. It's true that our cook is off for a couple of days." Her voice trailed, then came back on a strong note of exasperation. "If he'd just gone for an hour for a nosh at McDonald's or a trip to the liquor store I wouldn't think twice about it, but it's been six hours now and maybe a lot more. Neither my stepmother nor our houseguest, our wine maker, saw him after ten last evening. Nor did I. Dad could very well have driven off then without anyone noticing he was gone."

"Eighteen hours."

"Maybe."

"All right, Jane. Give me the details—license plate number, your father's license number if you have it, distinguishing marks like scars or moles or tattoos. I can describe him. The clothes he was wearing when you last saw him, did you check to see whether they're missing?"

"No."

"Have Mrs. August do that. Leave a message for me when you know. E-mail a digital photo if you have one, or fax one. Also give me a list of people and places you've called to check up on him. Think about spas or resorts around here if there are any he likes to visit. Favorite restaurants. That sort of thing."

"I'll do it right away." She sounded relieved.

"Mind you, I can't send out a general missing person bulletin. It's too soon. I can ask the patrol officers to be on the lookout for the SUV, though."

She thanked him and hung up. He went off to see Beth in a thoughtful mood.

He found her in her office playing Scrabble with her computer and clucked his tongue.

"At my age," she growled, "I need to hone my brain. Three-letter word beginning with *X*."

"The Greek letter *chi* with an English plural."

"Will Scrabble take that?"

"Try it."

She did, it did, and she paused the game. "What's this about Judy?"

She was frowning by the time he finished. "If Jack's alarmed I'm alarmed. I haven't seen her since she escaped from the army—except at the funeral. She was such a cupcake."

"Cupcake? Bill Hough's daughter?"

"Hard to believe but true. She had a minor reading problem, attention deficit attributable to hormones. The boys swarmed like bees." Beth gave a reminiscent smile. She had loved teaching remedial English. Not many people did.

Rob figured that anyone who could teach remedial English and make the kids like it could run a thinly populated county with one hand tied behind her, as Beth did. "According to Jack, she's now channeling her father."

"That is not good. I'm so sorry for her."

"Because of Bill?"

"Because of Bill and her army experiences."

"You're a convinced feminist, lady. Be consistent."

"I'm not convinced that combat is good for anyone's head, male or female, and strictly speaking, Judy was not in combat.

She was a keyboarder, secretary we used to say. She was going through a marketplace with a patrol of security types—on her way to the office, so to speak—and was caught at the edge of a big explosion. What do they call them? Some hideous acronym."

"IEDs?"

"She behaved very well, saved several of her comrades and two Afghan civilians. Nevertheless, a dozen people died, many more suffered dreadful wounds, and Judy herself was hurt. There are some parallels with what happened to her father. I'm morally certain she and Bill both suffered post-traumatic stress, not to mention survivor guilt, but there's no way you nor I—nor anyone without similar experience—can know what's going on in her head. I hope the outcome will not be as tragic for her as it was for her father, but I'm not optimistic."

"That's quite a speech."

Beth's eyes sparkled with tears. "It makes me so angry. How can we do this to our young people, generation after generation, not to mention their families and all the civilian casualties?"

Rob thought the Taliban had some responsibility and said so.

"Plenty of guilt to go around. We're accumulating a mass of bad karma. It frightens me."

"Bad karma. And you a practicing Catholic."

"I hope I know an intelligent idea when I hear one."

Both of them sat silent for a moment, Rob thinking of his long-dead father. If Charlie Neill had survived the rocket attack that killed him, would he have come home as damaged as Bill Hough? It was not a comforting thought.

At last Beth sighed and said, "Shall I take Judy and Alice out to lunch?"

"Maybe you should make it one-on-one."

"I was afraid you'd say that. I'm scared. I think William Hough was poisoned by anger and fear. He very nearly destroyed his son. And now Judy—"

"Russell? Jack seems to think Russell is okay." Except for the minor matter of a missing foot.

"If he is, I'm happy. That was one very bright boy, a bright likeable boy, which is not a necessary combination. His father abused him verbally and probably physically until Russ walked away from his family."

"Is that what happened?"

"I don't know what happened." Beth ran a hand through her short white hair so that it stood up in tufts. "I only know what I heard, and the people I talked to, mostly high school teachers, had no reason to speak well of Bill Hough. He abused *them*."

"Biased witnesses?"

"Something like that. The boy didn't say anything about his father, good or bad."

"You taught him?"

"I did. Ten years before I taught Judy and just sophomore English, not remedial. I hadn't specialized at that point. He sailed through the class with no effort. I'm bound to say he didn't exert himself all that much for me, but he was outstanding at math and science."

"And Miss Trout taught him biology?" Miss Trout had taught Rob biology.

"She did. She had high hopes for Russell." Beth leaned toward him, eyes intent. "Where has he been all these years?"

"In plain sight. I Googled him. He attended Washington State in Pullman." Pullman lay far to the east, on the Idaho border. It was the main campus of the state's land-grant university.

"Good grief. But Bill—"

"Bill apparently knew nothing."

"And Alice?"

"I don't know. Russell has a master's in biology. Works for Eismann. Manages a vineyard. His website is minimal—it lists a couple of published articles, technical stuff. He's unmarried, and has no military or criminal record. I didn't have time to go into news archives. I'd say Jack is probably right about him. He'll be okay. Now about Judy—"

But Beth just shook her head. "I'll do what I can."

Rob decided he had pushed Beth as far as he should. He told her about Frank August's disappearance. She thought the banker was hiding out from the press.

When he called home, Meg thought so, too. She grumbled about errant bankers, which was not surprising. Rob had had a recent high-rent case. Rich folks were time-consuming, she said.

"You prefer me to entangle myself with poor suspects?"

"No suspects at all, please God. I like a peaceful life."

So did Rob, but he was in the wrong profession for that.

~

JANE had e-mailed a photo to the undersheriff along with the information he asked for. Now it was a matter of waiting. She was not good at waiting.

Libby was lousy at waiting. She paced. She whined. Sometimes she cried. She turned the kitchen television on and off. She jumped for the house phone whenever it rang, which it did fairly often because of the bank crisis. By the time the breeze picked up in the late afternoon, Jane was ready to throttle her stepmother.

"Libby," she said, "why don't you go do a little surfing? I'll answer the phone."

"Oh, I couldn't. Could I?"

"Of course. Go. Take Gerd."

Libby pouted. "Gerd said he was busy. I think he's mad because of his money. I told him, hey, I lost money, too."

"A lot?"

Libby's face closed. "More than I wanted to."

"I'm sorry," Jane said inadequately.

"Didn't you lose any?"

Jane explained that her financial people had avoided the August bank.

Libby sniffed. "Banks like that ought to have warning signs."

"Like cigarettes?" Jane laughed, but it wasn't funny. *Caveat emptor.* The people her father's bank trapped were vulnerable to their own greed. Or desperation. She had never in her life been desperate for money. She hoped Libby would not be. Frank had settled a generous sum on Libby at the time of their marriage with the understanding that she would then have no claim to his private fortune.

Libby was watching her with an expression Jane couldn't read. She turned away when Jane caught her eye. "I guess I'll take your advice and go surfing. Don't wait dinner for me. I'll eat something in town."

"Okay. Take your cell." Libby nodded and turned to go. "I'll phone you if anything happens," Jane called after her but her stepmother was halfway out the door.

Messages had begun to accumulate on Jane's phone, though none was from her father or brother. Reporters, alert to the bank's problems but not yet to Frank's disappearance, had left most of the ones on the landline. Those she deleted. She had received responses from the real estate agencies in Hood River on her cell phone, so she called and made two appointments for the next day. She wanted *out*. Where was Gerd? She knocked at the guest house door, but he did not reply.

By dark, Jane was trapped in a loop of "what ifs." At the top of the list, *What if Dad's dead?* filled her with horror. Around seven she made herself a sandwich then stood in the kitchen and looked at it. She had no appetite. And oddly enough, no thirst either. *A nice glass of wine? No? Warm milk? Aaargh.* She rummaged in the fridge for bottled water.

What if Frank had committed a crime of some sort connected with the bank's failure and made a run for Canada? He could fly anywhere from Vancouver BC, and if he'd fled, his head start was now twenty-four hours. The world was very small. *He may be in Rio already. If so, he abandoned his wife.*

What if he drove into the wilderness and ran off the road? What if he's lying unconscious somewhere or, worse, alone and in pain, unable to reach anyone because…? Where's his cell phone? He must have it with him. She dashed to his study and searched frantically without result. *No phone. Well, I knew that.* It wasn't in the bedroom he shared with Libby. Jane even went through the pockets of his jackets.

What would it mean if it were here and he was not? That would be much worse, she decided. Her burst of energy faded, and she slunk back to the kitchen with her feet dragging. By the time she got there she was crying from confusion, anxiety for her father, and loneliness. She poured herself a glass of wine and sat over it, sobbing, and at that inauspicious point Gerd returned.

He bounced through the door from the pool area and stopped short when he saw her face. "What is it? Is there news of Herr August?"

Jane sniffed. "No, I'm just afraid something's happened to him, something awful, and I hate waiting."

"It is very hard, Jane. I am so sorry."

"Thanks." *Sniff.* "Wine?"

"Yes, please."

"Where were you? I didn't hear you drive in." She poured him a generous glass.

"Oh, I, too, am forced to wait, so I decided to see if I could help Russell. After I checked in with Tom Dahl, I walked down and spent several hours with Russ in those fields across the highway. I ate dinner at the farmhouse. Mrs. Hough is a fine cook."

Jane thought Alice Hough's food was not the sole attraction. She hoped her stepmother wouldn't find out about Gerd's abrupt attraction to Judith. Libby in a temper was a jarring presence. Jane was glad Frankie had left.

"I did check in with Tom," he repeated. He sounded defensive. Thomas Dahl oversaw Frank's work crews. At this season about all they were doing was moving irrigation pipes early in the morning. In a few weeks, as the grapes ripened, Gerd would be busier than a three-tailed cat in a room full of rockers. Right now he had plenty of time to get into trouble with the boss's wife or the neighbor's daughter.

"How is Russell?" she asked by way of distraction.

"Relieved that the good leg is not broken."

"But?" Jane poured herself another glass of wine.

"Preoccupied. He's worried about something. Not the leg."

"And he hasn't confided in you?"

"No. And that worries *me*," Gerd admitted.

"What do you think it is? What's your best guess?"

The blond eyebrows drew together. "It could be something easy like money."

"Easy?"

"Superficial. Not weighty. For your father, money is weighty. Not for Russ."

She digested that. "And if it's not superficial?"

"His sister." He looked as if it hurt him to say the word. "Or his father's death."

"Or his sister *and* their father's death."

"That. Yes."

Jane said, "I'm sorry, I think she's...disturbed." *Such a euphemism.*

"She's so beautiful."

"Yes." Jane was an artist. She had to acknowledge beauty. She wished Gerd was not so vulnerable to it. *And what about Libby?* Her mind jumped sideways. *And Dad? Where is he?* She gulped wine.

5.

TIME PASSED with excruciating slowness. There was no sign of Frank the next day, no sign of the white SUV either. Jane had to cancel her house-hunting appointments. Around two, Robert Neill called her to report. She stuck by the phone, at least she did at first. Later Tuesday afternoon she took her Prius out through a cordon of reporters, including a television crew. Word had gotten out of Frank's disappearance.

She dashed to the grocery store and dashed back with enough food to last a week. Neill called again. No progress. He would come over in the morning to see if there was evidence of Frank's intentions that Jane had overlooked. Frankie left a message, asking whether it was true that their father had gone missing. Calling back, Jane was finally able to speak to her brother. Yes, of course he'd made his flight south to San Francisco. He hadn't seen Frank before he left. He sounded almost as baffled as Jane felt. He asked how Libby was holding up.

Jane's mother called and said kind, soothing, motherly things. As usual, Mary Sylvester avoided saying anything negative about her ex-husband. She never had when Jane was a child either. As an adult, Jane found her mother's virtuous reticence exasperating.

"For Godsake, Mom, give me a clue. You know the man. Why would he do this?"

"He wouldn't."

"Why not?"

"Go missing on purpose? No. Frank likes an audience for whatever he does."

"Everything?"

"Well, maybe not his fiscal shenanigans. Otherwise, yes. He plays to the gallery."

"You think his absence is involuntary?"

"I'm afraid I do."

Jane swallowed hard. "Then we have to look for his enemies?"

Her mother assented, adding grimly, "And right now they're all stirred up."

~

JUDITH heard her own voice rising. It was as if she were a ventriloquist's dummy, mouthing hateful words, her father's words. They weren't even directed at her mother and brother, who were also sitting at the kitchen table but not looking at her. Her rant was triggered by the television news. It showed events in Egypt.

"Butter, please." Russ took a slice of Alice's bread. She passed him the butter. "Thank you. Know all about Egypt, do you, Jude?"

"All I want to know." Judith had never been to Egypt. Neither had Bill Hough.

Russell buttered his slice with deliberation.

An advertisement for pain tablets brightened the screen. Another commercial, this time for mass-produced cheeseburgers, succeeded it, followed by another touting a cold remedy.

The television in the kitchen had been her father's brilliant idea. He would turn on the news at dinnertime and yell at the screen in a parody of conversation while she and Alice ate in silence. This was the first time they'd turned the television on at dinner since Bill's death.

The anchor, a man with a full head of reassuring gray hair,

moved to local news. He narrated scenes from a street shooting in east Portland, segued to a mention of Frank August's disappearance, and passed the story to his perky female collaborator. Russ gripped the arms of his wheelchair and leaned forward, intent, but there were no new developments.

Judith waited, only half listening to a clip from the public appeal Robert Neill had made earlier that day. A clear photograph of their neighbor appeared on the screen. The contact number scrolled across the base. She wondered who had driven the SUV into the orchard. Had Frank August done so himself? She would have to tell Neill about the incursion.

I can't tell him, she thought, panic closing her throat. *He'll ask me why I was out there so late.* When the sound bite ended and yet another commercial began, Russ clicked the set off. The silence rang.

"Pie?" Alice Hough used food as a form of communication. Since Russ's return she had been baking up a storm.

Judith shook her head *no.* So did her brother.

Alice looked disappointed but resigned. Russ smiled at her. "I'll eat a piece later, Ma. Right now I have to call Jack. I need a ride to Klalo tomorrow morning. The doctor says he'll give me a walking cast."

"It's too soon!" Alice, perturbed.

"I'll drive you." Judy, surprising herself.

The two women spoke together.

Russ looked from one to the other. "Uh, thanks, Jude, but you'd have to drive my Blazer. I can't climb up into the pickup."

"I can drive an automatic. I said I didn't like to, not that I can't." She heard the sharp edge of her words and winced.

Russ frowned. After a long moment he said, "Thank you. I have to be there at ten."

"Okay."

"I'll come, too." Alice rarely asserted herself. Both of her children stared at her. At last Russell nodded.

Judith wondered what it was like for him, after seventeen years without family, to be the focus of all this nurture. She almost envied him his long absence, but she thought it could not have been easy—even with Jack as a tenuous connection.

She had thought Russell dead. She was eight when he disappeared. Bill Hough had not attended Russ's high school graduation. Alice had—with Jack and Madeline. Jack brought Alice home. By that time Bill was drunk and asleep on the living room sofa, and Judith was hiding upstairs. She always hid when her father drank.

Next morning, when Judith asked for Russ, her mother said something vague about a party for graduating seniors. But he never came home. Would he have come home if Bill had attended his graduation? No, that was an eight-year-old's thinking. The trouble ran deeper. Bill had ranted and stomped around and finally gone out to look for his son. None of Russ's friends knew where he was. Or so they said.

Judith was still very angry that Russ had allowed her to imagine him dead. Alice claimed she had never believed he was. What had their father thought? In all those long years Judith had not heard him say Russell's name, nor did he mention his son in the short vicious message he left when he shot himself, the message Judith had destroyed. Bill had also believed Russ was dead. She was sure of that.

~

ROB Neill drove himself to the August mansion with Linda Ramos and the technical crew following in the van. It was nine o'clock Wednesday morning, and there was now no doubt that Frank August was a missing person. Time to take a look—but at what? There might or might not be a crime scene at the house.

Rob was more curious about the Houghs' place than the Augusts'. The August house was reputed to be spectacular but had no history, whereas the farmhouse was almost as old as the county. The Klalo settlement at Two Falls went back much farther than that, probably to the Missoula Floods. Rob reined in his wandering thoughts—it was August who was missing.

Mrs. August met Rob and the team of deputies at the monumental front door. She was tiny and blond with eyes of contact-lens blue. She bared ultra-white teeth in a welcoming smile. It faded a bit when Rob handed her what he trusted was an unnecessary search warrant. She toyed with it, then beamed again.

At first glance she looked young enough to be August's granddaughter, but once Rob got over the shock, he decided she was just well-preserved and probably on the shady side of thirty, young but not disgustingly young to be the wife of a man in his sixties. *Abishag.*

Jane August, slim and a hand-span taller, looked like big sister standing behind her. A classy big sister. Like her step-mother, Jane was fair-haired. Unlike her stepmother, born that way. *Lord, I'm catty,* Rob thought, as he introduced his inves-tigators and made polite apologies for intruding on the ladies' privacy. He was refusing tea, coffee, and other beverages when a Spanish-language wail issued from the back of the house.

"Oh, Jane," Mrs. August quavered.

Jane grimaced. "Our housekeeper, Irma Castro. She's threat-ening to quit because of the press cordon."

"I can imagine." Rob had driven to the house with the last mile very much on camera.

"Libby will show you around. I'll join you when I've derailed the crisis. It's mostly drama. I hope." And she slipped away.

Libby gave them the Grand Tour, twinkling at Rob as she talked. She didn't exactly lisp, but she was cuter than a bug's ear. She ignored Linda, though Rob told her twice that Sgt. Ramos would be taking charge of the investigation. He was there to observe. As a courtesy to a prominent taxpayer, though he didn't say that.

Linda maintained a look of polite interest through the great room, two of the "studies," and the first three bedrooms. Two techs left the tour at the study Frank August used. They drooped over his computer, emitting faint buzzes of satisfaction. The third deputy, Niles Larson, a new recruit, followed Linda and the lady of the house into the master suite. The bedroom was just a very large room with very large furniture and an unmade bed.

Libby glanced at the bed. "The housekeeper came late. Sorry for the mess. She's been off two days."

Linda said, "Can we hope she hasn't done the laundry?"

Libby picked up a garment that looked like a negligee and tossed it at the bed. "I imagine she did a wash Sunday before she left."

"Hmm."

"Well, that's the master bedroom. I'll show you the other wing, but it's just more bedrooms and the bookroom. Oh, and the media room. Gerd's staying in the guest house. He's the wine maker. Gerhard Koeppel."

Linda was nosing through a door.

"Hey, where do you think you're going?"

"Is this the dressing room?"

"What if it is?"

"It looks as if someone tossed the place. Have you had an intruder?"

"No! I was trying. To find. My leopard-print pants." Libby's voice went up half an octave with each phrase. "Get the hell out of my closet!"

Rob and Niles exchanged glances. Niles looked alarmed. Rob smiled at him and followed Libby into the next room. It was as large as most people's master bedrooms and featured two room-length walk-in closets with dressers against the interior closet walls. There was a sink and mirror in the dressing room proper, along with a loveseat, a dressing table with a triad mirror, and assorted domestic devices, one of which looked like a boot-jack and another like a pants press. Rob saw a treadmill and weights of the kind women used to tone their arms. Full-length mirrors hung on the closet doors as in a funhouse at the state fair. One closet gaped open. Garments strewed the floor and every other flat surface.

"You can't go into the bathroom," Libby protested.

Linda said something.

"No, that's *my* toothbrush. What are you doing in there? Come out! I'll report you to…"

Rob couldn't decide whether Mrs. August was thick as a plank or just distracted. Niles was still ogling the dressing room. He had recently built a house with his own hands. Seven hundred and fifty square feet of perfect living space. Its footprint would have fit into the dressing room.

Having tried outrage without result, Madam dissolved into sobs. Linda ignored her and kept poking away in the monumental bathroom. All she wanted were samples of DNA—toothbrush, hairbrush, ear pick. Rob let his eyes roam over the dressing room until he spotted what might be a laundry chute. He opened the little square door. Sure enough, an overflowing hamper lay below in what had to be a utility room.

At that point Jane stuck her head into the dressing room and snickered. "Wonderful room, isn't it?"

"A miracle," Rob said, "of rare device."

She laughed but sobered quickly when he mentioned their need for clothing her father had worn recently. Unwashed. "Irma's about to start the laundry. I'll go down and stop her, shall I?"

"Please do."

Jane vanished. Rob decided he liked her. He was willing to bet that she got along well with her appalling stepmother. Some people were born friendly. Nor did she twinkle or lisp.

Now that Linda was on course to do the job she'd come to do, Rob abandoned Libby to her. Linda meant to find out which of Frank August's garments were missing—the message Jane had sent Rob was vague about that—even if it meant going through everything in both walk-in closets.

Rob took Niles down with him to the utility room. They found Jane and the housekeeper, a plump woman of forty with flashing eyes, deep in conversation over the silent washing machine. Jane introduced them, and Rob thanked *Señora* Castro for her cooperation. He did a bit of twinkling himself, and it seemed to work.

When Niles had bagged the clothing Jane identified as her father's, Rob asked her to show them the garage. The garage was a last resort. The house showed no signs of a struggle, nor was it unnaturally clean as if someone had tidied up after a fight.

The garage was ambiguous. There seemed to be a lot of dried mud on the slab that led to it. It had rained before August disappeared. The three vehicles in residence were Jane's Prius, Libby's Jeep, and the wine maker's BMW. There were other means of locomotion, of course—mountain bikes hanging from the wall, a couple of snowmobiles, a golf cart, three wind-surfing boards along the wall and one atop the Jeep, a big rack of skis, both cross-country and downhill, snowboards, and a forlorn scooter of the kind Rob associated with little kids. A leftover from some visiting guest? As far as Rob knew, August had no grandchildren. An extra freezer and refrigerator stood along the side wall beside the door to the house, and the back wall featured a long work bench with tools hung neatly above it.

The spot reserved for the SUV lay between Jane's hybrid and the Beamer, with another blank spot for a guest car. Libby had parked her Jeep right beside the small door that led into the house. Rob stood under the wide, wide garage doors and squinted into semi-darkness to take an overview. When he knelt for a closer look at the concrete floor, Jane flipped the light switch on for him. Dried mud in two colors. A couple of stains.

He creaked to his feet after a long, futile scrutiny. It was late to find clear signs of movement in and out, but the techs needed to analyze the stains. The tread marks looked blurred, overridden. He would have liked to ask Jack Redfern to check the place. Jack was the best tracker in the county.

According to Jane, all the resident cars had come and gone since Sunday, the Jeep several times, and her brother's rental car, a Lexus, had left early Monday morning. Rob would need to talk to Frank, Jr., of course. He made a mental note to ask the young man whether the SUV had still been in place when he left for the airport.

He indicated the BMW. "I see Mr. Koeppel's car is here. We should probably interview him next. Then Linda will want to talk with you and Mrs. August at greater length." Rob explained that he had an afternoon court appearance.

"Oh dear, Gerd is down at the farm. He's a friend of Russell Hough. Russ had a medical appointment this morning, so Gerd is filling in for him across the highway."

"Filling in?"

"Supervising the work crew. They're harvesting veggies of some kind. Apparently Bill Hough was so erratic in his latter days that Russell had to recruit a whole new batch of workers after the suicide. He's training them. They're inexperienced and mostly speak Spanish. I doubt that either Russell or Gerd plucks onions, but somebody has to be there most of the time."

"Sounds as if Hough chose a bad time to sprain his ankle."

"He did. He's planning to remove the remaining cherry trees from the orchard, though that work's just beginning, but surely he won't drive a bulldozer himself. All of this is according to Gerd."

"Kind of Mr. Koeppel to help his friend. Doesn't he have work to do for your father?"

"He will in a couple of weeks, certainly. At the moment, he just confers with Tom Dahl, the vineyard manager, and keeps track of the ripening process—" She interrupted herself. "For heaven's sake, take whatever I say with a heap of salt. I know less than nothing about oenology."

"Me neither." Rob picked his way alongside the Beamer to the bike rack. "Who uses the mountain bikes?"

"I don't know. Let's ask Libby." She stood at his elbow, frowning at the bicycles as if they were a fresh jigsaw puzzle. "I guarantee you my father doesn't ride a bike. Libby may."

Rob touched the wind-surfing board atop Libby's car. "She's a real athlete."

Jane nodded. "She may be small but she's as strong as an ox. Shall I call Gerd for you?"

"If you will."

She led him to the kitchen, which was as wonder-making as the dressing room, and out via a short hallway to the pool enclosure. She showed him where the guest house was and left to find her cell phone and call the wine maker.

The guest house was a cheerful mess, unlike the master dressing room, which had been an ill-tempered mess. Since the search warrant was comprehensive, Rob didn't hesitate to go inside, though he left Niles by the pool. He saw no sign of Frank August's presence, and didn't expect to. He did find indications that a woman had been there. Lip-gloss on a glass, a long blond hair on the sofa, faint flowery scent in the air, and something heavier beneath that. Not exactly damning, but thought-provoking.

He considered Libby August's big blue eyes and Jane's natural ash-blond hair, but it could have been any other woman—visiting? snogging? The bed lay on a loft above the sitting room. Rob climbed the ladder. Churned bedclothes suggested it had been left happily unmade all during Irma Castro's absence. So—the techs should check the sheets. Just on general principles. He returned to the living room.

Koeppel was a reader—most of the books and some magazines were in German, but enough were in English for Rob to gather that the wine maker had a butterfly mind. Popular thrillers, histories, science fiction blockbusters, and books on cookery sat beside printouts of scholarly articles, some on viticulture, others on wholly unrelated subjects like archaeology and primitivist art.

Rob picked up a paperback tome on Pacific Northwest Indians, consulted the index, and found a scatter of references to the Klalos. A trading culture, very wealthy at one time, language Chinookian, art in the great coastal tradition. Exogamous. Klalos looked to marry outside the band they were born to, even outside the tribe. The culture was matrilinear and mildly matriarchal at one time. Exposure to other tribes, especially those from the east, as well as to Christian missionaries, had eroded that eccentricity somewhat, but maternal descent still counted for a lot, and boys in traditional families were guided to manhood by mothers' brothers, not fathers.

Rob reread the page that dealt with family structure. Jack and Leon Redfern were maternal uncles to Bill Hough's children. Rob wondered what Hough, something of a racist, had made of that. Have to ask Jack.

Back to business. Rob spotted a modest flat-screen television and a DVD player with red Netflix envelopes beside it and thumbed through other film DVDs. Some German, some French, one English. Three Coen brothers' films including his own favorite, *Raising Arizona*. Funny, he'd always thought of that as quintessential American humor. Maybe German humor was similar. Maybe Gerhard Koeppel was just trying to understand what made Americans giggle.

Koeppel showed up half an hour later, and Rob took to him immediately from his toes to the cerise crest of his hair. The reverse was not true.

The wine maker protested invasion of his territory. Rob showed him the warrant. Koeppel was covered in dust from the fields. Grumbling, he retreated to the shower while Rob waited politely in the sitting area. Koeppel returned, freshly clothed and still grumbling, and sat across from Rob in an armchair that, like the rest of the furniture in the tiny guest house, must have been bought in a lot at IKEA. The big house was more expensively furnished, though not more imaginatively. Apparently Libby August was uninterested in interior decoration. She was an unusual combination of conflicting stereotypes, some of them clearly cultivated for effect.

Rob gave the wine maker a conciliating smile. "What do you think has happened to Mr. August?"

Koeppel shrugged. "No idea. He pleases himself."

"Did you see him after dinner Sunday evening?"

"No." He shifted in his seat. "I heard him. A car came in about half past ten. It was probably Frankie, er, the son. I heard a door slam and after a time two male voices raised in argument. I didn't hear what was said, but one of the voices must have been Herr August's."

"Did you then hear a car leaving?"

He looked away. "No, I went to sleep."

"Alone?" Rob maintained a matter-of-fact tone.

Koeppel's mouth set. "I went to bed alone," he said with the precision of truth.

And you were joined later by the lady or the daughter of the house. Nice.

The wine maker flushed as if he heard Rob's thought.

Rob let it go for the time being. "Tell me about the next morning."

Koeppel and Jane had walked down to the farmhouse through the cherry orchard, he said. He seemed genuinely pleased to reconnect with Russell Hough but reserved his greatest enthusiasm for Judith who was, he said, an angel. And, as an afterthought, her mother was a good cook.

Rob was amused. He wondered what Libby August thought of Koeppel's fresh infatuation—if she knew of it. Judith Hough might not be an angel, but she must at least be a cupcake. Amusement faded. She was also a hero, as her father had been.

With a sigh, Rob turned his mind back to the cherry orchard. He had Koeppel show him and Niles the fallen bough and the route he and Jane had walked. The gate, now open, had been closed when the two of them started out, he said. Did that mean anything? Jane had opened it when she rescued Russell, and probably hadn't closed it, because she hadn't driven back up to the syrah vineyard. Rob glanced at his watch. Time to check in with Linda. Time to leave.

~

HE had just returned from testifying in court to his office in the courthouse annex when Jack Redfern called him.

"You looking for a white vehicle?"

"Frank August's SUV."

"I was hiking up the west bank of the Choteau, past the bridge. Spotted a flash of white in a blackberry thicket on the east bank. Want to take a look?"

"You think it's a car?"

"Looks taller than a car. May be nothing. Lots of debris in those thickets at the end of summer. Still..."

If Jack thought investigation was called for, Rob would take a look. He said so. Jack said he'd walk across the bridge and wait on the east end.

Rob checked the charge on his cell phone and left without further ado. It was nearly five. A little detour to Two Falls wouldn't make him very late for dinner. On second thought... He hit the speed dial for Home and left Meg a message of warning and apology in case she'd decided to prepare something time-consuming and delicious. It seemed the prudent thing to do.

6.

HIMALAYAN BLACKBERRY is the Northwest equivalent of kudzu. The smaller native blackberry is less aggressive. By the time Rob reached him, Jack had tracked the vehicle in question down from the road, across a bumpy stretch of brush, and into one of the largest blackberry thickets Rob had seen, and he'd seen a lot.

Close up, it was clear that the bushes had been penetrated, but vicious brambles had snapped back, obscuring the vehicle itself and its path of entry almost completely. Bits of white showed if you squinted. Drivers up on the road would see nothing amiss or imagine they saw sun reflecting from rock. Rob suspected that the car would be equally invisible from the air. It had to be the missing SUV. He groaned.

Jack gave him a sympathetic grin. "You'll need hedge clippers, friend."

Rob shut his eyes, drew a long breath, exhaled, and breathed in again.

"Yoga?"

"Take a sniff. Do you smell anything like the three-day-old corpse of a banker?"

"No. No, I don't." They stared at each other. Jack was

frowning. "Want me to edge around by the river? Might be able to see more from there. I caught a glimpse of white from across the way, remember."

"Thanks but no, I'd better call for the crime scene van. We'll cut a corridor through the blackberries." So as not to disturb what evidence there was of the vehicle's entry. "This is going to take a while." Rob sent for the technicians, then rang Meg's cell phone again and left another message. While he waited for his backup, he led Jack through his actions and reactions, step by step, and between them they came up with a formal statement. Jack was happy to leave when he'd signed it.

⌒

THE call from the undersheriff came on the landline just as Jane was about to turn in. Jane answered because Libby hadn't yet come home from the river, or wherever she was, and Gerd had already gone to the guest house. Alone. Probably thinking about Judith Hough's beauty.

Neill spoke rather formally, asking for Mrs. August.

It took a second, but when Jane recognized his voice, she shifted into formal mode herself. "I'm sorry. She's not home at the moment. May I take a message?"

He hesitated.

Jane's blood ran cold. "Have you found Dad? Is he...he's all right, isn't he?"

"We found the SUV around six. It's been towed to the county lot for forensic tests, but there was no obvious sign of your father in it. It's a puzzle, in fact."

"What do you mean by puzzle?"

"It was found just east of the Choteau bridge—the one on Miller Road." Miller Road was the name of the main road on the "scenic route." "It was almost in the river."

"But that's crazy. I must have driven over that bridge twice, coming and going, since he vanished, and I didn't see anything like the SUV. Was it driven there today?"

"We think it was abandoned a couple of days ago with the engine running." He explained about the obscuring blackberry thicket. "The gas tank was empty, and the driver's door was open—half-open anyway."

"And the front end was almost in the river? But how did the car get into the thicket? It doesn't make sense."

"Then you see what I mean by puzzle. The door's open, as if someone got out, but we found no footprints and no trace of anyone moving through the surrounding brambles. Finding footprints would be chancy in there at any time, but I think we would have found fabric and probably blood on those blackberry thorns if someone had tried to get out. They're as sharp as stilettos. We'll look again, of course, in daylight, but we did bring in lights this evening. We could see pretty well."

"Good heavens." Jane closed her eyes, trying without success to imagine the scene. "What do you think happened?"

He gave a heavy sigh. "I'd rather not speculate until the technicians have had a good look. Your father's a relatively small man. He may have shielded himself from the brambles with his jacket and slipped into the river."

"Suicide?" she croaked. She was having trouble drawing breath.

"Or confusion, if he hit his head. The airbag on the driver's side didn't deploy. The one on the passenger side did, which is odd."

"Dad hates airbags—an airbag broke his nose once in a minor wreck. He may have deactivated the one on the driver's side and forgotten about it, forgotten to warn me, I mean. I'm the one who usually drives the SUV."

"Yes, you did say so. Is it an easy car to drive?"

"Duck soup. It's all-wheel drive. Was it in Drive when it was found?"

"It was."

Jane felt a headache forming. "Maybe there was nobody in it when it crashed through the blackberries."

Neill made a noncommittal sound.

At least he didn't laugh at me. Jane's mind raced. "Are you going to drag the river?"

Neill gave another audible sigh. "I'm going to consult Jack Redfern first." He explained Redfern's record as a tracker and his special knowledge of the Choteau. "That's a white-water stretch, so dragging the river above the bridge would be pointless. Jack will know where to look."

For a body floating downstream. Jane took a gulp of air.

Neill was saying farewell phrases, again rather formal. He would call Mrs. August in the morning, he said.

"I'll warn her," Jane promised.

When he had hung up, she found a Post-it, wrote Libby a note, and stuck it to the master bedroom door. She needed someone to talk to, but when she looked out toward the guest house, she saw that Gerd's lights were off. For a brief mad moment, she considered calling Russell Hough. However, she saw no signs of life at Hawk Farm either. Their lights always went off early. Farmers' hours had to be the opposite of bankers' hours. Jane called her mother.

~

RUSS was finally asleep. His hands lay slack on the sheet. Judith stood in the darkened hall watching him through her night goggles. They gave everything in the living room a green cast. The farmhouse was dark. Her brother frowned in his sleep as if he were in pain or worried about something.

The wheelchair waited beside the hide-a-bed with the new walking cast sitting on it. The cast snapped on and off. In a few days, he would be able to use the artificial leg and move back upstairs. Right now, though, he was not much better off than he had been. She supposed that meant the wine maker would continue to hang around. She didn't know what to feel about Gerd.

She didn't know what to feel about her brother either. She'd been angry with him for pretending to be dead. No, he hadn't pretended. He'd allowed everyone to believe he was dead, which was almost the same. Or was it just that Bill Hough had believed his son dead, and the force of her father's conviction had persuaded everyone else? Except Alice. Except Jack.

Russ must have been in touch with their Uncle Jack all along—Judith had figured out that much. Why not with Alice? Judith turned a simple truth over in her mind. If Russ had wanted to vanish without a trace, he would not have told Alice where he meant to go, because she had never been able to lie to her husband.

What difference does it make? With an impatient shrug, Judith moved to the front door, which she had left ajar, and eased out of the house. The night was clear and moonless, the stars brilliant. A breeze kissed her cheeks. When she had crept soundlessly down from the porch, she made her way to her accustomed post at the back of the garage. Then she took out the pistol.

Her father had given it to her for her sixteenth birthday. It was a lady's gun, he'd said, pretty but useless, a .22, engraved, an antique with a grip of real ivory. They didn't make ivory grips these days, thanks to the spotted owl brigade. He would teach her to shoot it.

He didn't. He forgot. Her boyfriend, Denny, took her out one afternoon to pot beer cans, though. He said she was a natural. *Must be genetic.* She'd laughed at the compliment, if that's what it was. Denny didn't like her father.

Bill had shown him the door shortly after that, so she'd practiced on her own, on the sly, until she had confidence. The pistol was in no way equal to the AK-47 Russ had made her lock in the gun cabinet, but it was better than nothing. He didn't know she had it.

She checked the .22 to make sure there was no shell in the chamber, then began her surveillance. The August house was mostly dark. Dim blurs of light showed in the second story, night lights. The pool area was dark, too, and the guest house where Gerd lived. Nothing and no one moved. That was good. She wanted calm. No more incursions. This was her place. She would keep it secure.

She stopped as she neared the closed gate to the syrah vineyard. *Was that an engine?* The distant slam of a car door touched her hearing—and the faint rumble of the garage door mechanism. A light turned on in the August house. *Must be the hall light. Someone just came home. Mrs. August. Wait a minute. What if it's the old man? He's still missing, isn't he?*

Judith eased her grasp on the handgun as the distant hoot of a train reminded her of her earlier blunder. There would be no wild shots this time. She cocked her head, pistol pointing down. Another hoot. A pause. And the last *woo-woo* as the train rattled, passing through. She let out her breath with slow deliberation. The train was a long one. They were shipping coal these days, lots of it. *Stripping the nation of its natural reserves.* She could almost hear Bill Hough's rant.

A flare of light from the August house, above and to her left as she faced it, caught her unawares. She dropped flat, face down, but no blast followed, no deafening explosion, no anguished shrieks.

Shaking, she ripped off the night goggles and saw that the light was mild and steady. Just the lights from the pool enclosure, probably triggered by motion. She could hear, too. If there had been an explosion she would have been deaf.

But then a high piercing voice, female, rang out, and a lower voice called, making soothing sounds. A light switched on, this one in the guest house, and she heard Gerd's tenor calling. Then all the lights flashed on.

Eyes clenched shut, Judith squirmed her way downhill until she lay beyond the pool of light from the big house. She stood on quaking legs and holstered the pistol. Then she ran, stumbling and sobbing, away from the light, from the shrieks on the hill and the screams in her head.

Halfway down, she had to stop so she could throw up. She vomited until she tasted only bile. After that she walked and jogged, walked and jogged. When she reached the porch she knew what she had to do.

By that time she was making no attempt to keep quiet. Her breath came in rasps that tore at her throat. She let the door slam, bumped her knee against the hall table and howled at the pain, stumbled into the kitchen, and sank onto the nearest chair, not her chair at all, her father's chair, the one they didn't sit in. *Well, that was only right.* She raised the pistol to her temple. She could hear her heart beat. Thud. Click. *Empty chamber.*

"No!" she screamed. "No-o-o!" and felt the push of air behind her, someone shouting. So she pulled the trigger, and everything went blessedly black.

～

TELEPHONE. Maddie cocked a bleary eye at the alarm clock on her bedside table. *Past midnight. Emergency? Wrong number.* She listened to the second ring. *Not the landline, not her cell.* "Jack."

Jack slept the sleep of the just. She heard his even breathing, felt his warm bulk beside her.

She touched his shoulder. "Wake up. Answer your phone. Now!" It rang again, *brrng brrng.* Jack didn't like his phone to play music. In fact, he didn't like his phone at all. Maddie wondered why it was on. Something to do with the August SUV maybe. Jack would put up with the phone to oblige Rob Neill. She poked again harder.

He groped for the cell. "H'lo."

Maddie heard the rumble of a male voice.

"Ambulance?" Jack croaked, and the voice answered. "On my way." He sat up slowly, dug at his eyes with the heels of his hands.

"What is it?"

"Judy. Shot herself."

"That was Russ?" *Who else?* Maddie was too stunned to feel. Her mind turned to Alice. "I'm coming, too. Is Judy...?" She didn't want to say the word *dead.*

"I don't know. Alice called 911. I think Russ was crying."

It was half an hour before they reached the farm. They met the ambulance headed the other direction just east of Two Falls. It was running flat out, lights whirling. The siren bleated. Jack pulled off the road, and they sat without speaking until the emergency vehicle was a white dot in the mirrors.

Maddie cleared her throat. "A good sign."

Jack grunted and hit the accelerator.

When they got to the farm, he skidded the pickup to the porch steps, jumped out, and ran for the back door, which was wide open. The lights were on downstairs.

It took Maddie a while to undo the seat belt and climb out. A short hall led past the utility room to the kitchen. When she reached the swinging door she stopped dead.

The kitchen was awash in browning blood, and a chair and the wheelchair, both overturned, lay beside the round oak table. Jack knelt by his nephew. Russ was sitting on the floor propped in the corner between the wall and the refrigerator, both legs stretched out. The stump of his left leg and the Ace bandage binding his ankle were smeared with blood. A trail of dried blood showed where he'd dragged himself.

"She bled all over me." Russell sounded exhausted. "Ma rode with her in the ambulance."

Maddie understood Jack's alarm. The boxers and T-shirt Russ had apparently been sleeping in were stiff with drying blood. Both hands were bloody to the elbow, and his eyes looked like holes burned in a blanket.

"You sure you're all right, Rusty?" Jack hadn't called Russell by that affectionate nickname in at least two decades.

"I'm sure. And the EMTs checked." He shoved himself straighter, grimacing. "Will you help me into the wheelchair? I couldn't manage it by myself."

"You *are* hurt!"

"I bumped my foot on the way down."

"The way down? What happened?"

He shut his eyes and kept them shut. "I'll tell you every-thing, but let me clean up first." *I'm weltering in my sister's blood.* Maddie heard that as clearly as if he'd said it. "Will you drive me to the hospital?"

"Of course," Jack said.

Maddie looked around the desecrated kitchen. "Is there any reason I shouldn't mop up the blood?"

"It's not evidence. I don't think they prosecute attempted

suicide these days." Russ's mouth twisted. "It's not as if there's property involved. Even if..."

Even if she dies. The thought skittered among them like a rat in the pantry.

Abruptly, Russ changed his mind. "I'll call and ask if I can move the wheelchair. Phone's on the table."

The cordless phone was sticky with blood, probably from Russ's hands. Maddie wiped it clean on a napkin and gave it to him. After two tries, he poked out 911.

He explained who he was in a voice that sounded calmer than he looked, listening with a frown as the dispatcher responded. "Okay. No, my aunt and uncle are here with me. Thanks." He thumbed the phone off. "Patrol car on the way. Said we should wait for it." Hands still shaking, he set the phone on the floor. Tears leaked down his face. He made no attempt to wipe them away, was probably not aware of them.

Maddie said, "You'll need clothes, Russ. Where?"

"Utility room. On the folding table. Shoes on the floor in the living room." He gave a shaky laugh. "Leg on the floor in the living room."

"I'll take everything into the bathroom. What about Alice?"

"She's with Judy," he said stupidly.

"Yes. Does she need something to wear?"

"Oh. Yeah, she's in her nightgown. She was downstairs before the echo of the gunshot died."

"Suitcase?"

"My room. Upstairs."

It was a huge relief to leave the kitchen.

The patrol car took half an hour to come. Maddie had plenty of time to gather clothes together. She found Russ's small wheeled suitcase in the closet of the room that had been his when he was a boy, the room from which Bill Hough had erased every sign of his son's existence. Apart from a few clothes in the closet, a couple of paperbacks, and a technical journal—something about botany—on the night table, there was no sign that Russ had moved back

He doesn't want to be here, she reflected. She had assumed he couldn't wait to come home, but the room said otherwise. She wondered who and what he had left behind.

She was bumping the suitcase down the stairs when the patrol car arrived. Jack went out to meet the officers. She heard his voice in the yard. As she reached the hall, a young woman in uniform entered, followed by Jack and Maddie's nephew Todd Welch in plain clothes. Her sister's son. The uniformed deputy carried a camera, Todd a recorder.

Todd was a detective now full-time and had taken the sergeant's exam. He smiled at Maddie and gave her a peck on the cheek. She asked him why he was out in a patrol car in the middle of the night.

"I'm on night shift this week. I heard the first call and hitched a ride with Kitty." Todd introduced the uniformed deputy, Catherine Grant. She inclined her head but didn't say anything. "Judith shot herself?"

"Yes. Russ called Jack."

"I see. I'm sorry. She's a real hero." He rubbed his nose. "I don't remember Russell. He'd left by the time I got to high school. I guess we're cousins."

"Courtesy cousins. Russ is the son of Jack's sister." She said that, though Todd knew it. She was reminding him of the closeness of that bond, drawing Jack's protection around Russell, if he needed it. *Maybe he did. Of course he did. He needed any help he could get.*

"And the son of William Hough," said Deputy Grant. Todd grimaced.

Maddie said, "I believe Judith found her father's body. You ought to take that into account."

"Bill Hough also shot himself," Todd said. He was speaking to Grant, but Maddie said, "Yes."

Todd went to the kitchen door, took a deep breath, and walked in with Kitty Grant at his heels.

Maddie dumped the suitcase in the utility room, found Russ's clothes in neatly folded stacks on a table beside the dryer, and followed Todd to the kitchen, which was just as horrible as it had been when she left it.

Kitty Grant was taking pictures of Russ. She stood over him with Jack at her elbow. She said she wanted Russ out of the room, speaking to Todd as if no one else was there. Maddie wondered what was going on with the two cops. Jack cleared his throat.

"I could crawl," Russ said without sarcasm.

Grant turned to Jack. "Help him up, Mr. Redfern."

"He needs the wheelchair."

"Can't move it." She spoke with complacence. *I am the Law.* Jack frowned. Russell didn't stir. He'd shut his eyes again.

"Where's Wally's scooter?" Maddie interjected. *Russ wasn't thinking. Nobody was.*

"Living room." Russ opened his eyes. "Bring the walking cast and my leg, will you, Aunt Maddie?"

She complied. The living room bore witness to his haste in leaving it. Bedclothes bunched on the floor. The cast lay half-way across the room as if he'd hit it when he groped for the wheelchair. She found the prosthesis near the pillow end of the couch-bed.

She sat in the motorized scooter, drove it to the kitchen, stopping out of range of the blood splatters, and dismounted. The deputies gawked at Russ as he strapped on the artificial leg and snapped the walking cast around his injured foot. He ignored them.

Jack and Todd helped him to his feet. *Foot.* Maddie corrected herself. Though Russ was no more than an inch over six feet, he was the tallest one in the room when he stood. They installed him on the scooter, and he backed it out of the kitchen. Maddie brought his clothes to the huge, old-fashioned bathroom.

"Do you need anything else?"

"No. Thank you. Out."

"That deputy wants to interview you."

"Fuck her." He shut the door. She waited until she heard the shower.

She supposed bad temper was preferable to incoherent shock. Maybe Deputy Grant knew what she was doing, provoking him. Nevertheless, Miss Kitty set Maddie's teeth on edge.

Maddie went back to the utility room to double-check that she'd covered Alice's needs and decided she ought to pretend optimism and take clothes for Judy, too. That involved another trip upstairs. When she came down, Russell was still taking the world's longest shower, running the hot water out. If the strobing lights in the kitchen were an indication, Kitty was still taking photographs.

In fact, Todd, not Deputy Grant, conducted the interview. The two officers followed the scooter into the living room when Russ finally emerged clothed and wearing both the cast and the prosthesis—full armor. Maddie was prepared to join the party, but Todd waved her off.

She felt her own temper flare. "Russell is an enrolled member of the tribe."

"Since when?" The Klalos were emphatically exogamous, and everyone knew Bill Hough had been invited to enroll as Alice's husband, but he had declined to join the tribe and refused to enroll his children.

"Since the day he turned eighteen—by mother-right. His choice."

"We're taking a witness statement, Chief Thomas." Deputy Grant spoke with exaggerated patience.

Madeline gave her a sweet smile. "Exactly."

Owing to the sometimes uneasy relationship between the tribe and the police, the sheriff's department under the McCormicks had taken to allowing Klalos to call on the chief as a witness when they were subject to questioning in a serious matter. When Bill Hough killed himself and his wife and daughter were questioned, neither had asked Maddie for help, but the possibility had been there. However, back when Russell had left Latouche County seventeen long years before, relations between the Klalos and the department had been less cordial.

She was not surprised that Russell said, "I'd appreciate the chief's presence, and my uncle's."

"We won't interrupt," Maddie promised, though she knew very well that if she was moved to speak she would.

Miss Kitty opened her mouth to object, but Todd shrugged.

"All right." He looked around the living room, which was short of chairs.

Russ said, "All of you can sit if you toss the rest of the bed-clothes on the floor and put the bed back in couch formation." It was a hide-a-bed, and the springs sagged.

Jack helped Todd reconfigure the couch, and they were eventually all seated, Russell still on the scooter, Jack and Maddie on the couch, and the deputies in the two armchairs with the recorder on the small table between them. Bill Hough's gun cabinet lurked in the corner by the fireplace. Maddie noted what looked like a brand-new padlock.

Todd mumbled the usual date, time, and names. "Okay, Mr. Hough, tell us what happened. From the beginning."

Russ stared at him as if he'd lost his mind. Maddie knew what Russ was thinking. Judy was his baby sister. He'd been ten when she was born, the right age to find a baby funny or repulsive, certainly memorable. *That* was the beginning.

"What happened this evening?" Todd, patient.

"She s-shot herself. In the h-head."

"Before that."

Russell shivered. He cleared his throat. "My mother went up to bed around ten-thirty. I'd had a long day. I turned in, too, read for a while. Around eleven-thirty my eyes started to go out of focus. I read the same paragraph twice, so I turned the light off. I was out cold before midnight. Something woke me, maybe the train. The whistle is louder downstairs than up in the bedrooms. When the train stopped rattling, I could hear noises outside the house."

"Noises?"

"Someone gasping and sort of whimpering. I knew it was Judy, and…"

"How?"

"How… She's been in the habit of taking a walk in the dark. I didn't think twice about it until I noticed how quiet she was, coming and going. Last week I decided I'd confront her. That was after I'd hurt my foot, so I was already downstairs."

"Last week?"

"Yes. I heard her go out, and I waited in the dark—in the hall. She didn't notice me when she came in. She'd taken off her night-vision goggles, so I surprised her when I wheeled into the kitchen. She was armed."

"Armed?"

"She was carrying a Kalashnikov rifle, my father's famous AK-47," his mouth twisted, "and it was loaded."

"My God."

"Yeah. We had a talk." He swallowed as if his throat was dry. "I told her I could understand why she needed to check things out, but I thought I persuaded her guns were better locked up. I said I wouldn't tell anyone what she'd been doing. I had no idea she had another weapon. You know she was in Afghanistan?"

"Yes."

"Well, she has trouble sleeping—nightmares when she does fall asleep, and trouble falling asleep in the first place. She said it's been worse since my father's death, damn him to hell." He choked.

No one spoke. Grant stared.

At last he went on, dogged, "She got so she couldn't rest until she'd checked that the place was secure, the farmhouse, the garage, the orchard. She'd put on her night-goggles, take up the rifle, and go out like a sentry to patrol the grounds. She admitted she'd never seen anything suspicious."

"But she kept it up?" Todd asked.

"It's a compulsion. My father installed an electric fence when Mr. August built the house on the bluff. The Augusts never bothered us, you know, whatever Dad said. Neither did deer, after the fence went in."

Todd gave a faint smile. Deer are farmers' number-one enemy. Grant asked a clueless question about deer and Todd answered though the question had been aimed at Russell.

Russ rubbed at his forehead. When Todd didn't say anything more, he went on, "I decided to remove the orchard. It's diseased. My crew harvested the cherries last week. I'll be taking out the rest of the trees next week, so I turned the electric fence off. That's the only thing I can think of."

"What do you mean?" Grant asked.

"The only thing different. She saw something tonight that upset her—so much that she was running and crying, making a hell of a racket. She doesn't do that. When I heard her coming, I threw myself into the wheelchair and raced for the kitchen. I got there in time to see her sit in my father's chair and raise that dinky little handgun to her temple. She pulled the trigger. I could see her finger move, but the chamber must have been empty. If it hadn't been—" He broke off.

Nobody said anything. Jack was watching his nephew.

Russ drew a huge breath. "So I rammed her with the wheelchair. I was trying to jar her hand upward. I did—some."

"The EMTs—"

"They said the bullet tore across the top of her skull. The gun went off while I was grabbing for her, and we both fell, Judy on top of me. I guess the gun dropped to the floor, too. She was bleeding like a slaughtered pig. Christ." He buried his face in his hands. After a long moment, he pulled them down and said in a dead voice, "Is that all? I want to go to the hospital."

Todd took him through the story again patiently, and Russ answered, patiently. Todd asked a few more desultory questions. Grant was frowning at Todd. The frown deepened when he said Russ could leave, but she at least didn't contradict him.

Maddie had been thinking. She touched Jack's hand. "Can you drive Russ's car?"

"Sure."

"Why not take him in that? It's less cramped than the pickup. I'll stay and clean the kitchen for Alice. She shouldn't come home to this. Then I'll join you at the hospital."

Jack thought it through, agreed, and rose. He gave her the keys to the pickup and kissed her on the cheek. His lips were cold.

Todd was packing up the recorder. "You said Judith saw something that scared her?"

Russ nodded, shoulders slumped. "Must have."

"I wonder what was going on up the hill. We found August's SUV this afternoon." Todd shifted his gaze. "Hey, you know that, Uncle Jack."

Jack shook his head. "Seems like three days ago."

"Did you tell the chief about it?"

"Sure."

Russ was frowning. "First I've heard. Did they find the old man?"

"No."

Russ returned to Judy's flight through the orchard. "What were you suggesting, Todd?"

"Neill only got around to calling next of kin after he came back to the courthouse—after ten. If one of them was out somewhere this evening, they wouldn't know. They might have come in at midnight. There would have been lights and voices, lots of activity, for a while at any rate."

Russell shook his head. "I don't see why that would bother Judy, but I obviously don't do a good job of reading her mind. I'll call Gerd in the morning. He'll know what went on at the August place." He bit his lip. "He's going to be shaken. He's in love with Judy. Christ."

7.

IRMA CAME IN bright and cheerful that morning. Jane concluded that the press had not yet heard about the SUV. Their presence had dwindled. By afternoon, the full regiment would invest the mailbox again, banners flying.

Irma made batter for waffles and turned one out for Jane, who had wakened at eight, groggy after her stepmother's midnight theatrics. Gerd might be able to sleep in. Libby certainly would.

When Jane had eaten her waffle and said words of praise, she told Irma to expect the sheriff's department again and why. She half imagined the chef would walk out, but Irma was surprisingly sympathetic.

The two of them talked themselves hoarse over the bewildering discovery of the empty SUV. They had given up trying to make sense of it and gone on to plan dinner when Gerd stumbled in from the guest house. He was muttering in German.

"What is it, Gerd?"

"Russell…he called from the hospice, I mean the *Kranken-haus*, the hospital."

"Oh, no, has he hurt his foot again?"

"He says…said his *Schwester*—" He broke off, collapsed onto a kitchen chair, and began weeping onto his clenched fists.

"Gerd!"

"I quit, I tell you. I am going home." He wiped his sleeve across his nose. "*Verdammte Amerikaner!* You leave guns in the hands of children and *berserkers*. I wish you all in hell with your *verdammte* Constitution."

"Gerhard," Jane said gently, "please stop raving and tell me what happened."

"Oh, Judith, Judith." He pronounced the name in the German way. *Yudit, Yudit.*

When she figured out what he was saying, Jane's blood ran cold. "Tell me what happened to Judith."

"She tried to kill herself last night."

"Oh, no," Jane whispered. She was shocked, horrified. Ultimately, she was unsurprised. She thought of Russell and Alice and felt terrible, curdling pity. And there was nothing she could do. "Ohhhh…"

"She tried with a small handgun to shoot herself here." Gerd tapped his temple. "Infallibly fatal."

"She's dead?"

"Alive. Just." He choked on the words. "Russell managed to deflect her hand up. He cannot stand, of course. He uses…used the wheelchair to bump her and reached for her elbow. So." He illustrated. "The shot goes off. They both fall together to the floor. He is holding her, and she bleeds all over him."

Irma made a gasping sound and ran from the room. Gerd was crying.

"Did he say why—"

"I do not know," Gerd choked. "I turn off the phone. I am angry, you understand. I shall say something unforgivable, so I break the connection. Now I must go to the hospital. At once, Jane. I must apologize to Russ, and hear more of Judith. I cannot drive."

Jane volunteered, of course. He was in no condition to drive—or do anything else. He wanted her to take his BMW, but she insisted on using the Prius. *She* was in no condition to wrestle with an unfamiliar car.

She made good time to Klalo, in spite of the five minutes she took getting dressed to go out. She parked in the Emergency lot, but they soon found themselves on the second floor of the hospital in the Intensive Care waiting room. It was empty when they entered, and the nurse had told them they would not be permitted to visit Judith, so they stood and stared at each other until Jane couldn't stand it any longer. She went to the window—it gave on the parking lot—and looked out at the sunlit asphalt and the glittering tops of the cars.

She didn't hear Russell enter in the wheelchair.

"Russ!" Gerd's voice made her turn.

"Gerhard." Russell gave Jane a tentative smile. "Thank you both for coming."

She inclined her head, unable to speak. There had been no virtue in her coming. Gerd had dragooned her. All the same she was glad she'd come, glad to see Russ, even though he looked exhausted and beyond sad.

He turned to Gerd. "I'm sorry I dumped all that on you. I was too tired to think—"

"No, my friend, it is I who must apologize. Tell me how it is with your sister."

He thrust a hand through his straight black hair. It flopped over his forehead. "They operated to relieve pressure on the brain. The shot cracked her skull—like an egg, I guess. Hairline fracture, not depressed."

"That's good, isn't it?" Jane said.

"There was swelling. She's unconscious." He spoke in jerky phrases. "I have to go in soon. So Alice can get something to eat. But I need to ask you both. What was going on up there around midnight? Something spooked Judy. We don't know what it was."

"Spooked?" Gerd sounded bewildered.

"Startled," Jane suggested. Russ threw her a grateful smile. She smiled back. "Have you heard that Dad's SUV was found yesterday?"

"Yes. Jack—" He wheeled closer. "My uncle was the one

who spotted it. He fishes the Choteau. He told me about it when he drove me here."

"Oh, Mr. Redfern. Of course." Jane glanced at Gerd, but he was watching Russell with an expression of deep anxiety. She went on, "Robert Neill called around ten last evening, asking for my stepmother. He told me about your uncle and what they'd discovered, and I promised to tell Libby. I left a note for her when I went to bed. She came home at midnight."

Russell didn't look enlightened, but he didn't know Libby.

"When she saw my note, she let out a shriek…well, a series of shrieks. She shook the house, but surely the noise wouldn't have carried as far as your place, and anyway one of the trains came through around then. I got up to calm her. Gerd woke, too, and turned his lights on. When he came across to the house, he triggered the pool enclosure lights and turned on the hall and kitchen lights, too."

At that point a haunted-looking couple stuck their heads in the room and withdrew without speaking. Probably looking for the nurses' station.

Jane shook her head to clear it. There wasn't much else to say. "Apart from the hoorah, which didn't last long, that's all that happened last evening. Libby was just dramatizing."

Russell sighed. "And nobody saw anything going on down in the orchard?"

"Not that I know."

Gerd also said *no*. "I went to bed well before midnight. Until Libby began to scream, I heard nothing."

"I'll ask Libby what she saw," Jane promised. "Maybe her car lights picked something out when she drove in."

Russell thanked her, and he and Gerd talked a few minutes more about a message Gerd would convey to the crew at Hawk Farm. Jane and Gerd left shortly after that. There was nothing else they could do for the Hough family. For no reason, Jane flashed on her father. He would not have wanted her to do anything for them.

When they reached home, Jane found Libby up and drooping over a waffle.

There was a text on the phone from her brother. He was coming back. He'd reach the Portland airport a little after two and rent a car again. He must be maxing out his credit cards while they still worked. Jane supposed bankers had more leeway on the primrose path to bankruptcy than other people, a spiteful thought. She suppressed it. She was very sorry for him. It was interesting that he chose to contact Libby and not his sister. Jane wondered whether the hypothetical affair was ongoing.

~

AT two, Rob Neill finally sat down at his desk after a morning of to-ing and fro-ing. He ate the sandwich he'd brought from home, drank a cup of decent coffee some kind soul had got for him from Sufficient Grounds, and ignored the stack of routine papers in his in-box in favor of working his two jigsaw puzzles— the August MisPers case and Judith Hough's heart-wrenching attempt at suicide.

As he sorted through the files looking for the reports his deputies had submitted after they responded to Russell Hough's 911 call, he called his wife on the landline. He found Deputy Grant's photographs of the scene as the phone rang the fourth time and clicked to the message recorder. He left a brief greeting, hung up, and squinted at the all-too-vivid photographs.

About Judith Rob felt helpless rather than guilty. There was no case and would be no further investigation.

Like father like daughter. That was the big puzzle. Why would an attractive young woman who'd enjoyed flirting with the boys in her English class, the daughter of a beautiful and by all accounts virtuous mother, mimic her father at all? Even more remarkable was the extent to which Judith had succeeded. And yet her brother had apparently felt no urge to imitate either parent and could not wait to escape the old homestead with no regrets or apologies.

Rob backed away from that. That was the situation as it appeared. What had happened in reality was anyone's guess.

The phone rang. He picked it up. "Hi, sweetheart."

Meg laughed. "What do you say when the sheriff calls you? 'Hi, Mom'?"

"I have suitable endearments for all regular callers."

They talked for a while about nothing much. Rob basked in the sound of her voice. Finally he said, "How's your foray into classification going?"

The library was considering a partial or complete switch from Dewey Decimal to the Library of Congress classification system with its elaborate call numbers. Today Meg was giving *D*, the "World History Other Than American" classification, a run-through with two of her volunteers, public-spirited women who loved books. The Latouche Regional Library, like most public libraries, operated under fiscal constraints. Wise use of volunteer labor was one way to save money, but not necessarily an ideal way. Testing the possible switch-over seemed a good use of volunteers.

"My people are both here, saddled and ready to ride. Pity they couldn't have come this morning." Meg's voice took on a graver tone. "Have you had an update on Judith Hough's condition?"

"She's still alive. Apart from that, nothing. It's hard to figure out what set her off."

"Madeline called me."

Rob groaned.

"Now cut it out. She knows I'm discreet. She was very upset and needed to talk it through."

Rob sighed. "So what did she tell you, Deputy?"

Early in their acquaintance, Rob had sworn Meg in as a reserve deputy, mainly because he wanted to use her research skills, but he'd also wanted to have someone to talk things over with, someone not caught up in investigation. He found he liked that—and Meg—a lot, and that dialogue was a tool of insight. Now he listened to Meg's report with attention to detail.

"And Maddie cleaned up the blood in the kitchen after the others had left," she concluded.

"Er, unwise but understandable."

"The chief has all the right instincts, even when she's wrong."

"Maybe so. Do I gather she didn't like Catherine Grant?"

"You may safely say that." She hesitated. "She said she didn't think Grant was necessarily racist, just cold and self-satisfied." That seemed like a fair description of Kitty Grant.

Rob cleared his throat. "Time I got back to work. Good luck with your call-number experiment, my dear. I'll see you at a reasonable hour."

"I hope so. Will you stop by the store for a bottle of red? Cabernet will do."

He agreed to that, hung up, and shuffled Deputy Grant's photos of Russell Hough. Grief and stark misery. If Judith died—or wound up vegetative—would Russell also sink into the morass of self-destruction? Rob didn't know, but he was sure the man would have been better off never to return to Hawk Farm.

You tried, kiddo. Let it go. He wouldn't, of course. Rob still hadn't met Bill Hough's son. He wanted to, but there was no excuse for what would seem like harassment if the undersheriff of Latouche County showed up with questions.

Rob listened to Todd's interview and reminded himself to praise the young deputy. It wasn't brilliant interrogation, but, considering Madeline Thomas's formidable presence, it was clean, clear, and thorough, and Todd had given her no reason to interrupt. Though he was inclined to defer to his aunt, he didn't stammer or apologize. He was growing up. Rob read Todd's terse report and thumbed through Kitty Grant's. Grant sounded smug. Self-satisfied was the word. It was hard to see why. Apart from two sharp but pointless questions, she hadn't given much to the interrogation.

Time to look at Frank August. Rob pulled the file. Time to look *for* Frank August. The forensic reports were starting to come in. It began to seem as though a ghost had driven the vehicle into the thicket. So far they'd found no indication that anyone had battled his way out through the brambles. Nor were there signs of a struggle inside the SUV. There was a little dried blood on the passenger seat.

The car was clean—not spotless but free of clutter. One of the drivers, probably Jane, had the habit of stuffing gas station receipts into the pocket on the driver's-side door. Apart from an ice scraper, there was nothing else in the pocket. The glove compartment contained the driver's manual, the vehicle registration card, and a small box of tissues. A white plastic litter bag of the kind handed out by the DMV lay on the floor behind the driver's seat. It was half-full of used tissues and other oddments.

Something besides groceries had been carried in the back. The techs hadn't seen anything, but their vacuum had picked up hairs and fibers for analysis. Not necessarily cause for alarm. Anyone leaning over to place a grocery bag back there could have dropped a hair or three. As for fibers, people threw jackets in the back of their cars all the time or transported clothes to the dry cleaner. Still, if any of the hairs turned out to be Frank August's, that would suggest ugly possibilities. And there was a smear of some kind of oil on the carpeting. If someone had transported August in the back of the SUV, where had he been taken and why?

One thing struck Rob as especially odd. At some point, a substantial puddle of water had evaporated from the floor on the driver's side. He would have to ask Jane whether she'd spilled a water bottle there recently. Although the surface had dried in the days of ninety-degree heat, the techs were sure the puddle was recent and sure it was water, not coffee or soda or beer—or urine, appetizing thought.

"What kind of water?" Rob scribbled in the margin of the report. Water from the well that served the house would leave a distinctive mineral residue—unless the taps had filters. *Have to check. And compare the results with scrapings from the passenger side.* The technicians were already testing soil samples tracked in by shoes.

He thumbed through photographs of the SUV interior and of the freshly barbered bramble patch. All the clippings had been painfully collected. And none of this quasi-scientific effort said anything about Frank August's present location.

Jack Redfern had agreed to help the uniforms check out likely places for a body to wash ashore. The Choteau cascaded into the Columbia at Two Falls. The odds were good that the body in question would make a long-distance journey. But Rob wasn't convinced that Frank had gone into the river at all—or been thrown into the river. He was probably basking on the beach at Ipanema.

~

IRMA had fixed chicken with rice for dinner. Soothing, she said. Libby said boring.

"Dad's in Rio," Frankie insisted, stabbing a bite of *pollo*.

"Have you had a postcard?"

"Oh, Jane, cut the sarcasm." Libby was pouting again. She hadn't wanted to stay at home for dinner, but Jane had insisted. Gerd ate with glum concentration.

The four of them needed to talk. There was the small problem of the cost of running the house, not to mention paying the work crews who moved the irrigation pipes around the vineyards every morning—and paying Tom Dahl and Gerd their salaries. Not to mention Irma. The chef had departed, unpaid, as soon as she served the entrée.

When the silence became uncomfortable, Jane said, "How long are you staying this time, Frankie?"

"Don't call me Frankie. It's a baby name." He sawed chicken. "Dad calls me Frankie. My friends call me Gus. My mother calls me Gus. I hate Frankie."

Jane digested that. She really did not know her brother. "Okay, Gus, how long are you staying?"

"I don't know. As long as it takes."

"To find Dad?"

"To find out where we are."

"What do you mean?"

"I mean I need money. He's swimming in it. There has to be a way to get at it."

"Er, yes, but it's his money."

"It's his *estate*," Frankie, aka Gus, said with no emotion whatever.

Libby gave a small shriek.

"You think he's dead." Jane ignored another squawk from her stepmother. Gerd kept his eyes on his plate.

"I don't know where he is or what condition he's in, and I don't particularly care. I just know he left me with nothing to live on and no money to hire the lawyers I need to defend myself from the consequences of his greed and stupidity."

Greed, yes. Stupidity no, unless greed was stupidity. Jane said, "Did he say he'd help you when you were here last time?"

"No. But I knew he'd come round."

Jane didn't buy that. "He's pretty stubborn."

Libby snorted.

"You must call Tom Dahl, Jane," Gerd said in a lackluster voice. "Your father incorporated."

Of course. The vineyards. Jane wondered at her own idiocy. She went into the kitchen, picked up the landline phone, and speed-dialed Dahl, whom she only knew in passing. He answered on the second ring as she reentered the dining room with the receiver. She'd expected to reach a message tape.

"Uh, Tom, it's Jane August. You heard about the SUV?"

"I heard they, the cops, found it yesterday afternoon. That true?"

"Yes."

"Hell of a note," he said heavily.

Fifteen minutes later she knew she could relax a little. Dahl was registered to sign checks. He could draw on the corporate account for wages and other expenses related to the vineyard, and he said that funds were transferred to the account every month by direct deposit from her father's private resources. There was also a Visa card with a substantial credit line, and Dahl could access it. That was a little weird.

She thanked him and moved to break the connection, but he asked to speak to the wine maker. She handed Gerd the phone.

Jane didn't know much about the vineyard manager. If Frank had trusted him to that degree, Dahl was probably dumb but honest. She hated her cynicism, but there it was. It was Frank's cynicism, and it left an unpleasant aftertaste.

After a brief exchange, Gerd passed Libby the phone. She took it off into the kitchen, and they heard her side of the conversation, uninformative monosyllables that faded to nothing.

Gerd said, "Why is Tom still at the *cave*? He's usually home by this hour."

Both men looked at Jane.

Jane had no idea. She explained at unnecessary length how Dahl would be able to keep the vineyard work going and pay everyone's wages. She didn't mention the Visa card.

"You ought to contact Dad's lawyers," Gus said.

"Why? That's ghoulish." *Goulash. Gouache.*

"Maybe, but you need to be able to buy groceries." *And give me a loan.* He didn't say that.

"Why don't you contact them?"

"*You* can sweet-talk the lawyer. He'd charge *me* a hundred bucks a billable minute."

That might even be true. Jane sighed. "I don't know who his lawyers are or where they are."

"Whitfield and Schramm in Klalo." Libby had returned to the dining room without the phone. "Lewis Schramm is the one I met. They're Frank's local lawyers. You know, for the vineyard. He has this legal team in Seattle to handle taxes and bank stuff. Bye, all. I'm off." She abandoned her half-eaten dinner and disappeared into the hall that led to the garage.

They heard the Jeep leave, the sound of its engine muted as the door to the garage closed after her. Jane wondered, idly, why Dahl had asked to talk to Libby and what they had talked about. She couldn't imagine her stepmother concerning herself about the disposition of newly harvested or, for that matter, unharvested grapes.

Bank stuff, Libby had said. Jane thought she probably ought to call the Seattle money men. Schramm first, though. The lawyer was local.

Gus and Gerd helped her clear up after dinner. When they had gone off for the night, leaving her alone in the kitchen, she looked at the phone's directory. Sure enough, she could also speed-dial the lawyer, so she left him a message. She did not expect an immediate reply. It was well after business hours.

To her surprise, Schramm phoned her as she was preparing to go to bed. He sounded anxious. She apologized for calling him so late. He hadn't heard about the SUV. She told him what she knew and explained the awkward financial situation.

"And I need to be able to pay Irma—the housekeeper," she concluded. "What do you suggest? I've been buying the groceries myself and keeping the receipts, but my income isn't up to running a house like this one. Libby hasn't offered, and I don't want to wait seven years to be reimbursed."

He took the feeble joke seriously. "No, indeed. Hmm."

She summarized her reassuring talk with Tom Dahl.

"Yes, yes. That would be appropriate."

"I beg your pardon?"

"Er, ahem, I spoke out of turn. My apologies, Miss August. Er, the simplest course is to add your name to the vineyard instruments—the checking account and the Visa. Yes. Shall we do that tomorrow?"

When they'd made a ten o'clock appointment to meet at the bank, she disconnected. She got up to go knock on Gus's door with the good news, but it occurred to her that he didn't need to know Schramm's decision. Libby certainly didn't.

Gus would want his name on the checkbook, too. She didn't like to refuse him, but she was sure Frank would not want his son making free with the moneybags—not yet, anyway. Frank had quarreled with Gus over money. She didn't think that was fair, all things considered, but it would also not be fair to go against her father's wishes the minute he was out of sight. The long run was another matter. So far Libby hadn't asked for money.

So far. A headache began to form. Jane went to bed, took her Kindle from the nightstand, and called up the therapeutic comedy she'd been reading. Her thoughts drifted. She wondered how Judith Hough was doing and decided to drop by the hospital after her meeting with Schramm. She went back to her comedy.

Lewis Schramm turned out to be an amiable man, sixty-something, the senior partner in a three-lawyer office, Whitfield having retired some years before. Schramm and the bank manager had obviously communicated, because the process of adding Jane's signature went almost too smoothly. Both Schramm and the manager said kind, hopeful things about Frank and sent her off feeling relieved but puzzled. Why were they bending over backwards?

For all they knew, *she* might dip into the money and make a run for Rio. It was easy for them to check her bona fides, but she had expected the bank to impose a day or two of delay, just to be sure she would take it all seriously. Or to insist that they should be dealing with Libby. However, Jane was not about to complain. She repaid herself for the groceries and took out two hundred for incidental expenses. When her new checks arrived Monday or Tuesday, she could pay Irma from the vineyard funds. Since she couldn't access Frank's business files, she asked the banker to send her duplicates of the print records that were sent to Dahl as a matter of course. That seemed prudent.

～

ALICE was at the hospital. Her brother Jack had driven her over, she said. Russ intended to teach her to drive. She sounded frightened but determined to learn. Russ was working. He came to visit his sister evenings. Jane was disappointed not to see him.

Judith's condition was unchanged. The VA wanted to transfer her to a Hood River nursing facility in the near future. *Warehousing*, Jane thought, but she knew better than to say so.

As she was about to leave, Alice touched her arm. "I have a big favor to ask."

"Of course."

"The doctors are moving Judy into Recovery soon, so she'll be allowed visitors. Could you drop by and talk to her a little?"

"Talk to her?"

"They say it sometimes helps people in a coma. Russ has been reading to her, and I talk to her about things she should be able to remember when she wakes up, but I thought maybe you could talk to her about, you know, art."

Jane gaped.

Alice's dark eyes were earnest. "She likes you, and she's serious about her quilts, I mean hangings. See, I even forget to say the right word. I think of quilts as a way of using up old clothes, but she says the hangings are art."

"She's right." Jane wondered what she was letting herself in for. "Yes. Let me know when she's in Recovery. I'll try to drop in whenever I'm in town."

Alice thanked her, and Jane left. The Houghs' problems put her own into perspective.

The next six days passed with tortuous slowness. The reporters got bored waiting. Jane made her way through a much-diminished cordon and drove to Hood River on Thursday to look for a place to live. She viewed three apartments and a small house, none of them appealing. The next day Alice left a message that Judith was now in Recovery, so Jane drove to Klalo, ostensibly to replenish the liquor supply but in fact to visit the hospital. Judith Hough lay alone in a two-patient room.

She lay very still under a web of tubes that dangled fluids. The monitor flickered coded information and made tiny noises. A turban of white bandages gave her face an archaic cast. She was pale, of course, but still beautiful. Jane touched her cool, unmoving hand.

"Hello, Judith, it's Jane August. Do you remember me?" Jane felt as self-conscious as if she were auditioning for a play. "Your mother thought we could talk about art." *We, who's we here?* "Uh, I'm not so sure there's any point in talking about art. Art is something you do. Critics talk about it, artists do it. Does that make sense? Not much."

No response.

She rambled on, glad Russell wasn't in the room to hear her foolishness. "I never worked with fabric myself, but I can see the satisfaction—turning one artifact into another. With crazy quilts, artists have the freedom to find their own patterns, their own meanings." *Within the limits of a two-dimensional map.* "I saw the quilt you hung in the hallway, the red one. That's a meaning only you could find." Despair dragged at her throat. She was not making sense.

No response.

"How does it feel to work with your great-grandmother's treadle? I don't know anything about my great-grandmothers except their names and how many children they had. A lot of women are summed up that way. I suppose there are worse things to be remembered for. But to be remembered for our artifacts?" She thought about that.

Archaeologists summed up human lives in terms of artifacts all the time. *Look at the caves at Lascaux and Chauvet, or the petroglyphs in the Gorge, for that matter.* One of her art history professors was convinced the petroglyphs were a form of graffiti, expressive of boredom. *Really? They weren't boring.* The art was there, but the artists were beyond reach—like Judith Hough. "Maybe that's how we're supposed to be remembered."

No response.

Jane talked some more. Mostly nonsense. When she heard herself commenting on the weather, she stood up. "I have to go now." She glanced at her watch. *Ten minutes?* That was as much as she could bear, and Judith, at least, was not going to reproach her. Jane drove home in a funk. Where was her father? She wanted him. She wanted to ask him about his life before it was too late.

~

THE next day, Saturday, produced minor annoyances and one big surprise. After Gerd had discharged his mostly ceremonial duties at the *cave*, he drove to town to visit Judith in the hospital. He came back looking as shaken as Jane had felt, but he wouldn't talk about the experience. He snapped at her when she asked how Judith was doing.

Libby hung around the house all day despite a promising breeze. The weather was changing. It was still August but felt like September, ideal for surfers Jane thought, but what did she know? Libby and Gus bickered, almost like an unhappy couple. The tone of their interchanges set Jane's teeth on edge. It also led her to thoughts about incest.

Libby was only three years older than Gus. If she could conceive of a relationship to a man thirty years her senior, surely an attraction to a man a few years younger than she was would not be impossible—not that a bond between Gus and Libby would be real incest. After all, they weren't related. Nevertheless, the idea was much more distasteful than an ephemeral connection between Libby and Gerd. If Libby got her claws into Gus earlier, before they moved north, Frank's hostility to his son was much more understandable. Jane felt as if she were trapped in a soap opera.

Irma served a seafood *paella* for dinner. Summer was not prime time for seafood. Libby complained that the calamari were rubbery. They were a bit, but the flavor of the sauce made up for that. The two men ate heartily. Irma left as soon as she had served a dessert of melon balls with ginger crisps. Jane and Gerd did the dishes. She was about to retreat to her room for an early session with her e-comedy when the doorbell rang. Front door.

She grimaced. "The press?"

Gerd shrugged. "Or Russ. He said he might drop in after work."

After work. It was eight.

Jane threw her sponge into the sink and raced to the door. Sure enough, Russell stood there, stood being the operative term. He had parked his Blazer right in front. Not that that was a problem. They didn't have visitors these days. Just journalists.

Russ was vertical, with a metal crutch on his right arm, and straight from the shower if damp hair was an indication. He was wearing a Hawaiian shirt and tan shorts. The prosthesis gleamed in the slanting light of evening. *It* was wearing a deck shoe. Without a sock. The other foot, the real one, reposed in the snap-on cast.

"Hi," she said. "Good to see you, Russ. Come in."

"Jane. How are you? Any word on your father?"

She shook her head *no*.

He followed her nimbly enough through the long hall to the kitchen, where Gerd greeted him without surprise.

"You saw Jude?"

Gerd hung his head, as Jane had. Some things are better not said.

Jane cleared her throat. "I'm glad to see you perambulating, Russell."

"Yes, well, I'm stuck with the crutch for a while yet, but things are looking up, legwise."

Not otherwise. "I saw Judith yesterday."

He nodded. "So the duty nurse said. Thank you."

"I don't think I did much good."

"Thanks for trying. You can't tell whether she hears. That's the hell of it."

And it must be hell, she thought, remembering the cool, unresponsive mask of Judith's face. "I'll try again." She smiled at him. "You haven't met my brother, Frank, Junior. He and our stepmother are out by the pool." She led the way out to where Gus and Libby sat by the drinks trolley. Gerd followed, looking glum.

Jane watched Gus as he took in the Hough apparition. Libby stifled a gasp, hand to mouth.

Gus looked flustered but set his brandy down, rose, and stuck out his hand when Jane made the introduction. "Call me Gus."

"Sure." Russ shifted the crutch to his left hand with the ease of long practice and shook. "Bad luck about your bank."

Gus flushed. "Thanks. It was."

"Uh, and this is my stepmother, Libby." *Be good*, Jane pleaded silently.

Libby looked anywhere but at the fake leg. "H'lo."

"Hello. Sorry for your trouble, Mrs. August." Russell seated himself on the lounge chair indicated.

"Get you a drink?" Gus offered.

"Better not. I have to drive to Klalo yet tonight. I came up to explain about the orchard."

"Orchard?"

Russell glanced from Gus to Jane. Libby wasn't looking at him. "I sold the usable trees to a cabinetmaker from Portland. His crew will log the orchard tomorrow—a lot of dust and noise from the saws. When they're done, sometime Monday, a bulldozer will come in and knock out the stumps. We'll chip them."

"Are you going to burn slash?" Gus, with a good question.

"Eventually, but there's a burning ban on right now. Too much danger of a brush fire."

"Do you want to use the gate and the lane through the syrah vineyard?" Jane asked.

"I don't think that will be necessary."

Gus said expansively, "Feel free, Hough. A little dust won't hurt anything. What are you going to do with the land, sell it?"

"The estate won't be settled for months, maybe longer." Russell spread his hands. "Selling is up to my mother, not me. I'm going to put in blueberries and raspberries."

"Not a vineyard?"

"*Château* Choteau?" He smiled. "Naw, too much competition from the neighbors."

Gus gave a hearty laugh and took a swallow of his drink.

Gerd said, "Russell runs the Hackamore Vineyard for Eismann." Hackamore was one of the two Eismann labels, a red table wine.

Gus spluttered, but made a swift recovery. "Good thing you're a farmer, not a wine maker. It'd take you twice as long to stomp grapes."

"That has been pointed out," Russell said.

Libby stood and excused herself. She had a headache. Everybody made sympathetic noises, and she left. Russell had risen as she escaped and now took his leave, too. Hospital visiting hours ran until nine-thirty, he said, but he needed to grab a sandwich somewhere first.

The men made manly gestures of farewell, and Gus buried his nose in another glass of brandy.

Russ touched Gerhard on the shoulder. "See you in the morning."

Gerd nodded. "About Judith. I cannot look at her again, not like that. It is to me intolerable."

"I know, friend. I'm sorry."

"I, too."

Jane saw Russ to the door. "*I'm* going to see Judith again. Tomorrow. Your mother said you read to her. What are you reading?"

He rubbed the back of his neck. *"Swallows and Amazons."*

"What!"

"I was reading it to her when I took off for eastern Washington seventeen years ago. I decided to finish the book."

Jane was speechless. One of her favorite childhood reads.

"She was only eight when I left," he added, apologetic.

At that point Jane decided she was going to marry Russell Hough.

"Come to dinner with me tomorrow? Have mercy. I need to get away from all this...." He made a vague encompassing gesture.

"All right," she said without hesitation. "What time?"

He blinked as if she had surprised him. "Uh, seven?"

"Seven. Where are we going?"

"Hood River?"

"Good. You can show me the town."

8.

MADDIE TOOK the sheriff to lunch Sunday. When Mack McCormick died, Maddie had called the governor to suggest that his widow be appointed to replace him, so she felt a proprietary interest in Beth McCormick's well-being. For her part, Beth was friendly to Klalo needs and a good friend to Maddie herself. Both of them were concerned for Judith Hough, whose pale shell they had just visited. Though Maddie found her sister-in-law exasperating, she was concerned for Alice, too, and for Russell.

The two women ate their salads in silence, neither willing to say aloud what she thought of Judith's chances. The noon crowd in Mona's was noisy with after-church diners. At last, by way of distraction, Maddie said, "This banker who's gone missing, what d'you think happened to him?"

"He's hiding from the press, and probably from the feds. I expect they want to question him about his financial hanky-panky. Have you met him?"

"At the library lunch. Didn't like him." She launched into a full-blown narrative of Meg's garden party. "See what you miss when you skate out of town?"

"It was Beatie's birthday." Beatie was Beth's oldest granddaughter. Beth had a raft of grandchildren. Maddie told herself not to be jealous. They talked in a desultory way about the upcoming school election, but Maddie's thoughts kept drifting back to the Houghs.

"I'm worried about Russell," she said when the election lost its charm as topic of the day. "He should never have had to come home."

"I can see why he'd stay away while Bill was alive and squawking, but now—"

"Now Russ is stuck here. Alice is the next thing to helpless."

"And Judy *is* helpless. I see."

"Jack wanted to adopt him," Maddie blurted. She had never told anyone that.

Beth's eyes narrowed. "When?"

"When Bill started beating him. Russ was eleven."

"What happened?"

"I'm not sure why it started. Something changed. Maybe it was moving to the farm with no neighbors to hear what was happening. Maybe the baby coming along. Maybe Russ growing up, starting to look like a rival. Bill didn't like competition."

"I thought he was a great football player."

"I mean emotional competition."

The sheriff considered that.

Encouraged, Maddie went on, "The booze didn't help. Bill was always a drinker, weekend binges to begin with. That was about the time he started drinking every night, but whether it was cause or effect I don't know."

"And he took to hitting his son?"

"Yes. Jack had to intervene."

Beth was sharp. "Intervene?"

Maddie said cautiously, "He persuaded Bill to keep his hands to himself."

"Good God, how did he do that? I thought nobody could persuade Bill Hough to do anything he didn't want to."

Maddie eyed her friend. "Bill was a racist."

"Among other things."

"He was always talking about redskin savages."

"Insulting."

"And inaccurate. The Klalos are traders, not warriors—fishermen and traders. Jack just used Bill's assumptions. He sort of hinted that, uh, savage things would happen unless Bill changed his ways."

Their eyes met. Beth began to laugh. Maddie had to smile, too, but it wasn't funny. Jack was a gentle man.

She greeted the waitress, her cousin, who had brought the coffeepot. When Lena went off, satisfied that the relationship was in good heart, Maddie sipped her hot coffee. "Jack was sorry for Bill."

"Sorry for a child beater?"

"Sorry for a man whose good deeds were destroying him."

"You're confusing me."

"A man whose nightmares were destroying him. You can't forget Bill was a hero, Beth. He lied a lot, but not about that. Jack respected what he'd done."

"But?"

"But Jack loves Russell like a son, the way a man should love a son." *Like the son Jack never had.*

Beth was frowning. "All the same, how could he think of adopting him? Both parents were alive."

"When he was drunk, Bill claimed Russ wasn't his son, and, before you ask, no, that's not possible. Not Alice." They both knew Alice. "Bill had her under house arrest for all practical purposes, once they moved out to the farm from Two Falls. He wouldn't let her learn to drive, and he had a fit when she took the bus to Klalo."

"Bill was sick."

"Yes. And a bully. You can imagine how Jack reacted to Bill's allegation, drunken or not. It was insulting every which way. Jack was angry, but mainly he was afraid for Russell."

"Not for Alice?"

Maddie squirmed. "I guess Jack thought she'd made her bed. When Alice insisted on marrying Bill, Jack was already in the army. He didn't get a chance to talk to her about her husband's character before the fact. He's always felt guilty about that, but I don't think he could have changed her mind. She was in love with her idea of Bill."

"But Jack knew what Bill was like?"

"Goodness, Beth, we all went to school together. Jack was two years ahead of Bill and Alice and three years ahead of me. Jack didn't like what he saw of Bill. They were both on the football team one year."

"Wait a minute. Alice is Jack's half sister."

"She is. His mother died in childbirth, and his grandmother raised Jack and Leon. She was a traditional woman. Jack's father remarried. Alice's mother didn't want to take on two boys."

"Cold."

"Yes. She was Catholic and didn't want *her* children to be exposed to 'pagan influences.' But she only had the one child." Maddie eyed Beth. "They weren't close growing up, Jack and Alice, hardly knew each other, but she's his sister. He was bound to feel responsible for her children, and he wouldn't tolerate violence toward her or the kids."

"No. I see." Beth understood Klalo customs better than most outsiders. "And Bill stopped using his fists on his son?"

"When he was sober. When he thought about it. It was a dangerous situation. We…Jack arranged for Russell to come to us after school. He told Bill he was teaching the boy how to track. Mostly Russ did his schoolwork on our kitchen table, but Jack was teaching him all right."

"Teaching him what?"

"How to be a man." The manhood trial was long and difficult. It had little to do with sex, a great deal to do with thinking things through, and among other skills, learning to master anger.

"Early," Beth said.

"Way early. Russ's voice hadn't even changed. I didn't approve." She hesitated, took a sip of cold coffee, and grimaced. "I feel bad about that. I think Russ believed I didn't like him.

He was too quiet. He seemed sly, but he was just scared. It took me a while to understand his reticence, and then it was too late."

"Too late?"

Maddie sighed. "Too late for him to think of me as a friend." *And maybe he was right,* she thought. *Maybe I'm not a friend.*

LOGGING the cherry orchard did produce noise, distracting but not intolerable. The worst whine of the saws hit the bluff and bounced back toward the river. The commotion had wakened Jane at eight, so she'd gone in to the hospital for a morning visit with Judith. She talked a little and read Judith an article on quilts she'd found on the Internet. When she left, she thought she saw familiar faces in the lobby. She'd met a lot of people at the library lunch and forgotten their names immediately. That was a bad habit.

With Frank gone, the Sunday schedule was shot. Libby went surfing, Gerd worked on the farm, and Gus slept off last night's brandy. He got up late and grumpy. Jane fixed him coffee and a sandwich, against her better judgment. Now she and her brother stood beside the low wall at the top of the bluff, taking stock. She glimpsed Gerd's cerise crest bobbing in the billowing dust. Russell's leg man. She thought Gus was watching Gerd, too.

Jane had gathered that Judith opposed removing the orchard. It was fortunate Russ's sister didn't have to witness the trees coming down, if there was anything fortunate about Judith's condition. Jane made a mental note not to mention the orchard's fate next time she visited the hospital. The swift destruction going on seemed ruthless. Trees, even cherry trees, were a life form, after all, and right now a bunch of them were being killed before Jane's very eyes. She supposed a farmer would have to have a streak of ruthlessness. And she was complicit with orchardists, fond as she was of cherry pie. The thought made her uneasy.

"Efficient s.o.b." The voice that growled at her elbow was

so much like her father's that she flinched. Gus squinted against the rising dust.

"Do you dislike Russell?"

"I thought he was damned insensitive yesterday, barging in here."

"The shirt was a little garish." Jane thought she caught a glimpse of Russ, and maybe she did because the Blazer drove down past the house and onto the highway. She watched it out of sight.

"He should not have let that metal contraption hang out for everyone to see. I thought Libby was going to be sick."

Jane turned. "Heavens, do you mean Russ's leg? It was a hot day, Gus. You were wearing shorts. Why shouldn't Russell?" Her eyes narrowed. "And what's it to you, whether Libby's delicate feelings are offended? She's about as sensitive as a lump of granite."

"She hates physical imperfection."

"Then she needs to toughen up. The world is full of imperfection, including her tendency to sob and shriek when things don't go her way."

"I don't know what you're talking about."

"You will. Stick around."

A shout and a crack indicated another tree was coming down. Jane winced.

"What's for dinner?" Gus said sullenly.

"I don't know. Irma will fix you and Gerd something, I'm sure. Speaking of insensitivity, Libby is dining with a 'friend.'" She made quotation marks with her fingers. "Me, too."

He gaped at her. "Who?"

"Russell, not that it's any of your business." She turned back to the scene below to hide a smile. She wished her father were there, blustering and ranting. She would have enjoyed it.

"Montagues and Capulets." Gus sounded disgusted.

"O, Romeo, Romeo," Jane bellowed over the whine of the saws, "wherefore art thou Romeo? Deny thy father and refuse thy name, or if thou wilt not, be but sworn my love, and I'll no longer be a stinking Capulet." She had played Juliet in a high school production. Mostly sitting down. She had been half a head taller than Romeo.

"Cut it out."

"Why? Nobody can hear me."

"Everybody in two states can hear you."

Jane laughed aloud.

After a long moment, Gus smiled. "All right, it's not my business. Though what you can see…"

"One man's meat is another man's poison."

"Well, that's true. Why so literary all of a sudden?"

"You're the one who brought up Shakespeare. I feel good. The sun's shining. I'm going to get out of the house this evening. And you, my dear sibling, can do the dishes." She left him staring down into the dying orchard and went to look for an outfit that would convey her state of mind. She wound up in a sundress she hadn't worn since she came north.

Russell showed up a few minutes after seven. Jane was a little disappointed that he wasn't wearing shorts. In fact he'd had a haircut and looked more than respectable in tan twill pants and a navy polo shirt. He was using a cane, a rather dashing one with a bronze head in the shape of a bird of prey. She admired it.

He held the door of the Blazer for her. "One of my father's souvenirs." He tossed the cane into the backseat and inserted himself on the driver's side with a slight grimace. He wheeled out onto the long lane that led to Miller Road smoothly enough, though Jane wondered whether she ought to volunteer to drive. *Probably not.*

When he had turned down to Highway 14 and settled into the straight stretch to Two Falls, he said, "Thanks for visiting Judy again."

"You've seen her already?"

"Yes, this afternoon. I took off when the loggers really got going. I hate watching trees come down. It's depressing when you think how old they are."

"Well, at least the cabinetmaker will use the wood to make something beautiful."

"On the other hand, cherry wood makes a beautiful fire."

Jane laughed. "True. I don't know how many fireplaces there are in Dad's house, but I've never seen a fire in any of them. I have the feeling they don't get much use, even in winter."

"Why did he build such a big house?"

"I don't know. He's a puzzle." They both fell silent. Frank August was a puzzle in every way.

"Shall we not talk about our families?" Jane blurted.

"It's a deal."

She let out a long breath. "So tell me how you came to work for Eismann. That's a company Dad finds very interesting. A role model for him. Oops, there I go talking about Dad."

"Watch it," he growled, and smiled when she blinked at him like an owl. "Eismann. Well, I worked summers at the Eismann vineyard near Pullman while I was at the university."

"Pullman. Is that Washington State University?"

"That's the one. Emphasis on science and engineering. Pullman is the main campus, though there are others now, including the one in Vancouver."

"And you studied agriculture?"

"No." Perhaps he thought his response too cryptic. After a pause he added, "I majored in biology."

"Microbiology?"

"Nope. I don't get along well with microscopes. I remember one early lab. They put us at the microscopes and told us to draw what we saw. I thought I did a pretty good job—very detailed. Then the instructor told me I'd drawn the surface of my eye as reflected on the lens."

Jane laughed. "You made that up."

"It's the unvarnished truth." He stopped at the light that signaled the approach to the Hood River Bridge. Jane found driving on the metal grate of the bridge uncomfortable, but Russ seemed used to it. He drove onto the drawbridge section without hesitation. "Take a look downriver."

She did. "My God, what a view of the Gorge. It's a Chinese painting."

"It's the best view anywhere, but I can't stop to let you appreciate it." The two-lane bridge had narrow shoulders and heavy traffic.

Jane's fingers itched for her pen and sketchbook. "I don't suppose you'd drive me across ten or twelve times so I could capture it. Look at the surfers!" The wind surfers and parasailors swooped and danced downstream at the confluence of the Hood River and the Columbia—like so many butterflies.

"Uh, my eyes are on the road. Is your cute little stepmama out there?"

"She may be." Jane wondered whether she ought to apologize for Libby's obvious revulsion at the sight of the prosthesis and decided Russ must have known what the effect would be. She cast him a sidewise glance.

His mouth quirked at the corners. "When Gerd took the job, he fell in love instantly and wrote me about her at boring length."

"He's very romantic."

"Incurably." He handed the bridge attendant a dollar bill and the little gate lifted. Neither of them mentioned Gerd's passion for Judith.

Russ was following the lane beneath the interstate that led across China Gulch into the city of Hood River. The railway station, now a museum, lay at the east end. It would have been the main entrance to town in the nineteenth century. He chugged along the main street, leaving her to admire Victorian storefronts she had only glimpsed when she drove herself.

"It's a handsome town," she muttered, "but not quite real."

"Too much tourist money?"

The Blazer made its way up an incline to a three-way stop. Portentous Victorian townhouses looked down on the river. "Might be the opposite," Jane replied. "Way too much agricultural and industrial cash. Not enough civic responsibility."

"You're thinking of the library."

The library had closed, briefly, when a levy failed. "Is it a nice library?"

"It has a reading room with a billion-buck view of the river and Mount Adams. They could auction off viewing tickets to the general public. Night gawp fifty dollars. Daytime goggle a hundred. Seventy-five for a view of the sunset. Nobody allowed to read while the sun sets on the river."

"It doesn't set on the river."

"Splinters of it set on the river." He wheeled, sharp right, into what looked like an old gas station, and parked.

Jane was trying to figure out where they were. She had driven through town twice from the other direction, but she didn't remember this area. "Where's Walmart?"

"West." He looked at her. "You like Mexican?"

"Er—"

He laughed. "Just kidding. I know Irma gives you classy Mexican food all the time. This is Thai."

"It is? It looks like Texaco."

"O ye of little faith."

Fortunately, the inside of the small restaurant did not look like Texaco. Someone grew orchids. The absurd flowers glowed against the dark wood of a tall bar. The tables had real tablecloths and real flowers. Though the place was almost full, it was quiet. She tried to figure out how they'd managed that. A clue—there was no canned music.

After weeks of Irma's experiments, Thai food tasted glorious. Jane drank beer with hers. Russ drank water. Pain meds, he said. He was driving. She asked him about his work again, and he told her a couple of stories, including one in which a rattlesnake struck his prosthesis while he was strolling though the vineyard.

"Knocked itself cold."

Jane shuddered. She was not fond of snakes. Neither was Russ, it turned out, though he said he didn't kill the rattler. Snakes eat vermin. He left it to recuperate and consider its sins.

He said he liked his job, but he didn't seem passionate about it. She gathered that while he enjoyed training and working with his crews, he found viticulture a little boring. She wondered why he stayed with Eismann, but decided it was too soon to ask probing questions.

He had no such inhibitions. "So tell me about your art—not just painting, apparently."

"Mixed media. I'm a painter by training, but I like to experiment." She found herself telling him about her fascination with Mount Hood and her plans for it.

The waiter broke in, poured water, and asked if everything was all right. "Everything's fine." She scowled after him. "I wish they wouldn't do that."

"Interrupt? It's an instinct with waiters. 'Those folks are enjoying themselves. Get in there and ruin it for them.'"

Jane laughed. "Well, I am enjoying myself. How come you know the right questions to ask an artist?"

"I'm jest a country boy—"

"Cut it out."

He gave an impish grin. "I took art history."

"You what? That's a course for art majors."

"I know, but the alternative was Art Appreciation."

"I don't follow."

"Any course labeled 'appreciation' is for people who don't want to be there. Appreciation of Poetry. Music Appreciation."

"Math Appreciation."

He smiled. "Nobody appreciates math. I just meant that science majors have to take a certain number of credits of humanities in order to graduate, and most of them don't want to do that. The appreciation courses in science are labeled 'Introduction to' instead of 'Appreciation of,' but they're full of cranky English and history majors. I figured it all out with a little help from my roommates. I wanted to be in classes with people who liked the subjects."

Curious, she took a verbal step backward. "Your roommates?"

"I went to Pullman the day after I graduated from high school. I had to find work fast. After a week in a hostel, I rented a vacant room in a houseful of science and engineering types—seniors and grad students. They eyed me askance."

"Nobody says that."

"Askance," he said firmly. "I was wet behind the ears—just eighteen because I'd skipped a grade, but they were kindhearted and decided to adopt me."

"Lucky."

"It was. I'm still in touch with them, though they're scattered all over the country now. I lived in that house the whole time I was at the university."

"Hmm." Jane had lived in her mother's sorority for a week before moving back home. Later, when she was at Mills, she had her own apartment. "So you decided not to take easy classes."

"Biology was easy, and so was math. Art history was hard. I had to learn a whole new vocabulary."

He'd done more than that. He had a good grasp of what artists might try to do within their aesthetic traditions and how the traditions limited what they could see, and he seemed to understand what she meant by magical realism when she talked about her mountain. What was even better, he was interested. She wasn't imagining that, she told herself.

She plunged happily into a discussion of the Missoula Floods and how an artist might convey the immense power of the river as it battered and rebattered the basalt landscape until it gave way.

That took them through the green curry chicken and the shrimp pad thai. They talked—or Jane talked—a long time.

"Dessert, madam, sir?" The pesky waiter removed their empty plates.

"Good heavens, no," Jane said without thinking. She blinked at Russell.

"I'll have a triple banana split."

The waiter gaped.

Russ grinned. "Joke. I think we're ready to call it quits."

Looking disappointed, the waiter whisked off in the direction of the cash register.

As soon as Russell said *quits* Jane recalled what she had to deal with at home. Her stomach churned.

"What's wrong?"

"It's been a good hour since I even thought about Dad." Guilt locked her tongue.

"*Tsk.* Dad me no dads."

"They might need me." That was feeble.

"Who?"

"Libby and Gus, who else?"

He cocked his head, watching her.

Her shoulders slumped. "I'm afraid..."

He waited.

"Afraid they don't really care," she blurted. Her eyes teared, and she dabbed at them with her napkin.

The intrusive waiter appeared with the check. Russ was ready. He dropped a credit card on the plastic tray, and the waiter went off with it.

"I should get that, or split it with you."

"Nope. Next time."

Her hand dropped, and she turned back to her preoccupation. "They care, of course. At least Gus cares about Dad's money. And Libby? I don't know. She signed a pre-nup, so there's no question of her inheriting, but what if she wants to be free to marry someone else? I'm afraid she'll tangle Gus in a cheesy affair that will damage him emotionally—more than he's already damaged." She bit her lip, unwilling to voice her suspicion that the affair had already taken place.

"You're not responsible for what they do, Jane." Russ's voice was so nearly harsh she stared at him.

He was frowning but not at her.

"More water?" The waiter laid the tiny tray with Russ's card and the receipt on the table. Russ took the proffered pen, added a tip to the bill, and signed.

"Let's go." He retrieved his walking stick from the back of his chair. The waiter smirked and covered them with thanks.

It was cooler outside, almost chilly, and the air smelled different. At the car, Russ looked up at the sky and drew a long breath. "Rain coming."

"How can you tell?"

"Feel it in my bones," he said in a creaky voice. She smiled at him, liking the self-mockery. He ushered her into her seat and got in the driver's side.

"That was a lovely dinner. Thank you very much."

"You're more than welcome." The engine started. "If you're cold there's a jacket on the backseat."

Jane was cold but not, she thought, from the night air. She pulled his light jacket around her shoulders and fastened the seat belt as he backed onto the street. They rode in silence. Jane's mind turned to thoughts of her family.

Her focus was so inward it took her a moment to notice that he'd turned off just short of the bridge. "Hey! I want to go home."

"In a few minutes." He drove along with the river on his right beyond what looked like public buildings. There was a sign for a museum and another pointing to the marina.

"Is this where Libby comes?"

"Probably. There's a spot down on the Washington side where some of the surfers like to go, but most of them come here." He pulled up in a small lot that lay only yards back from the water, lowered his window a few inches, cracked hers, and killed the engine. There were two other vehicles left in the lot, one a van. Surfers were busy outside the van, peeling off wetsuits, shouting to each other, and laughing.

"Nice view of the bridge."

"I like the river at night." He touched her hand. "Call home."

"What?"

"You'll go on brooding if you don't." He got out of the Blazer, took his cane from the backseat, and went for a walk along the esplanade while she fumbled in her purse for her phone and called her brother.

Gus sounded half-drunk. She was surprised he'd answered at all. There was no news. She didn't talk long and sat a while admiring the dark, mile-wide swell of water with the bridge lights twinkling above it. She watched Russ. He walked without limping, but he stayed on the paved path. If she hadn't been wearing strappy sandals with three-inch heels she would have joined him. Gradually her jaw muscles and those at the base of her neck eased, and she began to relax.

He got back in the Blazer. "No news?"

"No. Gus is drunk, Gerd has gone to bed, and Libby's still out on the town."

"All accounted for." He started the engine and backed out.

"I was watching you walk. That must have been a very bad sprain. It's taking forever to heal."

He headed back the way they had come. "I tore a ligature."

"A what?"

"Gerd was convinced ligament was the wrong word."

She laughed. Ligature sounded like Gerd. She was revising her perception of Russ's injury. "Won't you need surgery?"

"Already had it. The sawbones on duty tacked it down the first afternoon."

"Yeow."

"Well, yes. It's coming along though. Another week or so." He paid the toll and swung the car onto the bridge. He drove carefully, peacefully. Jane felt much better.

"Tell me something."

"If I can."

"Tell me why you really took art history and all those other courses."

He dipped his lights as a car approached on the bridge. "I had what's called a full-tuition scholarship. The state hands them out like lollipops to graduating seniors with good grades and test scores. It's an investment, I guess. You can use the scholarship at any of the state colleges or universities. It covers up to twenty credits every term, but the normal academic load is fifteen. I didn't want all that free credit to go to waste, so I decided I'd take a course every semester that was just for me—something I was interested in or curious about, something my major didn't require."

She thought about that. Her own undergraduate experience had been boring. She had wanted to be elsewhere, painting up a storm, but her parents had insisted that she take a bachelor's degree at least. She had done minimal work and earned Bs and Cs. "You must enjoy studying."

"I enjoy learning. Studying is just the price." He hesitated. "You get what you put into it. I admit I dropped a couple of those courses within the requisite two weeks."

"Two weeks?"

"You have two weeks to drop before a course becomes part of your record for that semester."

"Ah. And you didn't want that."

"Not if I was going to flunk. I had to keep my grades up." When he reached the end of the bridge, the hum of tires on metal stopped abruptly. He eased the car into the right lane and turned onto Highway 14 at the light. "And not if I was bored. That didn't happen very often."

"Did you enjoy grad school?"

He didn't respond immediately. At last he just said, "Part of it," and left it at that. He took the short route home. She supposed his motorcycle accident must have happened while he was a graduate student. That would have taken the joy out of learning.

When Russ drew up at the front door, Jane said, "Would you like a drink, now that you're almost home?"

"I'll take a rain check, Jane. The loggers will drag me out at the crack of dawn."

"Well, thanks again. I enjoyed the meal. And I really enjoyed talking to you. You may have noticed. Sorry if I babbled." She leaned over to give him a kiss on the cheek at the same moment he turned. She hit his nose.

He laughed and gave her a peck on the lips that turned into something much hotter.

When they finally came up for air, they stared at each other, neither of them smiling. She thought he was startled. She was.

She cleared her throat.

"Um, good night, Jane."

She slid out of the Blazer and through the unlocked door to the house in a state of blissful confusion. She was grateful not to find anyone up and about.

9.

THE SLOPES of Mount Hood were visible but not the peak. Loggers had finished cutting the trees in the cherry orchard, hauled the trunks off, and chipped the stumps. They were clearing up debris by the time Jane woke Monday morning from the best night's sleep she'd enjoyed since her father disappeared. The workers made separate stacks of firewood and slash.

It had rained that night, as Russ had said it would, just enough to settle the dust. The day dawned clear and cooler. They'd soon be in September, and she would have to attend the faculty orientation across the river. If she could. If she weren't stuck here.

Perhaps an hour after the loggers had loaded the firewood onto two trucks and driven off, a heavy-equipment hauler brought in a bulldozer. The dozer made its fat way down to the east end of the orchard where it began bumping and shoving debris toward the slash pile. The pile lay some distance east of the garage, to minimize fire danger.

She saw Gerd but not Russell. She supposed Russ was already working across the highway. Her mind shied away from him. She didn't want to analyze her startling evening to death. For now, it was enough to know it had happened. She hoped Tom Dahl was getting Frank's money's worth from Gerd. The wine maker seemed to be having a good time down in what had been the orchard.

When the mail came around noon, the new checks were there with her name printed on them, hers and Dahl's. She paid Irma, who took the rest of the day off. Gus hadn't gotten up yet when Jane drove the Prius into Klalo for a load of easy-cook groceries, and she hadn't seen Libby either, though Libby's car was in the garage beside Gus's rental. Jane drove to the hospital first, half hoping Russ would be there. He wasn't but Alice was—praying.

Jane retreated to the cafeteria for a cup of coffee. Why shouldn't Alice pray? If Judith had been Jane's child, Jane would have spent the past week on her knees whether or not she believed. She thought of her father, or tried to, but all she could conjure was the image of his face. She had so many questions for him—and no answers.

The cafeteria was almost deserted, as it deserved to be. When Jane reformed health care, she would start by hiring four-star chefs to re-create hospital food, including coffee and the Jell-O inflicted on patients. She took a swallow from her cooling cup and gave up. She could not drink it. She bused the cup, went out to the elevator, and rode up to the second floor. Alice was standing by Judith's window looking out at the parking lot. She turned and smiled, the smile rather forced.

"Thank you for coming, Jane. You're very faithful."

Jane felt herself blush as she groped for something to say. "How is Judith?" was pointless because she knew the answer. She settled for "How are you, Alice?"

Alice burst into tears.

Jane helped her into the deathwatch chair, patted her, made soothing noises—all the right things. Nothing seemed to reach the older woman. Maybe the emotional collapse was overdue.

Over the buzz of embarrassment in her head, Jane could hear Alice saying that she was a bad mother, that it was all her fault. This was nonsense. Alice had made mistakes—marrying Bill Hough, for one—but Judy's situation was clearly the result of her decision to shoot herself. For that, blame could lie at Daddy's door—and all the presidents' doors and the Viet Cong's and the Taliban's—and firmly on the Second Amendment. And on Judy. Blaming was futile.

Jane had had very little experience of death. One of her childhood friends had died of leukemia, a teacher had been killed in a traffic accident, and her Sylvester step-grandmother had died of a wild-card aneurysm—that was all. She'd read about the stages of mourning, of course, enough to know that weeping and self-blame were healthy and normal. But they were very hard for bystanders to bear, especially those like herself who tended to cry when someone else did. As she stroked and murmured and patted Russ's mother, tears rolled down her own cheeks. Her nose was probably red. It was certainly runny. She grabbed tissues from the bedside table, handed a fistful to Alice, and scrubbed her own face.

But Judy was not dead. She was lurking there. Maybe she was listening.

"Judy," she said, "it's Jane. Your mother is being very foolish. I'm sure you'll agree. I think you're being foolish, too. It's time for you to wake up."

She broke off and bit her lip. What was she thinking? As she turned back to Alice, she thought she saw the fleeting wraith of an expression on Judith's face. She held her breath and watched.

It must have been an illusion. Judy lay as still and silent as ever. The shuddering woman in the chair gave a last sad gulp and blew her nose. "I'm s-sorry."

"Alice…"

"You're very kind." As Alice blew her nose, she added, "And sympathetic. I'm sorry I made you cry."

Jane explained her weeping problem. "It's contagious. Like yawning. I don't dare attend a movie if I know people in the audience are going to cry. My mother says I was terrible when I was small. I used to howl."

Alice sniffed, then began to giggle. Jane had to laugh, too, but she was embarrassed. Perhaps Alice realized that. She talked about the change in the weather. Neither of them said anything about Jane's speech to Judith, and Jane was careful not to mention the ghost-expression she'd seen. *No use raising false hopes.* At last, rather shyly, Alice begged a ride home so Russ wouldn't have to come for her. Jane said she'd return to the hospital when she'd finished grocery shopping. Alice said she ought to shop a bit, too. Could she come?

She could and did. Shopping ate up half an hour. They rendezvoused at the checkout stand, both with laden carts. It looked as if Alice meant to do some baking. The Prius held everything. Just.

On the way back, Jane chattered. She was not about to allow Alice the opportunity for an emotional relapse. Alice talked about the cherry orchard's demise cheerfully enough. Russ had agreed to keep two of the healthy trees near the garage for household needs, and he was going to plant berries to replace the orchard—blueberries, the domestic cousins of huckleberries, and raspberries. Alice approved. Maybe the yellow jacket population would dwindle.

When that topic ran dry a few miles east of Klalo, Jane asked how the driving lessons were going. This was fruitful of chatter because Alice had mixed feelings. On the one hand, she relished the freedom promised by a driver's license. On the other, driving itself terrified her. Russ had been taking her to the network of lanes across the highway to practice where there was no traffic to worry about. Apparently she had tromped on the accelerator rather than the brake more than once.

"And Russ didn't even yell at me," she confided.

"Maybe he couldn't speak." Jane regretted the ill-considered joke as soon as the words left her mouth.

Alice gave an uncertain laugh. The woman had spent more than thirty-five years married to Bill Hough, a yeller if there ever was one. To make up for her gaffe, Jane told tales of her own mishaps as she learned to drive, including the time she ran into a stop sign with the driver's ed teacher sitting beside her.

That took them to Two Falls. Chief Thomas's double-wide manufactured home, visible from the main street, showed movement in the kitchen. *Time to cook already?* Jane checked her watch. *A bit early.*

"Did you enjoy your dinner last night?"

"Um, yes. Nice food, good company." Jane did not want to talk about her evening out. She meant to hug it to herself. It was special. It was private. It was nobody's business but her own—and Russ's. Clearly he had told Alice something.

"Russ said 'good food, good company.' Do the two of you think along the same lines?"

Jane found the idea pleasing. "We must. Afterwards he took me down to the marina and showed me where my stepmother surfs. The river's beautiful in the dark."

Alice digested that. "It is beautiful. Maybe I take it for granted. He said you had Thai food. I've never eaten Thai food. Chinese, yes. How is it different?"

Jane was shocked and rather touched. Imagine never having eaten Thai food. She spent some time trying to explain the differences. On impulse, as she turned in to the farmhouse, she said, "I'll tell you what, Alice. When you pass your driver's test we'll celebrate by eating at that restaurant."

"Oh, could we? What a nice thing to say."

Jane set the brake and killed the engine. "You can drive me there."

"I knew there had to be a catch."

Jane stared at her. Alice was smiling. Jane helped her carry her groceries to the kitchen.

The rest of the day was uneventful. Jane cooked for Gus and Gerd. Libby went off with friends. Russ called after dinner, and he and Jane talked about nothing much for half an hour, happy to hear each other's voices. They made a tentative date for pizza later in the week. Jane took her Kindle to bed.

~

THE call came shortly after Rob Neill had settled into his office early Tuesday morning. The latte he had bought on the walk to the courthouse was still warm. He identified himself and took a quick gulp of coffee.

"My name is Russell Hough. I thought I should phone you directly." The caller coughed. "My crew just found Frank August's body in the cherry orchard here—at Hawk Farm, I mean."

Rob sat up straight and set his coffee down. "August..." He could hear voices shouting in the background and the noise of a heavy engine.

"Who else could it be? Who else is missing?" Hough's voice was ragged.

"Do you recognize him?"

Rob heard the man draw a steadying breath. "I've never met him, though I saw the photo you showed on TV. The thing is, the bulldozer—Hell, I have to explain." He made a bid for control and went on in a flat monotone, "I'm removing the orchard. They cut the last trees down yesterday and chipped most of the stumps. I had a bulldozer brought in to smooth things down. It's just finishing, up by the gate to August's syrah vineyard. The driver's blade brought up a human arm."

"My God, d'you mean the body's dismembered?"

Hough cleared his throat. More shouting in the background. The heavy engine stopped. "No. It's, uh, still connected." He cleared his throat again. "The blade was just skimming—shoving dirt around. Gerd saw the arm and shouted to the driver to stop. It's pretty horrible."

"Gerhard Koeppel. The wine maker?"

"Yes, August's wine maker. Gerd has been helping me out since I hurt my foot. I'm not supposed to walk on loose dirt."

"I met Koeppel," Rob interjected. "Keep everyone away from the site, that is, from the place where the body lies, but don't let him—or your workers—leave the premises. We need to question everybody. I'm sending a car from Two Falls now, and I'll bring an ambulance and the forensics van as fast as I can. The press will swarm."

Hough groaned.

"Get your defenses in place. They're not supposed to trespass. And keep to 'no comment' if they corner you. Let your phone calls go to voicemail. Since you called me directly instead of going through 911, they probably won't catch on for a while."

"But they will catch on."

"Yes. Take care, Mr. Hough." Rob disconnected. He and his team were almost to Two Falls half an hour later when it occurred to him that he had failed to tell Hough not to call his neighbors with the news.

~

JANE'S cell phone rang as she was staring into her first cup of coffee. When she saw that the caller was Russ, she answered it—on the third ring. It took her that long to find Talk.

"Jane—"

"What is it? What's wrong?"

"My dear, I'm afraid we've found your father's body."

She made a gasping noise, reaching for a scream, but her throat locked.

He went on, his voice dragging with sadness. He was saying something about the orchard and the bulldozer that she didn't want to hear.

The *no* in her head blanked out meaning. "I'm coming down."

"Yes. Drive. It's safer. The press—"

She disconnected and sat for a numb moment. She ought to wake Gus and Libby. When she thought of Libby's shrieks, her mind revolted. She grabbed her purse from the kitchen counter where she'd left it the night before, stuffed her phone into it, and ran to the door that led to the garage. She didn't even leave a note.

Russ was waiting and stood as she turned the Prius into the farmyard. He had been sitting on the porch steps with a crutch beside him. He stood without its aid, and Jane flew to his arms. He didn't say anything at all, but he held her, smoothing her hair.

When her shaking eased, he retrieved his crutch and led her up the steps. She could hear voices babbling in the orchard beyond the garage.

Russ said, "Let's go in. The patrol car will be here any minute."

"You called the cops?" *Dumb question.*

"The undersheriff. Neill. He sent a car from Two Falls and will be here with his crime scene investigators as soon as he can. He won't be happy that I called you."

"I had to know!"

"Yes."

Her brain began to work. "I suppose he wanted to see my reaction when I heard."

"Cops think that way." He ushered her into the dim hallway.

Jane's mind skittered, and she stopped dead.

"What is it?"

"Shouldn't I...view...uh, look at the body?"

"Someone will have to eventually, Jane, but he's still half-buried. The deputies will remove him from—"

"Then how can you tell it's Dad! Maybe it's—" She broke off. "How could you do this to me? He can't be here. He has to be, oh, in Brazil or Canada. Somewhere else. He can't be dead."

He was watching her, his dark eyes grave.

"You don't know him! You never met him. How can you tell—" She knew she was talking nonsense.

He took her by the arm and led her into the living room. When he had settled her on the sofa, he disappeared.

She didn't cry, but she was trembling again. She heard low voices from the direction of the kitchen. *Oh God, Alice.* Jane blew her nose. She could not make small talk with Alice. She had to collect her wits before the police arrived. All the scenarios that raced through her mind were appalling.

Someone had buried her father in the orchard. *That meant*

murder, didn't it? But who? The why was easy. Money, money, money. But what about vengeance? She thought of the woman Frank had insulted at the library fête. He went out of his way to annoy innocent bystanders. He enjoyed conflict. But surely he had not tussled with anyone in Latouche County long enough to provoke murder. Bill Hough was safely dead. And few of the people Frank had dealt with in California knew where he lived.

She didn't know that, not for sure. The bank employees—and the customers—had the strongest motive to harm him, but he'd left the banking scene well before things began to fall apart. If anyone, Gus ought to be their target, not Frank. But suppose the bank's victims did know of her father's move north, and did know of his role in the mortgage crisis? She could imagine some aggrieved victim of foreclosure stalking him via the Internet, moving to the area, lurking.

She buried her face in her hands. She was avoiding the worst scenarios. All too often, murder was a household matter. Gus, Libby, Gerd, even Irma. And down the hill. Here—where his body had been buried. Russ, Judith, Alice, and, just possibly, Tom Dahl. And what about the man who had found the SUV, Russ's uncle? Redfern, that was his name. Alice's brother. *Nonsense,* she told herself. *The poor man was the most innocent of bystanders.*

At that point she remembered something important, something wonderful. Russ could not have killed her father. The day Russ had torn the ligament in his foot Frank had been alive and blustering about lawsuits at the dinner table. She would never have believed Russ could kill her father, but her confidence was not just sentiment. Russ *could not* have taken Frank's body to the orchard and buried him. No way. Even cops would have to see that.

For at least a minute, she basked in the joy of knowing there was someone she could trust, and, above all, that it was Russell. Misery swept back over her. How was she going to live in the same house with people she had to suspect might have killed her father? If only she'd found a place to rent in Hood River and moved out. If only.

Russ returned with a mug of coffee. He was leaning hard on the crutch and juggling the cup in his left hand. He set it on the end table beside her. "Black. No sugar. Right?"

She nodded, mute.

"I told Ma you wanted to be alone with your thoughts."

"Thanks. I can't t-talk."

"It's okay. If she tries to thrust coffee cake on you, just say no. She won't be offended. I have to go back out there now and soothe down Gerd and the kids."

"Kids?"

"Three of my regular crew were helping to clear the orchard. They're scared they'll be deported."

"And will they?"

"Not if I can help it. I think they're okay." He didn't sound sure. He cocked his head, frowning. "Siren. Must be the patrol car."

"Do you have to tell the police I'm here?"

The siren wailed, cut off, gave a yelp.

"I'll have to if they ask. The undersheriff is bound to, but he won't get here for a while."

She heard gravel crunch as the patrol car turned in to the farm.

"Drink your coffee, Jane." Russ touched her hand. "And don't think too much. We don't know what happened." He stumped off, leaning on the crutch. She hoped he hadn't damaged his foot walking in the orchard.

~

ROB drove the new four-wheel-drive car from the courthouse in Klalo. He didn't drive patrol cars that often. He preferred to use his time more productively riding shotgun, but Linda Ramos wanted to consult her notes. She needed to bring him up to date on the missing person investigation, now that the person was no longer missing. Niles Larson crammed himself into the backseat. The forensics van followed, and an ambulance was coming, too.

The state patrol had rounded up a medical examiner who would drive out from Camas.

Rob accelerated past the Highway 14 sign on the east side of town. "So tell me about backgrounds—the son and the wife first."

Linda spent some time reviewing her notes before she replied. "Neither Mrs. August nor the son has any kind of police record. Francis, Junior, is twenty-seven, has an MBA from Wharton."

"Hmm. Pennsylvania."

"He's unmarried. Mrs. August attended UC Santa Barbara for a while, never graduated. I don't think she declared a major."

"Not surprising."

"No. This was August's fifth marriage, her second. Her former husband was a senior executive at the August bank."

"I gather she was not a widow."

"No. And she divorced *him*. No-fault. She got a big settlement. There were no children."

"How old is her first husband?"

"About the same age as Frank August."

"That's interesting. She would have been young for the man when they married."

"I suppose so. She's thirty now, three years younger than August's daughter."

"That all?"

"I need to dig deeper," Linda said with resignation. "The son you know about. He's hiding out. The bank failed a week ago, but it's been shaky for at least a year. He held thirty-five percent of the shares—a controlling interest—and his father made him CEO before the bank went public. Speaking of young."

"Frank, Senior, must have been looking for trouble."

"Why do you say that?"

"Leaving an inexperienced kid in the driver's seat. Handing over all those shares. I wonder…"

"What?"

"There's the daughter, Jane. If her father gave the son what amounted at the time to a fortune in shares, what did he give his daughter? If nothing, she has a real grievance."

"And that makes her a suspect."

"Pity. I like her."

"Yes. Me, too. Better than I like her stepmother." Linda sniffed.

"Did you look into Jane's background?"

"Some. Her BA is from Mills, and she took an MA at San Francisco State—no, it was an MFA, master of fine arts. Never been married. Her paintings are beginning to sell, though not sensationally. She has an independent income from investments in real estate and what are supposed to be safe stocks, not the August bank. From my viewpoint, she's rich. From her father's, not. She seems to be on good terms with her mother and step-father. Her half brother from that marriage is a law student at Hastings in San Francisco. That's all I got. I wasn't looking at her hard."

"No reason to, at the time."

"I wish I had more on the stepmother, Libby August. I talked to a couple of the surfers."

"And?"

"They said she's a great athlete. They don't like her much. Both of them are women, by the way."

"Which means what?"

Linda shoved her glasses up the bridge of her nose. "It usually means a woman has no time for other women when guys are around—and lots of guys surf."

"So women don't like her."

"That's about it. Other resentments popped up. She flashes her money in everybody's face, for one thing."

"For another?"

Linda wriggled against the seat belt. "The women I talked to are convinced she sleeps around, though she's discreet about it."

"Names?"

"They didn't give me names. They clammed up."

"Okay. Look into it. What about the wine maker?"

"I got a lot off the Internet, but half of it's in German."

"Bummer," said Niles from the backseat. He was sitting forward, listening.

"Rhys is looking for a translator," Linda said. Rhys Howell was the desk sergeant.

They were coming up on Two Falls. Rob wondered whether Maddie and Jack had caught wind of something happening. Probably. Local news traveled fast. He groaned when he thought of Jack Redfern. Of *course* Hough had called his uncle. And Koeppel had probably called Jane August.

Rob braked for the stop sign at the center of the tiny village. Not a soul in sight. He eased on through the intersection and out of town.

"I know a little about him." Linda meant the wine maker. "He's thirty-six. August hired him early this year and paid him a signing bonus. He just got back from a tour of Northwest vineyards—buying grapes for the first vintage. He's an old friend of Russell Hough."

"Yes." And that was an interesting coincidence, if coincidence it was. Time for another talk with Jack. Interesting it might be, Rob reflected as Linda gave him Koeppel's history in the U. S., but what possible connection could there be between Russell Hough and Frank August?

Judith. Of course, Judith. The night Frank August disappeared, her brother had caught her coming in from a "patrol." She'd roamed around the area where August's body was found, and she was armed. If she'd seen him as an intruder, if she'd shot him and buried him, would she have been overcome with remorse? That made sense of her suicide attempt. Unfortunately, she was not up to answering questions.

"Uh, boss? You're leaving the van behind." Niles was peering out the back window.

Rob slowed the patrol car until the van reappeared in the rearview mirror with the ambulance now close behind it. *If Judith was the killer, who drove the SUV into that thicket of blackberries?* The question hung in the silence.

The August vineyard with the unfinished *cave* came into view. Rob could see workmen in among the vines. A man stood in the doorway that led to the tasting room. The men turned to watch the patrol car pass. *Nothing like a little excitement next door.* The farmhouse lay just beyond the vines. He turned left and parked behind a blue Prius abandoned at the front steps. A cluster of men in work clothes watched from the porch. They were drinking from coffee mugs.

The tech van and the ambulance stopped closer to the garage. The drivers stayed at the wheel. The EMTs and the deputies from the van emerged, and one of the EMTs lit up. As Rob got out, Niles popped from the backseat in a blur of cramped limbs. Linda took her time. The other patrol car was not visible—up near the gate at the top of the orchard, Rob supposed. He hoped it hadn't obliterated the tread marks of other vehicles.

How had Frank August's body got to the burial site? Maybe he'd gone for a midnight stroll in the orchard, and Judith had accosted him where he now lay half-buried. If so, there should be no tire tracks leading to or from the syrah vineyard. Rob had seen the three-barred gate from the pool enclosure the day the MisPers case became official, the day he and Linda "searched" the August house. He had gathered from Koeppel that the Houghs didn't use the gate at all, and he and Jane had only opened it to walk down to the farmhouse. It was pretty far off for an elderly man to walk to in the dark of night.

Elderly. Listen to me. August was in his mid-sixties. Not all that old. Gloomy thought. Rob was pushing fifty. He went to the van and indicated to the driver where he ought to take the crew. The first order of business, assuming the first responders had done their job, was to disinter the body. He would have to take a look before they moved it, but they wouldn't need him for a while.

He turned back to the farmhouse and the men on the porch. Three of them were very young and looked to be Hispanic. The fourth had to be Russell Hough. Not a brilliant deduction—he was older, and he looked enough like Bill Hough to be a clone rather than Bill's son, despite the black hair and dark eyes. He was thinner than his father had been, and his default setting seemed to be sadness rather than anger, but there was no doubt at all that he was Bill Hough's son. He stepped forward, and Rob saw that he was using a metal crutch, which cinched the I.D. if proof had been necessary.

"Mr. Hough? I'm Robert Neill. I assume that Koeppel and the driver of the bulldozer are up at the site with the deputies I sent from Two Falls."

"Yes. These guys are part of my regular crew. They were helping to clear away slash and didn't see much." He introduced his men. They nodded to Rob. One of them muttered, *"Señor."* The other two kept silent. "They don't speak English well. Or at all, in one case. I can translate for you."

"That won't be necessary. Sergeant Ramos can translate when the time comes." Rob indicated Linda, who was listening intently. "Right now I need to talk to you. After that I'll go up to view the body *in situ* so the ambulance crew can move it. We'll wait for the medical examiner. It will be some time before we get around to interviewing other witnesses."

Hough frowned. He started to say something, then shook his head.

"What is it?"

"I appreciate that that's your usual procedure, sir, but I was hoping you could talk to them as soon as possible—"

"So they can get back to work? Understandable, but I'm afraid murder takes precedence."

"Yes, of course it does. The thing is, they're scared, and I think they may decide to bolt. I tried to reassure them."

"Are they illegal?"

"Not to the best of my knowledge, but they're afraid they'll be deported anyway."

"We don't operate like that."

"I'm sure you don't, but *they're* not sure." He drew a breath. "As I have reason to know, an interrogation can be an alarming experience."

"I can't believe Todd Welch threatened you. In fact, I listened to the tape—"

"Todd? No. *He* was okay." He shrugged, turned to the three young men, and began speaking to them in rapid Spanish.

Kitty Grant had also been present in the aftermath of Judith Hough's suicide attempt. Deputy Grant was not noted for tact and diplomacy. What had she done? He remembered the graphic photos of Hough covered with his sister's blood. He had looked understandably distraught. In those circumstances, questioning must have seemed brutal. Rob doubted that Kitty had done anything incorrect, but she enjoyed the power she had a little too much. He wondered whether she realized why she would never make detective as long as he had a say in the matter.

Rob turned to Linda. "What's he telling them?"

She ducked her head. "He's just reassuring them, saying not to worry and to wait for him here. He says he won't be long, and that his mother will be fixing lunch for them. He's kind of jollying them along."

Rob changed his mind. "Niles, get over here." Niles had been chatting with the EMTs. "Mr. Hough?"

Hough broke off in mid-sentence.

"Sergeant Ramos will interview your workers here while you and I talk. Then they can go. She'll want to see them one at a time. Do it in the patrol car," he said to Linda, who stared at him. "Niles can assist you." Niles had some Spanish.

Hough said, "Thank you. I don't suppose—"

"No, you can't sit in on the interviews, damn it. Don't ask." Rob tried to imagine Bill Hough concerning himself for his work crew. *Interesting character difference.*

Hough gave a sheepish smile, turned back to his crew, and let loose another burst of Spanish. They looked relieved, though they were clearly still wary. Murmuring among themselves, they settled down on the surface of the porch, which wrapped around the side of the house. Linda beckoned to the youngest-looking one, and the two of them went off to the patrol car. Niles followed.

"Want a cup of coffee? We can talk in the kitchen. My mother went upstairs to change sheets."

"Lead the way," Rob said.

Hough preceded him around the side of the house and down a short hall to the kitchen. It was bright and charming, and in it, at the round oak table with her back to them, sat Jane August. She whirled, saw Rob, and put her hand to her mouth.

"Oops." Hough sounded resigned.

"Hello, Jane," Rob said. "I'm very sorry for your trouble."

"Mother?" Hough said.

Jane nodded. She'd been crying, and an untouched piece of coffee cake sat on the table in front of her. "She was so nice. She said she was going upstairs to make the beds and wouldn't bother me. I didn't have the heart to say no."

"You have to be firm with Ma." He sounded teasing and affectionate. She gave him a tremulous smile.

Rob wondered what the relationship was. As far as he knew, Jane had taken Russell to the hospital the day he hurt his foot. No one had said anything about closer ties.

She turned to Rob, earnest. "You mustn't blame Russ for calling me. I know you wanted to see how I'd react when I heard—"

"That's a minor consideration." He was lying. "Have you called your stepmother?"

"No. I...they're not awake. What time is it?" She looked at her watch. The clock on the wall said 9:32. "Oh God, Libby. Gus will sleep until noon, but Libby—"

"Who is Gus?"

"My brother. Francis, Junior. He prefers to be called Gus."

So the son had come back.

"He drank a lot last night. And the night before that. He'll sleep off his hangover, but Libby is bound to be up by now. I'll have to call her. She'll shriek like a banshee—" She broke off and began to cry.

Rob said, "You know, Jane, one of the reasons we prefer to notify survivors ourselves is to make sure there's someone present who can help them. I want to wait until your father's body has been disinterred before I let them know what's happened."

She mopped her eyes with a wad of tissues. "But what if they see for themselves? The area around the gate is visible from the pool deck. I would surely have seen it...the bulldozer, I mean, and the patrol car, and my...the body. I go out on the deck to look at the mountain every morning. I would have *seen*. Russ wanted to spare me that."

"That makes sense," Rob said. "But, since you're here now, I'll have to ask you to stick around until I can take a statement. Then we can both go up and break the news to your family."

10.

JANE WAITED in the kitchen. She could hear Alice creaking around upstairs and Russ's workers on the porch muttering in Spanish. Neill had taken Russ with him to view the body, interrogating him on the way, she supposed. She was glad Russ hadn't had to walk through the orchard again. The two men had ridden up in the patrol car, leaving Sgt. Ramos behind to conduct the last of her interviews.

Sitting there in the kitchen, staring at the unmoving clock, it occurred to Jane that there was one person she could call. Neill could surely not object if she called her mother. She got out her phone, poked the speed dial, and took the phone into the living room because she could hear Alice coming downstairs.

Jane's mother answered on the seventh ring. Mary Sylvester was suitably shocked and even cried a little for old times' sake, but she didn't sound surprised that Frank was dead. She had expected that. "Surely it was an accident, not murder."

"He's buried in the orchard, Mom. Buried. Get it?"

"Does that mean someone at the farm killed him?"

"No!" Jane drew a breath. "I know Russell couldn't have, Alice wouldn't, and—"

"The girl is in a coma. I see." Mary took her time. Jane thought she was drinking tea.

Judith could well have killed Frank. Jane didn't point that out. Nor did she explain why she knew Russ was blameless.

"You'd better come home, Jane. Right now." By home, Mary meant the Sylvester house, never mind that Jane had lived in her own little house for more than ten years.

"I can't."

"The police won't let you?" Indignation sharpened Mary's voice.

"They haven't said anything yet. I have a job. I have to report for duty next week."

"Ha." Mary was not impressed by Jane's contract to teach art part-time. The pay was derisory, and most of the students would turn out to be crafters who wanted to learn how to paint baskets of kittens.

Her mother was right, but Jane needed the stimulus of other viewpoints, and there was nothing like a classroom to provide that. Also, teaching classes in the area would give her an entrée to the community her father didn't have. The thought of her father blotted out what Mary was saying about coming home.

When her mother wound down, Jane said, "Well, I can't come back now, so tell me what I ought to do."

"Call Frank's lawyers."

"But surely the police will do that, or Libby."

"Don't be simple, Jane. Find out who has your father's will. You're bound to be an heir."

"Oh, God." A chill ran down her spine. "Then I'll automatically be considered a suspect. I'll have to stay." It struck her that no one, least of all the very sharp undersheriff, would believe she hadn't thought about the will, though she hadn't. Gus's blunt reference to Frank's estate had repelled her. She had pushed the whole question of inheritance aside, as if it didn't matter. *Nothing like denial.*

But it did matter. She thought of the huge house with the stirring of hope. She could pass its management back to Libby and Tom Dahl, find herself a place across the river, and what?

Invite Russ to come to her there? She liked the idea of living next door to him, but her father had been buried here, probably killed on the farm. That fact would change everything.

Mary was urging her to find a criminal lawyer.

"I have to go now," Jane interjected. "I called because I wanted you to know what's going on, but they're coming back soon, and I may have to identify Dad."

"Oh, darling—"

"Yes. Then I'll have to go with the undersheriff to tell Gus and Libby." *If they haven't already figured out what's going on in the orchard.* She wondered whether Libby's shrieks would be audible at the farmhouse. *Would she shriek if nobody was around to hear her? If a tree falls in the forest...*

Mary said motherly things and hung up, sounding worried. Jane set the phone on the end table and put her head in her hands again. Should she call Lewis Schramm? Not yet. She was innocent. She wanted to look innocent, which was a different matter. Calling a lawyer, any lawyer, was surely premature.

~

FRANK August's body had lain in the good volcanic earth more than a week, so there were maggots and other signs of nature taking its course. Rob had never learned how to look at a corpse with equanimity, not even at open-casket funerals. He managed not to throw up.

He heard the words that pronounced August dead and the voices of his forensics crew as they moved the body from its fetal crouch in the dirt to a body bag and from there to the flattened gurney. Rigor long gone, the arm the bulldozer had caught flopped. The driver sat frozen on his vehicle. The first responders had taken a statement from him. Rob sent him home and sent the extraneous deputies back to Two Falls.

The EMTs moved the gurney to the ambulance. Beside Rob, Russell Hough shifted on his crutch and murmured something in a language other than English.

Rob cocked his head. "That's not Spanish."

"Klalo."

Rob turned to him, blinking.

"The equivalent of rest in peace. You can see Memaloose Island from the east end of the bluff." Hough didn't meet Rob's eyes. He was looking upriver. Memaloose was an ancient burial ground. "I'll have to ask Maddie to conduct a purification."

Rob had attended several such rites and found them moving, but it surprised him that Bill Hough's son thought along those lines. "Your parents were Catholic. Didn't your father have you raised in the church?"

"My father didn't raise me. Jack did. Excuse me." He made his careful way over to his friend, Gerhard Koeppel, who *had* thrown up.

Hough touched his arm and said something too quiet for Rob to catch. Koeppel nodded and wiped his mouth on a blue-spotted bandanna. The wine maker had known August better than anyone else there and had agreed to make the formal identification of the body, so he had been standing close enough to the gurney to get a strong whiff of death. The stench hung on the air, barely tolerable. Rob walked over to the two friends.

"Can you identify the deceased, Mr. Koeppel?"

The wine maker nodded. "It's Herr August."

"Thank you. I'm sorry you had to go through that." Since Rob had met August at the library luncheon, he could have made the identification himself—the face was recognizable—but it was always better to have a family member or a friend do it. Rob thought Koeppel had obliged so Jane wouldn't have to. Kind of him.

Jane was the sort of woman men would always want to take care of, though she seemed unconscious of the fact. She was probably going to be wealthy. Rob hoped that wouldn't ruin the connection he sensed between her and Russell Hough.

Romanticist, he chided himself. It was time to get to work. The M.E. the state patrol had sent came over to him and drew him aside.

"I suppose you want to know the time and cause of death."

"I do, but I don't think you're going to tell me."

"No. He wasn't shot, if that's what you were thinking. The blows to the head probably killed him." He tapped the back of his own skull. "But he might have died of a heart attack. Or he might have smothered."

Ugly thought. Rob's stomach lurched.

"As to time," the M.E. continued, "a week, ten days, your guess is better than mine. I'll conduct the autopsy this afternoon at the hospital."

"I'll send a deputy to observe."

"Two o'clock." He strode off to his car, full of his own importance, leaving Rob to wonder which unfortunate deputy he should pick on for mortuary duty. Niles, he supposed, poor kid.

As the ambulance made its way down the hill to the farm-yard, Rob pulled out his phone and called the sheriff. She liked to know what was happening, and too often he forgot to call her. When he finished his brief conversation with Beth, he found that Hough had returned to his side. The wine maker was walking toward the farmhouse, head down.

"I can tell you why August was buried where he was," Hough said.

Rob stared at him. "You can?"

His face was impassive. "I felled a diseased tree here when I first came back. I removed the debris and dug out the root ball—didn't have a chipper. The stump left a sizeable hole. I burned the roots but didn't get around to filling in the hole. Whoever buried August just put him in it and shoved the mounded dirt over him. It wouldn't have taken five minutes."

"That's interesting. The workers who harvested your cherries would have seen the hole."

"Yes, and it would have been visible from August's pool deck."

"And to anyone who walked down to the farmhouse from that gate," Rob observed. "And vice versa."

"A lot of people."

But only people who knew about the orchard and the gate to August's property, not bank clients in California. Rob turned the fact over in his mind. "Did your sister know you'd cut the tree down?"

After a long, revealing silence, Hough said she did, his voice lifeless. "She knew. She didn't want to admit the tree was diseased. I'd told her I meant to remove the orchard if it was infested."

"Removing dying trees seems reasonable."

"It is. She doesn't want things to change. She grew up on the farm, but thanks to my father she knows nothing much about farming." His mouth twisted. "'Not women's work.'"

That sounded like Bill. What Russell said corroborated what Jack Redfern had already told Rob about Judith.

"We argued some, Judy and I. I was going to have to take out the trees, but I didn't like to disturb her. She was still very upset about Dad's suicide, in addition to her other problems." Hough bit his lip. "You don't need to know that. It doesn't bear on August's death."

"No."

He gave his head a shake. "My sister knew the tree was gone. She told me she walked up to the gate and checked that entrance to our property every time she went out 'on patrol.'"

"So she would have noticed if someone had filled in the hole."

"Probably, though she came up here in the dark. She wore night goggles and didn't use a light."

"August wasn't shot." Rob didn't know why he wanted to comfort this man. "The M.E. thinks he was killed by blows to the head."

Hough took a hasty step toward him. "Are you sure?"

"That's what the M.E. told me." It was just possible the pathologist might have missed a small-caliber gunshot wound in his perfunctory look at the body, but Rob doubted it.

"Christ!" Hough rubbed his hand over his face. "Christ, that's wonderful. I mean that he wasn't shot, not—"

"I know what you're saying. Your uncle told me your mother was worried about Judith, afraid she might kill someone."

"Jack told *you?*"

"We're friends." Rob left it at that. He wasn't insulted. He thought Hough's surprise was genuine. "When you found she'd been carrying a rifle around the place at night, you must have been worried, too."

Hough gave a choke of unamused laughter. "Worried! I was shit-scared. Damn Dad, and damn the VA. They have all these vets suffering from post-traumatic stress, and they don't give them the help they need. So my Catholic mother gets to deal with two suicides in the family." He sounded as if he didn't believe Judith would recover.

"How is Alice? I haven't seen her since the funeral."

As they walked over to the patrol car and drove down to the house, Hough told him a little about Alice's coping techniques—baking, cooking, canning, stewing, freezing—and about their daily visits to the hospital. He spoke with affection. They had painted the kitchen together when he first came home. He was teaching his mother to drive. Rob was struck again by the character difference between father and son. Maybe Jack *had* raised Russell. Family dynamics never ceased to be amazing.

Jane August was waiting on the porch when they reached the house. So much for Hough family dynamics. Now for the family of Francis August, deceased.

～

JANE had returned the Prius to its spot in the garage and saw that the Beamer, Libby's Jeep, and Gus's rental were still in place. Reluctance dragged at her ankles as she trudged to the front door to await the undersheriff and his sergeant. The deputy who had come to the farm with them had gone off to witness the autopsy.

Jane felt queasy. Despite everyone's protests that viewing the body wasn't necessary, she had looked at it. She told herself she had to verify that Frank was dead. He was. She vomited.

Rob Neill and Sgt. Ramos came up to the house sooner than

Jane expected. Libby was up, taking a shower from the sound of it. If Libby shrieked when she was told, Jane thought she might strangle her stepmother. Breakfast debris cluttered the kitchen. Could Libby not clean up after herself?

Jane gritted her teeth and saw her two visitors to comfortable chairs on the pool deck. Then she went to wake her brother. It took some doing, but when she told him the third time that the police wanted to see him, he stirred and sat up, groaning.

"What's it about?"

She had been asked not to tell him, which was okay. She didn't want to. "We'll be waiting for you by the pool. Hurry up and get dressed. Do not go back to sleep, Gus. I'll get Libby."

She heard him grumbling questions as she went off to the master bedroom. Libby's shower was still running. Jane waited in the hall. When the water continued to flow, she marched into the bedroom, strode through the dressing room, and banged on the bathroom door.

Libby shrieked.

"Police, Libby." Jane made a swift withdrawal. Maybe that was malicious.

She brewed a pot of coffee. Gus would need it. As she waited in the kitchen and listened to the pot burble, she watched the two cops. They were talking, and both of them looked grave. It must be difficult, having to inform a family of a murder, because your natural sympathy for someone else's pain would be poisoned by the suspicion that one or more of the family might deserve no sympathy.

The image of her father as she had just seen him flashed across her inner vision, and her stomach twisted. She gripped the edge of the sink, willing herself not to vomit again. *Oh, Dad.* She had barely known him. He had not been a good man or even a likeable one, but he hadn't deserved to be murdered and slung into a hole in the ground.

Memory kicked in. *A hole in the ground.* That was what had changed in the orchard. There had been a gaping hole near where she'd driven the SUV from the syrah vineyard the day she took Russ to the hospital. She had swerved to avoid the hole. The next day, when she and Gerd walked through the orchard to the farmhouse, the hole had disappeared. Another wave of nausea clutched at her. She swallowed bile. Had she walked over her father's body? The horror of that froze her where she stood clutching the sink.

The coffeepot gave a final burp. She poured the black fluid into a Thermos jug and fiddled awhile fixing a tray. Eventually her hands stopped shaking. When Gus and Libby still hadn't come, she took the tray out and poured three mugs of black coffee. That left perhaps three cups in the Thermos, so she went back in and started another pot. Gus stumbled into the kitchen unshaven, in shorts, a T-shirt, and flip-flops.

"They're on the deck." She didn't meet his eyes.

"Who?"

"Undersheriff Neill and Sergeant Ramos."

"Haven't met them." Gus sounded hung over, his consonants blurred.

She didn't respond to that. "There's coffee on the tray outside."

He slouched out. Jane followed. Neill and the deputy fell silent. Jane introduced her brother and sat where she could watch him. Her drink was lukewarm.

When Gus had slurped some coffee, he said, "What's happening?"

"A lot," Neill said. "Let's wait for Mrs. August."

The silence stretched, more and more uncomfortable. At long last Libby twinkled onstage. Her hair fell into its perfectly cut shoulder-length bell. Her makeup—minimal, Jane had to admit—enhanced her unnaturally blue eyes, and the figure of Kokopelli danced across the bosom of her turquoise T-shirt. Denim cutoffs bared waxed legs. Her toenails glittered in turquoise sandals. When had she found the time to be waxed?

Neill had risen when she came out. "Mrs. August—"

"Mr. Neill. I'll call you Rob since we're old friends by now. Sergeant."

Sgt. Ramos nodded.

"Please sit down, Mrs. August." Neill gestured to a chair.

Libby sat, still twinkling.

He resumed his own seat. "We have very bad news for you all."

Jane waited for the shriek, but Libby just stared, wide-eyed.

"Frank August's body was found this morning buried in the Hough orchard."

Libby may or may not have shrieked. Jane didn't hear her, because Gus turned curd white. He slid from his chair onto the deck in a dead faint before anyone could move to catch him.

Jane dropped her mug, slopping coffee, and jumped from her chair, but Neill beat her to Gus's side. He knelt and took a pulse. Jane could never find a pulse let alone take one.

"He's all right," Neill murmured when he had checked Gus's head for injury.

"All right!"

"In good health," Neill amended. "Strong heartbeat. Didn't hit his head."

"I hope you saw what you wanted to see," Jane snarled.

Neill didn't reply.

"Go away!" She took Gus's clammy hand and stroked it. "Frankie, c'mon, honey. It'll be okay." *Why am I uttering nonsense?*

Her brother moaned. "Hate Frankie—"

"Gus, then. Come on, Gus. Buck up. You're all right." *You have the undersheriff's word for that.* She had the feeling none of them would be all right for a long time.

Libby was sobbing. When no one paid any attention to her, her sobs dwindled to sniffs. Sgt. Ramos scribbled in her notebook.

After a minute or two, Gus groaned and sat up. He blinked at his sister. "Dad's dead then?"

She nodded.

"Thought he was in Rio, poor old bugger." He shook his head as if to clear it. "Or drowned in the river. Here all the time?" Libby gave a halfhearted shriek.

Neill said, "We don't know."

So Jane told him about the disappearing hole in the ground. Sgt. Ramos scribbled furiously, and Gus stood up and fell back into his chair.

"Thanks, Jane," Neill said. "That helps establish the time line. The medical examiner was coy about it."

"Have you arrested him yet?"

Everyone turned to Libby.

Her face contorted. She looked almost ugly. "That Hough man with his tin leg. The cripple. His father hated my h-husband." Her voice broke on a sob.

Jane choked out a protest.

Neill said, "If you mean Russell Hough, he could not have buried anyone, not in the orchard. He injured both legs the previous morning and had surgery on his foot. He was using a wheelchair that couldn't negotiate loose soil."

"Who says?"

"Jane, among others. I imagine his doctors will confirm it when we ask them. He didn't know your husband, Mrs. August, nor was he on such terms with his father that he'd be likely to continue his father's quarrels. I advise you to be careful who you accuse." He added, in a conciliatory tone, "A murder investigation is disturbing to everyone, especially to the victim's survivors. I'm sorry for what you're going to have to endure."

Libby snorted.

He went on, almost as if he were pleading with her or perhaps with all three of them, "The loss of privacy, the feelings of anger and suspicion, above all the grief—I'm not indifferent to all that, believe me, but society also has a stake. The first right the Declaration of Independence lists is the right to life. When a life is taken, the perpetrator has to be found and punished. Since the punishment in this state is severe, we're careful where we lay the blame." He looked straight at Libby. "And so should you be. I understand that you were the one who insisted that Mr. August was missing."

"I knew something had happened to him," she said tragically. "I just *knew* it. A woman's intuition. No, a *wife's* intuition. Jane laughed at me."

Thanks a lot. Jane clenched her teeth. Unfortunately, Libby had a good memory.

"Should we call a lawyer?" Gus had been so quiet, Jane started when he spoke.

Neill said, "You can call a lawyer at any time."

"Yes, yes. What do you advise?"

The undersheriff turned to Sgt. Ramos. She closed her notebook.

"You have a lot of rights," Neill said, "most of them listed in the first ten amendments to the Constitution, and that includes the famous right to remain silent when you're questioned. We can't force you to speak if you choose not to. Right now you're all suspects. As far as I know, you were here during the time in question—between, say, ten P.M. on the Sunday he disappeared and six or seven the next morning."

"Not me," Gus said. He had flown to San Francisco before seven A.M.

"Not Gerd," Libby pleaded.

"Gerhard Koeppel is a suspect. At Hawk Farm, Alice and Judith Hough. In addition, we have to look at anyone who worked here at the house or down at the farm or in the two vineyards adjoining the farm—not because they had any reason to kill Mr. August, but because they could have known about the burial site and could have entered either property unseen during the crucial time."

"Tom Dahl?" Libby's voice squeaked. Jane was surprised. She wasn't aware that Libby knew Dahl well enough to be concerned, but of course it was logical that she would.

"Irma?" Jane asked.

"Yes to both, and the farm workers, Russell Hough's and Mr. August's. In practical terms, only someone with a possible

motive is apt to be looked at closely. That's where our questioning is likely to irk you. I met Mr. August. He struck me as a
man who liked to provoke conflict. That made him interesting,
but it can be a dangerous trait." He let the silence lengthen
then turned to Jane. "Is there a room we can use for private
interviews?"

Dumb question in a house this size. "I'll show you the nearest
study."

"The one your father used?"

"Yes, his computer's there."

"Good. I know where that is. What I want to do today is
to take a preliminary statement from each of you. After that my
forensics crew will search the house and grounds. Or begin the
search, at any rate."

"Do we need a lawyer?" Gus asked again in tones of
exasperation.

"Probably not," Neill said coolly. "Since I don't know what's
on your mind, I can't say. What you tell me will be recorded. You
can stop the interview by asking for an attorney."

"You're wasting valuable time," Gus grumbled. "You should
be looking for the perpetrator."

"I am."

That took a moment to register. Libby gave a shriek

"I don't see why we should cooperate!" Gus fumed.

"I can think of one reason," Neill said. "Most relatives of
murder victims want to know who killed them." He waited for
their protests to die. "I'll take you last, Jane. Mrs. August, if
you'll go with Linda, I'll join you in a moment."

Libby and Sgt. Ramos went off. Neill looked from Gus to
Jane. "Please don't discuss this while you're waiting. With the
best will in the world, you'll end up altering each other's perceptions of what happened."

Gus sniffed. Jane said, "All right. I'm going to my room for
my sketchbook."

She occupied herself well enough as she waited, though the
mountain wasn't fully visible in the slight haze.

Gus watched her. At last he said, "You *knew*. You were down there when Dad's body was found."

"Not when it was found. Russell called me after he called the police."

"Why didn't you let us know?"

"You were both still asleep."

"You should have wakened us."

"I didn't want to hear Libby shriek," Jane confessed, inserting a hawk into her skyscape. "And I was in no hurry to carry bad news. Forget it, Gus. You know now."

She flipped the page and began to draw a larger hawk from memory. Beautiful birds, hawks, but predatory, no doubt about it. Russell might be a Hough, but he was not a hawk. So what kind of bird was he? She sketched birds—ravens and crows, swallows, meadowlarks, woodpeckers, jays, robins, gulls. Birds—an alien species. Dinosaurs, some of them anyway, were probably very large birds or bird-ancestors. She wondered what the area had been like when dinosaurs walked the earth. No Gorge then.

After a good half hour, Linda Ramos came out to fetch Gus. Libby didn't return. That was a relief. Jane was still in a mood to scratch out her stepmother's eyes. *Cripple, indeed.* What would it be like to demand that everyone be perfect, physically or otherwise? Maybe that was why so many actresses were interchangeable. They'd all gone to the same cosmetic surgeon, the one Libby had used.

She sketched Libby's perfect face, altered the cheekbones, and added a wart to the end of her nose. *Much more interesting.*

Gus's ordeal didn't last long. He'd gone off to shower and shave, Linda Ramos said. She led Jane to the study and sat behind Frank's desk to tend to the small video-recorder. Neill sat in an armchair beside the empty fireplace. Jane took the vacant seat beside him.

"How are you holding up, Jane?" Neill's tone was kind, not at all suspicious.

"Well enough, thank you. Better than my brother."

"Sorry about that." He didn't sound sorry. He sounded as if he were a hundred miles away. When he had got her permission to record and intoned the ritual phrases that began a formal interrogation, he said, "Take me through the time in question."

Jane complied. She thought she was accurate. Her voice didn't shake.

When he lost interest in her account of Frank's disappearance, he said, "Do you know the terms of your father's will?"

"No. I assume he split what he had among Libby, Gus, and me with some bequests to causes. He was a man with strong opinions. As far as I know Gus and I were his only blood relations."

"It wouldn't occur to him to return the money to his failed bank?"

She considered that. "I doubt it. He thought of the bank's clients as suckers. And he took his money out more than three years ago when the bank went public."

"Made a clean getaway?"

She looked at him. He met her eyes, unsmiling. "Something like that. I don't understand money, Mr. Neill. I'm glad I have some, of course, since that means I'm free to focus on what does interest me."

"And your brother?"

"He's anxious about it now, because he lost what he had when the bank failed. I don't think money was ever a passion with him. He plodded through the MBA—"

"What does he care about?"

She sighed and thought of her brother's faint. "I don't know Gus well."

"What of your stepmother, the current one?"

Jane squirmed. "Self-focused. I don't think she's obsessed with money. She signed a pre-nuptial agreement, and she apparently made out well when she divorced her previous husband. I find her boring, and I think Dad was beginning to." She was tempted to tell him her suspicions—that Libby had slept with Gus at some point and with Gerd more recently—but the thought was so distasteful it was easier just to stay silent.

"We'll have to contact your father's lawyers—"

Jane interrupted to tell him about Lewis Schramm and the tax lawyers in Seattle. When she had done that, Neill stood up and disengaged, warning her not to leave the county in a polite, unthreatening way that was somehow more chilling than if he had shouted at her.

11.

I T WAS NEARLY eight when Russell called Jane. He said he'd tried earlier but the line was busy.

"I was on the phone all afternoon—mostly with my mother who wants me to lawyer up and come back to San Francisco, like yesterday."

"You don't need a lawyer. Maybe she's right about going home, though."

"I have a Job!" Jane howled. She'd been repeating that to deaf ears since nine-thirty in the morning, or so it seemed.

"You also have a life. Save it. Move down to the farm."

"What are you saying, Russ?"

He mumbled something about swimming and sharks. She could not have heard him correctly. In fact, she was having a hard time hearing him at all.

"Are you talking and driving?"

"Yes, and I don't like to. I'm on my way to the hospital to pick Ma up. Jack drove her in after lunch, while I was still dealing with the cops."

"Oh, God, I promised Judy I'd see her today. Apologize to her for me."

He was silent. When he spoke again his voice was warmer, less harassed. "You really believe she's listening, don't you?"

"Yes, and so should you."

"Okay, Jane. I will. Pizza tomorrow night?"

"I can hardly wait." They agreed on half-past seven. He said he'd drive. "We can look in on Judy afterwards," Jane said.

"Or beforehand. I don't like to watch the clock when I'm talking to you."

"What a nice thing to say."

"I am nice."

He laughed when she sputtered. She made him hang up at that point lest he run the car off the road while they babbled away. She disconnected, smiling. If Russ had asked her again to move down to the farm, she might well have done it.

The smile faded fast. It occurred to her that they would probably wind up talking about her father's will over their pizza.

Lewis Schramm had called her while the forensics people were still in the garage. Though the Seattle attorneys handled her father's fiscal affairs, Frank had left his most recent will in Klalo. Schramm had checked with the other lawyers in case they'd drawn up a later one. He said he'd bring what he had out to the house after lunch tomorrow.

Libby and Gus would be there, yes, indeed. They had made dinner hideous with their speculations. Jane thought Gerd was as repulsed as she was, but he and she had seen the body. Her brother and stepmother hadn't. She told herself that accounted for their coldness. After a nightmare-plagued sleep, Jane determined to resume her online house hunt.

The next day Irma was set to vacuum the east wing, do the weekly laundry, and cook. Jane could avoid domestic chores. She and Gerd ate breakfast together and didn't talk about her father. Gerd looked like a man who was about to say *I quit*. She did not want that to happen on her watch.

She wanted to talk to him about Libby. And Judith. Jane really didn't understand his kind of romanticism. Within easy memory he had fancied himself in love with both women. She herself could not see the attraction to Libby, but she hadn't understood her father's marriage either—her father's serial marriages, for that matter. Common sense, or maybe self-preservation, suggested that she stay away from that topic, so she drew Gerd out about Germany and got him talking about the trip he'd taken with Russell on the Rhine. Unlike most Americans, he said, Russ wasn't interested in castles.

"He wasn't?" Jane had loved the Rhine castles.

Gerd grinned. "He said they depressed him. They were prisons. He wanted to know about the rivers as trade routes—the Moselle and the Rhine, the vineyards, the Hanseatic League, how the area was settled all the way back to the Celts. His mind is fresh. Is that the right word?"

"Unusual?"

He considered. "Uncommon."

Jane was happy to think about that. After breakfast Gerd went down to the *cave* as usual to report to Tom Dahl—the *vendange* might come early that year, he said. Jane wondered if Dahl's brief flirtation with unlimited wealth had gone to his head. Until the bank had registered Jane's signature, he had been the only one with a hand on the August wealth. Repressing the unlikely thought, Jane went on the Internet.

Schramm was punctual that afternoon. Jane wondered whether his fee was tied to the size of the estate. She envisaged him sitting in his car out on Miller Road among the lurking press until four minutes to two, then driving up to the front door as the clock chimed twice. She let Irma answer the bell.

They assembled in Frank's study, though it was on the small side for four people. Gus brought in a third armchair, so the three heirs sat in a semicircle, facing the desk. Schramm occupied Frank's ergonomic office chair. He looked what, wary? Not complacent, at any rate.

Schramm extended his condolences and explained that Frank had had him draw up the will toward the end of July. Frank meant to keep his copy in the house in the safe Jane didn't know how to open. The square metal box was built into the wall of the study behind a framed photo of Mount Adams. Schramm had the combination. He opened the safe and removed the contents.

"My diamonds," Libby murmured, looking soulful. "He kept them for me when I wasn't wearing them."

"I'm sure he did." Schramm drew out a printed list and read it. "Yes, I see. Mrs. August's jewelry. Two boxes." He handed them to her. "He gave the diamonds to you outright?"

"My diamonds are mine. From my first marriage. My other jewelry is in the small safe in the master bedroom."

"He doesn't mention jewelry in the will. Jane, Francis—"

"Gus."

"I beg your pardon, Gus. I take it neither of you disputes that. Perhaps Mrs. August should keep the diamonds elsewhere. I suggest a safe-deposit box at the bank." He had to mean Frank's local bank.

Libby clutched the boxes but looked puzzled.

"There is some cash here. We can count it later." He removed it and a stack of papers, shut the safe, and riffled through the papers. "Deeds to land, house, cars. Passport. Ah, yes, the will." He drew it out. "Yes. Unchanged. Dated July twenty-seventh." He set the rest aside. Then he took a document from his brief-case. "My copy. Shall I read it to you formally or summarize?"

"Summarize," all three of them said in wonky chorus. They looked at each other.

"Very well. There are two large bequests outside the family." He named a small-government think-tank Jane would not have given a nickel and The Nature Conservancy. Both would no doubt receive the handsome gifts ecstatically, and the estate would enjoy a tax break. Schramm set the will down and folded his hands. "Mr. August, Gus, your father explained to me that he had given you enough shares in his bank for you to have a controlling interest. I believe the share transfer occurred almost five years ago. Your sister received no such gift. Is that correct?"

Gus nodded, his expression sullen.

Schramm looked at Jane and Libby. He named the sum the shares had been worth at the time then turned back to Gus.

"Frank was emphatic that he had great affection for you. For that reason, he also left you the condominium in San Francisco, the one you've been living in, and half a million dollars in stocks and bonds."

Gus's mouth set but he didn't speak.

Schramm frowned, then gave a slight shrug and turned to Libby. "In your case, Mrs. August, he explained the generous settlement he made on you when you signed your prenuptial agreement. He showed the document to me, and there's a copy here." He tapped the stack of papers. "It leaves you with no further legal claim on the estate. Because of his affection for you, however, he also left you half a million and what he referred to in conversation as his Sundance house, a lodge he owned in Montana."

Libby sniffed. Schramm gave another shrug and turned to Jane, whose heart had sunk. "He left you the balance of the estate. Unconditionally. I am the executor."

Jane burst into tears, and they were not tears of gratitude. Her first panicked reaction was that her father had hijacked her life. What was worse, he'd saddled her with a house she'd begun to loathe. She saw now why Schramm and the banker had been so eager to let her sign checks on the vineyard account. They had known she'd inherit.

She was conscious that Schramm was talking quietly, or rather reading. She blew her nose, but the tears kept flowing. Gus or Libby must have asked the lawyer to read portions of the document. She didn't blame them. She was also sure now that Gus had cuckolded his father and that Frank had known about it. Frank was too smart to leave the culprits nothing. What he had left them was a small portion of the estate, but lawyers attempting to overturn the will would have a hard time proving bias.

The will was insolent, ill-tempered, the opposite of love. Frank hadn't loved Jane. He'd used her to get back at his son and at his wife. If he had lived longer, he would no doubt have changed the will. But he didn't live, and it testified to his resentment.

Jane's tears dried up. She mopped her face. Neither Libby nor Gus had said anything. When Schramm finished reading the section that dealt with Gus's bequest, Jane's brother rose.

Schramm raised his hand. "A moment, Gus, if you please."

Gus sank back down.

"I need to remind the three of you, first of all, that settling the estate will take time—given its complexity at least a year, perhaps two."

Jane could read Gus's thoughts. He needed money now.

Schramm looked down at the will lying on the desk. "If Frank August's death resulted from murder, whoever killed him can't inherit from him. I'm confident the killer was an outsider, but the question of murder will also delay things." He looked up, dead serious.

Libby gave an indignant squawk. Gus grimaced.

Jane decided to put them out of their misery. "Meanwhile, what do we do for money?"

"Rely on your own resources."

Gus groaned. "Thanks to my father, I have no resources."

That was probably true, or close to true. With deep reluctance, Jane said, "You can stay here if I have the means to keep the house open."

Schramm said, "That won't be a problem. When I file the will, I'll suggest to the court that the monthly sum deposited to the vineyard account be continued for maintenance of the house as well as the vineyards. More will be needed, but you must let me know how much—utilities, food costs, the housekeeper's salary. Document it."

"Then we go on as we have been?"

"Yes." He rose, gathering the papers to return them to the safe. His hands stilled on the stack of cash. "You can borrow on your expectations, Gus, once the will is filed."

Gus gave a sour laugh. He wouldn't be able to borrow much, not enough for a top-flight defense attorney. Given the lawsuits that were bound to be filed in California, top-flight was what he needed.

Jane stood, too. "None of us can leave until the police say we can. You may as well stay here during the investigation, Libby. No point in setting up another household." *And I won't be moving to Hood River any time soon.*

Libby stared at her, face unreadable. Jane was grateful to be dining with Russ.

Schramm counted the cash in their presence, two thousand three hundred and fifty dollars, then put everything back in the safe, and closed it. When Libby and Gus had gone off, he wrote out the combination for Jane. She walked him to the front door, and they shook hands.

He said, "You ought to make a will as soon as possible."

"I had one drawn up the first time I traveled abroad. I left everything to my mother."

"Good. You should tell everyone that. I think you're not pleased with your father's arrangements."

Jane gave a shaky laugh. "Perceptive of you, Lewis. I'm appalled. So would you be, if you knew that everyone including the police was going to suspect you of parricide."

"I'm sorry," he said.

The income of many states and some countries was smaller than Frank August's fortune. He had not reached the Bill Gates category, but he had been a very wealthy man. She didn't explain to Schramm that she was afraid of her father's money, because she knew Schramm wouldn't believe her. Who would? Russ? She wasn't sure.

So she wouldn't tell him. She couldn't bear to.

It would come out, of course. She'd given permission for Schramm to take a copy of Frank's will to the undersheriff. Neill would be discreet, but after a will was filed it became public property. When the press caught on, her name would be mud. She wondered whether to warn the college.

~

THE desk sergeant ushered Lewis Schramm into Rob's office as he was re-reading the results of the search of Frank August's house. At his direction, it had concentrated on the garage and cars. It was almost five. Rob was thinking about going home.

Schramm left before six, but Rob sat frozen in place. The will had knocked his thinking into a cocked hat. *Jane August the heir? Impossible.* He had had three viable suspects in the August case with motive, means, and opportunity—Judith Hough, Gus August, and Libby August, though Judith was shaky as to motive and means. Now, with Jane, he had four. Gerhard Koeppel was a fifth possible culprit, though Rob couldn't imagine what his motive might be, unless he'd lost a great deal of money when the August bank failed. Rob made a note to check on that—for Koeppel and for the others.

The autopsy had revealed that the victim died of one of two sharp blows to the back of the head at the point where the spine reaches the skull. There were bruises on both upper arms. The murder weapon had a smooth narrow surface—cylindrical metal like a pipe or a tire jack, or conceivably, the barrel of a rifle. Rob meant to search the house and garage for it again. Now, however, with Jane atop the list of suspects as far as motive went, he had to reconsider everything.

His thoughts circled, angry. What did the SUV mean? Who had driven it into the thicket? "Why" was less baffling—a successful attempt to lead searchers astray, to prevent a serious search of the houses and grounds that might have led to earlier discovery of the body. "Who" and "how" remained puzzling.

He went home with a headache. Meg wasn't there yet. He put a pot on to boil, took out frozen stew neatly stowed in a vacuum-packed bag, and threw the bag into the bubbling water. Dinner would be ready in half an hour. He wondered how much longer they could keep up the fiction that he was cooking as often as she was. She had made the stew.

He changed into a track suit and had drunk a beer by the time Meg came home. As it turned out, she was almost as frustrated as he was.

She unburdened herself on the dining room table, the universal repository, and went off in the direction of their bedroom.

She returned in a pink track suit that made her look like a bonbon and peered into the boiling pot.

"Ah, the stew."

"Yup."

"Good thinking."

"I'll put a salad together. Beer?"

She made a face. "I want a scotch. My Library of Congress volunteers are driving me nuts. They keep stopping and getting lost in a book. Last time I checked their progress they were frozen somewhere between the Ephesians and the Etruscans."

"Uh, DF?"

"DE. 'The Greco-Roman World.' They promised to come in tomorrow morning to make up for lost time." She accepted the scotch-rocks he'd poured for her, took a ladylike sip, closed her eyes, swallowing, and opened them. She smiled at him like sunrise on the river. "What's the news with you?"

So he told her about Jane August's good fortune.

Meg shook her head. "Good God."

"Motivation," he said gloomily.

"Nonsense. She wouldn't harm a fly."

He'd forgotten that Meg had met Jane. "Maybe not a fly, but her father was substantially more irritating."

~

RUSSELL arrived a little late for their pizza date, his hair still wet from a shower. Jane deduced that he'd just gotten off work.

"Did your crew show up at the farm today?" She clicked her seat belt into place.

He maneuvered the Blazer back onto the drive. "All three of them, plus a friend who wanted to meet Sergeant Ramos."

Jane was startled into laughter.

"They were very taken with her." His mouth quirked at the corners. "An Older Woman, a Mother, her eyes like stars, her voice like the cooing of doves."

Older woman indeed. Linda Ramos was in her thirties, *early* thirties. "You like them, don't you?"

"Yes. They're good kids—smarter than I was at that age. How are you, Jane?"

Not a question she wanted to answer. "Um, okay."

He crossed the much-depleted press cordon and headed onto Miller Road. He didn't turn down to Highway 14.

As they approached the bridge over the Choteau, Jane said, "There's the famous thicket. That's such a puzzle, the SUV. How did it get there? Why?"

"I don't have answers or even a good guess. Did Neill tell you the medical examiner let Judy off the hook?"

"What are you talking about?"

"Yesterday, after we found your father's body, I had several bad hours imagining she'd shot him."

"Shot him? But he wasn't shot."

"No."

"You'll have to explain."

So he told her about Judith's attempts to "patrol" the farm, of the AK-47 he'd taken from her, of the small-caliber pistol he hadn't known about, the one Judy had used to such devastating effect.

Jane was horrified. She had been afraid of Judith, but what she had feared was something more like suicide than homicide. And her fear had been right on target. She winced at the grisly exactness of that thought. Judy's "patrol" made a kind of sense. She had been trying to protect her family from the monsters her father and the war had conjured in her head. And Frank August had been monstrous, indulging his anger.

"She could have shot him," Jane murmured, "but she didn't."

The car nosed up a long hill with a blind corner at the top. It shifted down, and down again, always a bit late as automatics tended to be. But they were handy if you had only one foot. Russ drove with assurance.

"You never told me how you came to wreck your motorcycle," Jane said. She was looking at his tough, long-fingered hands on the wheel.

Russ was silent.

"I don't see you as a biker."

"A motorcycle is cheaper—to own and insure—than a car. I would have preferred not to own either one, and I didn't when I was an undergraduate. Zipping around from classes to the labs I was teaching, to weekend jobs and to summer work at the vineyard required more flexible transportation than my bicycle or the county bus system."

"Oh." Jane's stepfather had given her a BMW hardtop convertible for her eighteenth birthday. Red. Built like a tank, Dan said.

"It was New Year's Eve," Russ said, "and there was a party. That was ten years ago, give or take."

"What? Oh, your wreck. I see."

"No. You don't see. I was stone-cold sober." He cleared his throat. "It was my girlfriend, Karen, who got drunk." He pronounced the name *Kah-ren*. This was the first Jane had heard of her.

"I was scheduled to work a twelve-to-eight A.M. shift at a convenience store on New Year's Day. I'd worked in the store Christmas and New Year's for five years. The boss paid time-and-a-half on holidays."

Jane thought about that. "And Karen wanted to stay for the rest of the party."

"Yes. She was pissed both ways, pissed as a newt. I told her she could stay and hitch a ride back with somebody else, but *I* was departing at eleven-fifteen, come what may." His voice took on tones of conscious virtue—blatant exaggeration.

"So you got into a fight. And she stayed behind…"

"No," he said, quieter. "She didn't. She came with me, and we bickered. Halfway to town the cycle hit a patch of black ice and spun out. Karen was thrown onto the guardrail and killed instantly. I was pinned under the bike."

"Oh my God."

He said nothing to that. Jane was thinking in platitudes. Her eyes stung. She closed them. "I'm sorry," she whispered at last.

"Yes, me, too. I loved Karen, sort of. We'd been together a year. D'you know what I loved most about her?" His voice was calm, sad but not agitated. It was a subject he had thought about. An oncoming car lowered its high beams. Russ reciprocated.

"No." That came out like a squawk. She tried again, "No. Do you mind telling me about her? Don't if it bothers you."

"It bothers me, but you deserve an explanation." They were coming up on the Two Falls stoplight. It turned green as they approached. Russ negotiated the tiny town with its cross streets. Lights shone in Chief Thomas's manufactured home. When the Blazer moved beyond the pink street lights into deepening dusk, he said, "What I loved about Karen most of all was that she was a good fighter. Most of the time when we fought, we wrangled for the fun of it. She never held a grudge, and she played fair, but she did argue."

Jane stared at his profile.

"You know my mother. Don't get me wrong. I love Mom. She's a sweet lady. She's also a total and complete wuss."

"Uh, did you know why you were attracted to Karen at the time?"

"Not a clue. Took me five years after her death to admit I loved her because she was *not* like my mother."

"That's not the whole story."

"No, of course it's not. The wreck knocked me flat emotionally. It was like I was put on Pause."

"Russell—"

He smiled. "Okay, dumb metaphor. I have a tangled psyche, as you may imagine. I spent large portions of my childhood and teenage years blaming my father for everything that went wrong in my life from poverty to athlete's foot. I owe Karen a lot. In a way, her death freed me from that whiny pattern, because there was no way I could blame Dad for the wreck."

"I hope you didn't blame yourself."

"I tried to. Karen's parents kept insisting I was a drunken

Injun, that I'd murdered their child. I'm lucky the cops did a blood test and very damned lucky I'd stuck to coffee all evening. I might not have. I don't drink much, because I don't like what booze did to my Anglo father, but I've been known to chug a beer now and then. If I'd had a teaspoon of alcohol in my system, Karen's parents would have convinced everybody, including me, that I caused the spin-out."

"People who stereotype—"

"I felt sorry for them, God knows, along with myself, but they pushed me too far."

"You lost your temper?"

"I came to a rolling boil." He pulled the Blazer around a slow-moving pickup and barreled down the highway. "Anger was refreshing. It energized me. That and the job offer."

"Job?"

"Lennart Eismann came to the hospital and offered me a job."

"Wow."

"Mind you, he'd been nagging me to work for him full-time for a couple of years. My first job in Pullman was at the small Eismann vineyard there. Syrah grapes like the vines near your house."

"And you'd worked there and understood the grapes."

"I'd worked there and understood the work crew. Literally, since I speak Spanish. Lenny liked that. I translated for the manager when he couldn't make the crew understand him and vice versa. I didn't think about it, but he saw the advantage right away and offered me a slight raise in return for my services. When I entered grad school, I thought about quitting Eismann and teaching summer labs instead. Adjunct pay is lousy, as you know. Teaching assistants are cheap labor. When I explained that to Lenny, he offered another pay raise. I kept on working for him summers."

"But the job he offered you when he came to see you in the hospital, that wasn't in Pullman, was it?"

"No. It was way west, past Richland and perilously close to

Dad's territory, but I was in a reckless mood. Lenny's manager was going to retire, and he promised me I would replace the old guy."

"And you jumped at the chance."

He gave a wry smile. "Insofar as I was capable of jumping, yes. I did. I was going to have to quit school anyway."

"Why?"

"My dear Jane, I know you live a sheltered existence but think about it."

"No medical insurance?"

"I had crap student insurance that covered about half the damage."

"Oh."

"Oh, yeah. You ought to hear Gerd's opinion of the American health care scene. Oops." He hit the brake in good time to prevent a collision with the car ahead of them.

Jane squeaked.

"Sorry. Let me put my mind to driving. You can figure out the rest of the story anyway."

"Not really," Jane protested. "In fact, it's getting even more interesting. Did you stay angry?"

"Not forever. I started working at Hackamore in May. By that time I could get around well enough on my peg leg."

"Peg leg!"

He smiled. "Okay, so it was the Maserati of artificial limbs. I was still mad at the world in December when I went back to Pullman and took the written exams for the Ph.D."

"I thought you quit."

"I did, but they encouraged me to take the exams anyway and gave me honors to boot. Doing the exams meant I was ABD."

"All But Dissertation?"

"Right. I suppose the dean thought I'd work a year or so then come back, retake a bunch of classes, and finish my research."

"Retake?"

"Things change fast in biology. I kept on with my research,

but I thought I'd better clear off my debt as fast as I could or I'd spend my life paying down the interest."

"Huh. You could've filed for bankruptcy, couldn't you?"

He clucked his tongue. "When I was sound of wind and artificial limb? Nonsense." A pause ensued in which Jane reflected on the difference between individual debt and that of large fiscal institutions, such as investment banks. She wondered what Russ thought of her brother, but it was better not to ask. She thanked Russ for giving her what had to have been a painful account, and they lapsed into silence, meditative on her part.

They went directly to the hospital.

Jane talked to Judith for a while about the studio she had just decided to set up in the house. *Now that I own it.* She didn't say that.

She talked about wanting northern light and about the small room in the turret above the library. The room was unused and faced north, but it was a long way from anything else in the house, including Jane's bedroom. At least it had a half bath, so there was water. She spoke of Judy's own workroom as inspiration, and of the need to remove the carpet and replace it with tile so the inevitable blotches of paint wouldn't damage the floor. The windows didn't open—a ventilation problem if Jane were using oils.

Eventually she wound down. Setting up a studio would be a commitment to a house she didn't want to live in. She did not say that.

Russ told his sister a little about Alice's flurry of cooking the day before but not the reason for it. Then he read her a chapter from *Swallows and Amazons*—near the end, when the going gets exciting. Jane liked the way he read—not attempting a British accent or dramatizing the voices, just letting the book be what it was, a good adventure yarn. Though he must have been hungry for dinner after a long workday, he kept impatience out of his voice. When they left at last, he said good-bye to Judy as if she were listening and kissed her on the forehead. The turban of bandages was gone and her hair was coming in curly. She looked almost like herself again.

It was starting to get dark by the time they reached the parking lot of the hospital where they wandered, looking for the Blazer. Russ leaned on the cane. He didn't say anything, and neither did Jane. When they found the car at last, he held the door for her. She thanked him and got in.

"Are you set on pizza, Jane?"

"Hmm. I'm just hungry."

"I was going to introduce you to KP. It's the best pizza joint in town, but it's a tribal enterprise."

"Isn't that okay?"

"Sure, but half the customers will be my cousins, and the last time Ma and I ate there, Judy was with us. They're bound to come over and ask how she's doing." He drew a breath. "And I'm not up to lying about her once, let alone repeatedly."

"How about the Red Hat?" she ventured. "I could murder a steak. Oh, please, tell me I didn't say what I just said."

He bent and kissed her on the mouth. When he drew away, neither of them was smiling. "The Red Hat?" His real question had nothing to do with the restaurant, and Jane knew it.

She nodded.

The Red Hat had a great view of the river and pleasant but unremarkable food. When they had ordered, they sat at ease, each with a beer, and watched the eternal river bypass them. Finally Russ looked at her and smiled. "Tell me about your studio."

"What I told Judith is a pretty good summary."

"Maybe so. But it implies that you're going to stay in the house for a while."

"He left me the house."

"And the vineyards?"

"Yes." Jane hoped he wouldn't probe further, and perhaps he read her mind, because he was silent a long time, just watching the river.

The waiter brought their salads and some bread. Russ raised his glass to her. "Wal, howdy, neighbor."

"Howdy back." Jane took a gulp. It was good beer. IPA. She picked up her fork and stirred the Caesar salad. "What do you know about money?"

He speared a crouton, ate it, and set the fork down. "'You load sixteen tons and whaddya get? Another day older and deeper in debt.'"

"Oh, come on."

"Huh. Well, when I'm working—"

"You're not working now?"

"Not for pay."

Of course, not for pay.

He waved a fork at her. "I hardly ever see money, which is the way I like it. My paycheck goes into the credit union once a month, *ker-chunk*, direct deposit, with taxes removed. Couple of days later, things come out. Medical insurance, phone, utilities. If I'm in town, I stop by the ATM. *Ker-chunk.* More comes out. What's left over sits there breeding interest until I blow it. That's what I know about money, lady."

Jane did not dignify his account with comment. She ate her salad, which was tasty. The bread took the form of rolls with crusts so hard she needed a steak knife to crack them.

Russ said, "If you're asking about theory, I'm a biologist, not an economist. Maybe you're wondering about my reaction to the August bank failure."

Jane wasn't. She blinked. "Er, yes."

"I stay away from banks. They're run by compulsive gamblers. At least with a credit union, there's some possibility that the money is being invested for the benefit of members. That may be utopian, but I like to think it's true." He finished his salad and laid the fork down. The waiter materialized and removed the plate.

Jane dug in. "Banks invest for the benefit of shareholders."

"Come on. Sub-prime mortgages? The fuckers, I beg Gus's pardon, the investors were gambling, and gambling stupidly."

Jane laid her fork down with a sigh. The waiter removed her plate. "You're angry."

"Not very. More like annoyed. Now my father could have given you a good rant on bank failures and government bailouts. I try not to rant."

"Do you think money is dangerous?"

"Good God, Jane."

"I know it's a stupid question."

"Lack of money is dangerous, too. That I could rant about. Everything's dangerous." Their steaks arrived, sizzling. "Eat up."

So she did. They did. With relish. Frank August might have thought the Red Hat pedestrian, but the chef did well by steaks. They didn't bother with dessert. Russ didn't fight over the check either, Jane was relieved to see. He left the tip.

When they reached the house, it was dark. Gus had apparently gone to bed. If Libby was still out, she would see Russ's Blazer parked at the front door when she came home. *Let her.*

Jane led Russ straight to her bedroom with happy results. It had been a while for both of them, and the first engagement involved some fumbling. It was also over-eager and left Jane unsatisfied but thrumming like a guitar. So she climbed on top, and the fun began. The thrum rose to a crescendo and crested again. Jane had thought she might find the missing leg obtrusive. She forgot about it.

Both of them drowsed. And woke. Or Jane did. She teased Russ awake, too. When he made sleepy sounds as if he ought to leave, she said, "Not yet, tiger." He groaned and laughed, and she teased. This time their lovemaking was languorous and very, very sweet. She fell into sleep as if she had fallen in the river. When she surfaced, at eight in the morning, he was long gone.

Satisfaction had just given way to anxiety when her cell phone rang. It was Russ, and she could hear the smile in his voice.

"Good morning, sunshine. I knew you'd be awake by now."

"Mmm. Just."

Both of them started to speak at once. Both laughed. Jane said, "I want to move down to the farm, but I can't scandalize your mother."

"You can try."

"Russ!"

"Your stepmother didn't come home last night."

"She didn't?"

"Her car wasn't in the garage at four A.M. Are you going to send out a missing person bulletin?"

"Well, well, well." Abruptly Jane's sins caught up with her. "Russ—"

"What's the matter?" Alarm sharpened his voice.

"I have to tell you." She gulped and told him the truth about her father's will. It took a while. He didn't interrupt. "So you see, Libby's angry. And Gus is, too."

"And you invited both of them to stay on." He sounded dazed. She heard voices in the background speaking in Spanish.

"I had to, yes. The will is vicious. I'm afraid—"

"You should be." He covered the mouthpiece and said something to someone. When he spoke to her again his voice was sad and tired. "I think you ought to take your mother's advice. I hate to say it, but you're not safe up there in that mausoleum. Go home to San Francisco, Jane. Or fly up to Seattle to consult the tax lawyers. Hide out in a hotel." He didn't say *you can afford it.* Didn't have to.

Pride kept her from saying, "But what about us?" She was not going to give him up, not after last night. "I want to stay here until I know who killed my father. I'll fix up my studio and teach my classes and visit Judy. That's what I'm going to do. Give your mother my regards." She disconnected.

The phone rang. It was Russ. "Let's make a deal. We don't hang up on each other."

"Okay. I'm sorry."

"And I'm sorry if I sounded like I was giving you orders. It's a scary situation."

"Yes."

"I just wanted to say one thing."

"What's that?"

"You're beautiful."

"I love you," Jane whispered.

"Back at you," he whispered. Both of them laughed. Spanish voices in the background provided the chorus.

Jane said, "We're a pair of clowns in the middle of a Renaissance tragedy."

"That's okay. Clowns win in the end."

She sobered. "I hope you're right."

~

MADDIE came back to the kitchen and placed the landline receiver on its cradle. "He wants a purification."

"Russ?" Jack took a bite of his smoked salmon sandwich. He'd risen at four-thirty to go fishing on the Choteau, so he was more than ready for lunch. "Of the cherry orchard?"

"Of the orchard because of Frank August, and the house because of Bill and Judy. I told Russ I don't perform for audiences, 'specially not audiences of reporters."

Jack took a judicious swallow of cider. An apple orchard the Klalos had recently inherited produced excellent cider. Unfortunately it was too cloudy to sell on the commercial market. Another problem to solve. Easier to solve than the problem represented by Russell Hough, with or without his cherry orchard.

Jack took another swig. "What did he say to that?"

"'When you can, Aunt Maddie.'"

He chuckled.

"All very well for you to laugh. Nobody's going to call *you* quaint."

At that he laughed out loud. "Russ never said that!"

"No. That's what the blasted reporters would call me if I was foolish enough to conduct a religious ceremony in their presence. Do you know how many reporters have been hanging around Hawk Farm?"

"Half a dozen. It's that dead banker," Jack said comfortably. "They'll get bored again when the sheriff keeps giving them no comment. They'll go away."

Maddie sighed.

"What's the problem?"

"Russell is the problem. He's been gone seventeen years, and he wants to slide back into the tribe as if he never left."

"You know why he left."

"I don't *blame* him, Jack. Not for leaving. Bill was impossible. It's all that secrecy. When did Russ let you know where he was? And his poor mother. He abandoned her to the tender mercies of Bill Hough." It was something they had never really talked about. Russell had always been a touchy subject.

Jack set his glass at the top of his plate, centering it. "My sister married Bill of her own free will, and you know how her mother raised her. Alice would never have left Bill, not after Judy was born, and the real trouble started then. Leaving Bill was the only way she could have protected Russ. She was not going to leave. It's a wonder she asked *me* to do something, and she didn't till the bastard broke Russ's collarbone. Alice had what she wanted."

"Did Russ hate her?"

"No, of course not. He loved Judy, and he could see Alice had to protect *her*. But he knew Alice wouldn't lie if Bill asked where his son was."

"So he saw to it that none of us knew where he was."

"That's it."

"He didn't trust *you?*" Maddie could see the pain in Jack's eyes.

"By the time Russ left, he didn't trust anybody."

"He let you take him to the train the day he went."

"Yeah, but he already had his ticket, so I didn't know where he headed, 'cept it was east."

"Spokane."

"Or even Seattle. He could have changed to a northbound train. I had a bad few weeks. I thought he'd call."

Russ hadn't called. He'd sent a card postmarked Las Vegas—must have given it to a friend to mail. All the card said was that he had a job and a place to stay. It didn't say where, or that he meant to go to college.

Jack rubbed the back of his neck. "I thought he'd join the

the question of the SUV. How cc
driven it from the garage, even su
the garage? And why? No, she v
had to be a major witness. And s

Rob turned back to his evic
was a trove of meaningless, unre
irrelevant, and the ski poles, the
narrow and not heavy enough t
wind-surfing paraphernalia and t
Ditto the snowmobiles. The gc
while. None of the four cars sh
anyway Gus's car was probably a
he'd been driving when Frank c
to check that. He was glad the S
pound. Another car on site woul

The tools hanging above
touched in months, maybe not s
left the bicycles, and the freezer a
supplementing the appliances in
held white wines, champagne, anc
ale, and IPA from a variety of micr
ice. Not cubes, which the refrige
continually, but blocks. Why? Sor
he supposed. No other possibilit
Irma Castro.

The bicycles hung shoulder-
stuck out from the back wall of t
on one of them came from the
bike was shiny-clean otherwise. T
and hung up clean some time agc
Since there was no way of knowing
been ridden, the mud on the tire
though, that bicycle had been st
Bizarre. Also bizarre was the fact
passenger seat of the SUV did not
from anyone Rob suspected of th

army. Dumb thinking on my part. He knew why Bill was the way he was. That was the last thing Russ would do."

"And the first thing Judy did," Maddie murmured.

He didn't respond to that, and she was sorry she'd said it. He felt very bad about Judy. He finished his sandwich and rose. "You'll do what's right, Chief. Sooner or later. Sooner might be better."

When Jack called her *Chief,* he was almost always joking, but not always.

A MASS OF inform[a]
forensics—from th[e]
the Hough gun collection,
thicket, and from the Augus[t]
an afternoon meeting for his
Thursday morning sifting th[rough]
to make sense of it.

He'd had Judith Hough[
he corrected himself—and t[
man. Nothing. It had been c[
from the shot she was know[n]
as a whistle. The only fingerp[rints]
consistent with his having ta[
gun cabinet after cleaning it[
barrel of the rifle had been [
was nothing to exclude it. K[
Judith used in the suicide atte[
Bloody from her head woun[
The diameter of the barrel w[

Rob had nothing against[
made his life simpler if she'd [

reached for the stapled sheets that summarized Kitty Grant's report on Judith Hough's suicide attempt. As he thought, the blood came from Russell, from Jane's mercy mission.

If it hadn't been carried on the passenger seat, the corpse could have been taken to the site of burial in the back of the SUV. Fibers on the rear carpet came from tweed fabric, not likely to be Jane's garment in summer. She had taken clothes to the dry-cleaner, she said, but that had been two weeks before her father disappeared. The bicycle detritus lay atop the fibers. Now that they knew what Frank had been wearing, the fibers could be retested for a match. Might as well retest the bike, too. It had been checked for prints and the mud analyzed. A more thorough look at the seat cover and crossbar might reveal something.

When Rob tried to visualize the bike, he couldn't remember whether it *had* a crossbar. Mrs. August had said she was the one who used the bikes, she and her friends. Women didn't ride bikes wearing skirts these days, especially not mountain bikes. Did mountain bikes for women have crossbars? Surely they did. Mountain bikes were supposed to be sturdy, and lack of a top tube would indicate structural weakness. His brain had turned to sludge, speaking of structural weakness. Madam Twinkler *said* she used the bikes.

The phone rang. Meg asked him to join her for lunch.

He was tempted but didn't see how he could spare the time if he was going to have to work with only half a brain. He said so and why.

Meg laughed. "When I was a kid I used to wonder why my bike didn't have a crossbar. I was told it was so I could ride wearing a dress. Guys wore pants and could fling their legs over the bar. Since I didn't want to ride in a dress, I didn't see the point."

"Hmm. I suppose you never heard the term nutcracker?"

"Not at the age of six. Even to my maiden ears, nutcracker made no sense for riders such as myself with no nuts to crack."

"Stop. Stop right there."

"Oh, my dear, be B, but not BF."

Rob whimpered. "Are you talking Library of Congress?"

"B is Philosophy," she chortled. "BF is Psychology and would include studies of madness."

"I'm not crazy," he said with dignity, "just stupid."

It turned out that she was very chirpy because she had decided not to change classification systems. The benefits of the change didn't outweigh the exasperation, and anyway, ninety percent of the public libraries in the country used the Dewey system.

Meg was basically a good-hearted woman, so she got sandwiches from the bakery and brought them to Rob's office. They had a brief picnic on his desk amid the evidence files.

~

JANE volunteered to take Alice to the hospital to save Russ the trip to Klalo. It turned into a driving lesson, with Alice, shaken at having to deal with the Prius instead of the Blazer, creeping along Highway 14. Jane didn't distract her with conversation. Somewhere past the turnoff to the Hood River Bridge their speed reached fifty. Alice's knuckles showed bone-pale where she gripped the wheel.

She parked in the lot behind the main entrance to the hospital, set the brake, and turned off the ignition. "Did it stop?"

Jane laughed. "Oh, yes—it's a very quiet engine. You drove well."

"I'm getting braver. Russ says it's a matter of practice."

That was an interesting thought. Jane wasn't sure she bought it. However, the idea of practicing courage seemed to cheer Alice, and that was what counted.

Jane watched as the older woman gathered her purse and jacket and climbed out. "I'll be here for you at half-past three." Alice had said she wanted to spend the evening at home for a change.

Jane raised a hand in farewell and made for the entrance. She drove back to the bridge. She meant to shop at Home Depot in Hood River for tiles and other odds and ends for her new studio. After that, she was set for lunch in Klalo followed by another signing session at Lewis Schramm's office and a trip to the bank. She would have about an hour to kill afterwards. Maybe she should spend the time with Judith, too, though she didn't have much to tell her and nothing to read.

As it happened, the shopping and the signing both took longer than Jane expected, so she spent the fifteen spare minutes in Judith's hospital room. Alice was willing to leave a bit early. Jane drove back—Alice looked relieved when she saw she wouldn't have to climb into the driver's seat—and Jane drove and listened as Alice assessed her daughter's condition.

Judith was better, her mother thought. She was showing some sense of circadian rhythms, though she didn't actually wake. She was off the ventilator. The VA wanted to move their patient to a nursing home after Labor Day, and Alice was not happy. Indeed, she was near tears as she told of her encounter with the VA doctor that morning. They were giving up on Judy, she said. It wasn't fair.

As Alice described the doctor's perfunctory examination— "How can he know from *that*?"—and countered with her own hours of observation, Jane let her mind drift. If Judith were released to a nursing home in Hood River, Russ's day would stretch even longer. She would never see him.

"You *must* get your driver's license, Alice," she said in the first long pause. She felt a little ashamed of her selfishness but not much. She was really thinking of Russ. *Oh yeah.*

~

"SHAKEN child trauma?"

"If I recall correctly, that's what the M.E. said." Niles squirmed in his chair. It was almost four in the afternoon. They were in Rob's office, working up to the investigation meeting, Linda in a corner taking notes, Rob at his desk.

"He didn't give me that in his summary."

"He was sort of mumbling to himself when I heard him," Niles said.

Rob's mind raced. The M.E.'s postmortem comments had had the usual fog effect generated by too much medicalese. The good doctor could not express himself in words of less than three syllables, at least not when he spoke to Rob. Rob called him. They talked, and Rob hung up in a thoughtful mood.

"Shaken child. What child?" Linda looked up from her keyboard. Her grasp of English was excellent but she had some trouble with idioms and figurative language.

Rob said, "I think Doc meant somebody shook August, as if he were an annoying child. Bashed his head against something." *Against what?* Shaken infants could die from the jolting alone— no blunt instrument required—but adults? Frank August was short, sixty-ish, and not heavy, but he looked tough. Rob closed his eyes, visualizing.

"What?" Linda said. *Echo chamber.*

"The bicycle," Rob said. *The crossbar of the bicycle to be exact.*

Both deputies were asking questions, but their words didn't register. Rob could see it—somebody had grabbed the exasperating man by his biceps and yelled at him, punctuating each remark with a shake that slammed the back of his head against the crossbar. The tube hung at the right height to smack his skull. The bike had probably fallen off its pegs during the assault—that would explain some of the bruising on the body—but it had been cleaned and put back in its place.

Who? Rob pushed himself to his feet and wandered to the window, his hands grasping, opening, closing, in half-conscious imitation of the perpetrator. He stared out at the courthouse parking lot.

Had Russell's injury not taken him out of the running, he would have leapt to the top of Rob's list of suspects. Whatever Hough's scholarly accomplishments, he was a very physical man. Rob thought of the metal crutch. Hough had to have a strong grip. But no, not possible. Gerhard Koeppel, then—short but a little taller than his employer, and a skier, an athlete. Good. Never mind that his motive sucked. What about Gus—Oedipus the Kid? Rob groaned. What about Jane? Her stepmother?

He turned around. Both deputies were staring at him. "Sorry. Light on the road to Damascus."

Linda and Niles exchanged glances.

Rob translated. "I think I just figured out what happened."

Their faces brightened. The lack of a working hypothesis had been dragging them all down. They cheered up when he explained, but Linda pointed out that they still didn't know whodunnit.

~

"RUSS is out in the garden." Alice covered the telephone receiver with her hand and gestured in the direction of the garage.

Jane nodded and backed out of the farmhouse kitchen, though, in fact, she had come to speak to Alice rather than Russ. *Garden? What garden?* She meandered out to the garage and peered around it. Sure enough, there was Russ, up to his knees in weeds where there might, at one time, have been a vegetable patch. She thought she saw beans and maybe broccoli. He had his back to her, and she spent some time admiring the view. *Excellent shoulders, truly fine butt, hair in need of brushing.*

She gave a piercing, sexist whistle, and his head whipped around. "It's yourself."

"Right the first time."

They grinned at each other. Last night in Jane's bed had been more than agreeable. He had been gone when she woke at eight.

She said, "I have no actual prejudice against morning canoodling."

"Is that a word?"

"It is now. Do you prefer 'post meridian sexual congress'?"

He picked his way over to her and gave her a leisurely kiss. "Let's filibuster."

"Oh my." After a long delicious moment she added, "Can't. I'm speechless."

A phone rang. His. He made an exasperated noise, pulled it from his pocket, and answered it. A male voice quacked at length, and Russ said *uh-huh* several times. He consulted his watch. The voice quacked again. "Okay. Half an hour. No problem." He disconnected. "Sorry. My assistant is a little anxious. We have a conference call scheduled, but one of the participants hasn't showed up."

A conference call explained why Russ wasn't across Highway 14 tending to the ongoing harvest. *What were they doing now, broccoli?* "Your assistant." *Gerd?*

"Uh, at Hackamore. Things are heating up east of the mountains."

"I thought you were on leave."

He gave a rueful smile. "I am, but Max is freaked out, and I promised to hold his hand during the *vendange*. I have a big mouth."

"I hope you're charging Eismann double-overtime," she grumbled.

Russ laughed.

She looked around. "Tell me about the garden. That's what Alice called it."

He sobered. "It was my grandmother's, my father's mother. Grandma baby-sat me when I was little—whenever Ma was teaching in the Two Falls elementary school. I used to bring my Matchbox cars out here and create magnificent traffic jams in the dirt while she gardened."

"Sounds like paradise."

"It was." He hesitated. "As I got older she taught me to identify the plants in their different stages of growth."

"So you wouldn't pull up spinach instead of weeds?"

"Exactly. After my grandparents left the farm and we moved out here, the garden was my domain."

"Your mother..."

He sighed and led her to the porch. They sat on the edge, feet dangling. "My father was a curmudgeon—cozy term for bully. He wouldn't let Ma teach once he took over the farm. She was supposed to stay home and keep house for him, so she developed subversions. I think they were unconscious. Refusing to tend the garden was one of her strategies."

"Did it work?"

"It provoked some of their loudest arguments. I wound up taking care of the garden. I was afraid—" He broke off.

"Afraid he would injure her?

"Yes. He always used violent language. When I spoke up for her, he hit me."

Jane sat up straight. She didn't say anything but she felt as if every part of her body was listening.

After a short silence, Russ went on, "So I guess I was right to be worried. What I didn't know was that my grandmother had been diagnosed with breast cancer."

"Oh no," Jane said softly.

He cleared his throat. "She'd skimped on the mammograms, I guess. It took her a long time to die, and she went through all the torture cancer victims suffer. They lived in Arizona by then, so I didn't know what was going on, just that I was scared for her. I think it was very hard on my father. He did know."

"And he took it out on you."

"On me and Ma. He didn't hit her unless she tried to pull him off me, but he was verbally abusive—in the style he's famous for. It's hard to take when it's directed straight at you."

Jane shuddered.

"Ma had to put up with it, or thought she did," Russ said. "As for me, if it hadn't been for my uncle, I would have been dead by the time I got to high school, or Dad would have been."

"How could your uncle help?"

"He stopped the beatings cold. I don't know how. He's a kind man with a sly sense of humor, but very quiet. I have trouble imagining how he could even get Dad to listen to him. I don't know what Uncle Jack said or did, but after Ma called on him to come to the rescue, Dad didn't raise a hand to either of us, not when he was sober."

"And drunk?"

Russ shrugged. "When he was drunk he was easy enough to evade. I'm bound to say he never beat Judy at all. Insofar as he was capable of loving anyone, he loved Judith."

Jane sat very still thinking of her own father. He had had his faults, but he wasn't violent, and he wasn't incapable of love. At last, she said, "Did you forgive him?"

"No." He rubbed his left knee. "I kept trying. From time to time I felt sorry for him—when Grandma died, for instance—but just when I got to the point where I could reach out, he'd do something, and *wham*, back to square one." His telephone rang. "Yeah. Okay, Max, call me again. Five minutes."

Jane got to her feet. "I'm going in. I need to ask your mom about that bread recipe. Come to dinner?"

"I...okay."

"Your uncle must be a good man."

His mouth eased in a smile. "He's a proper uncle. Mother's-brother. There's a Klalo word for that."

"Dinner," she repeated. "Seven-thirty, in your honor. I'll make the roommates wait for it." Somehow it was easier to deal with Gus and Libby if she thought of them as non-paying roommates. Lately they had seemed to be not so much conspiring together as conferring. She would come across them talking, and they'd break off, eyeing her. She hoped to God they weren't getting together again. Was a stepsister-mother like a sister-wife?

The cell phone rang again, so Jane bent down and gave Russ's hair a rumple, as if he were an errant child. When he swatted at her, smiling, she ducked into the house by the side entrance.

Alice was wringing her hands, a gesture Jane had thought purely literary. "Oh dear, he's still on the telephone, isn't he? I can't get used to all these phones. The hospital wants me. They think I should talk to Judith. Now."

"That's very good news," Jane said. "I'm sure Russ will be as quick as he can." *Or he might take hours.* There had been false alarms. A look at Alice, anguished but hopeful, stirred Jane's sluggish conscience. "Would you like *me* to drive you to Klalo?"

"Oh, my dear, yes. You're so kind, Jane."

One of nature's saints.

Jane had been on her way to town to sign something for Lewis Schramm. She and Alice reached Klalo in record time and found Judith as pale and still as usual, though the head nurse showed Alice what she said was an interesting set of readings from earlier in the morning.

Alice settled down to watch her daughter. Jane went off to sign papers. She meant to drive over to Hood River afterwards, to take course outlines to the college print shop, but she found the Prius nosing back into the hospital parking lot without conscious direction from the driver. That was eerie enough. As she got out of the car, she spotted Russ striding into the hospital, almost running. How could he do that? He'd re-injure the foot. He didn't see her, and she didn't call. Something had happened.

She locked the car and dashed for the entrance. He'd disappeared by the time she reached the lobby, and the elevators were in use. She ran up the stairs and raced down the long corridor to Intensive Care and Recovery where she saw a cluster of nurses and civilians in the hall outside Judy's room.

She made herself slow down. She didn't see Russ or Alice in the group, nor did there seem to be a doctor in attendance. The low murmur of the nurses' voices assured Jane there was no emergency, whether good or bad. Still, something must have happened to attract the cluster of watchers. As she approached, she recognized one of them, a comfortable middle-aged LPN named Myrna, who smiled at her.

"Did Judith wake up?"

"We think so. She's sleeping, but we're pretty sure it's real sleep not coma. Lots of brain activity."

"Exciting," Jane offered, puffing a little from emotion and her run.

Myrna beamed at her. "Wonderful. Her mother can't stop crying."

"Oh, dear. Is Judith's brother...?"

"Just got here." Her lip curled.

"He was working," Jane said. *A lie. Unless marathon phone calls can be classified as work.* "*I* brought Alice this morning."

"Oh, yeah."

"He comes almost every evening." Why was she defending Russ to this woman?

"I guess." The nurse did not work evenings.

"Can I go in?"

"She's in Recovery. It's visiting hours. Sure you can."

So Jane went in. Alice was sitting on the chair beside Judith's bed, sniffling, with Russ bending over his mother and patting her shoulder. He looked up and gave Jane a fleeting smile. He seemed, what, disquieted?

She went to him. "What is it?"

"Ma said she spoke."

"That's good, isn't it? I mean, that's wonderful."

He nodded, frowning, eyes on his mother.

At last Alice said, "Oh, Jane. You came back." Her voice was hoarse with anguish.

Jane knelt by her side and patted the arm that hung down. "So I did. What did she say, Alice?"

Alice burst into tears again.

Russ gave her shoulders a squeeze and straightened. He walked to the door and Jane followed, abandoning Alice to her grief with a backward glance.

"What's the matter?"

He leaned against the doorjamb, eyes closed, and shook his head. At last he said, very softly, "Word salad."

13.

RUSS WAS clearly not going to be able to join Jane for dinner. She was a good enough person not to pressure him but not good enough to swallow her disappointment. She considered sticking around the hospital herself, but that didn't make sense. If Judith did start talking again—even babbling— doctors and nurses were bound to rush in and out, and they would need to consult Alice and Russ. A non-relative would be redundant. So Jane gave hugs all around and took off for home.

There was no one but Irma inside the huge house, but as Irma hastened to tell her, the police had just left. They had spent more than an hour in the garage, and when they'd gone at last, they had taken one of the mountain bikes. That was weird. She gave Jane the receipt. "The *señora* was furious. She left immediately, driving very fast."

"Why would she care?" Jane's question was the sort no one could answer. Irma didn't try. "She may have sped off but she didn't drive far. Her Jeep's at the *cave*."

"Oh well, just Tom Dahl," Irma said.

Jane nodded. The puzzle of the police presence rattled around Jane's head, though. The cops had taken nothing anyone would miss from the garage. Yet Libby had reacted with rage. *She's on edge. We all are.*

Irma pulled vegetables from the hydrator. "So how many is coming to dinner?"

"Is Gus still here?"

"Out by the pool."

"Then three. Unless Libby comes back. She probably won't."

"No more? Not Russell Hough?" Irma looked sly.

Jane told her about Judith, and she sobered, clucking her tongue. "This word salad, it's like language chopped up?"

"Yes. I think Judy also has trouble pronouncing words. As if her tongue is too big for her mouth."

"The poor child. I pray for her every night." She crossed herself.

"Very kind." Jane was embarrassed. "I'm going for a swim."

"Do it while you can. They're saying rain for the Labor Day."

Jane could believe that. It was humid and hazy though not overcast. The mountain was nowhere in sight when she made her way out to the pool enclosure. It hadn't been there on the drive home either. She found Gus by the pool, not yet drunk. He didn't know that Libby had gone off—or care, apparently. Jane wondered whether she ought to tackle Gus about drinking. A good sister would have.

She changed into her bikini in the cabaña and went for a lazy swim. Gerd came home from the *cave*. He was still overseeing disposition of the first harvest of grapes from southern Oregon. Maybe Libby had rendezvoused with him there. He didn't say so, and Jane didn't ask.

He was back on the job. Russ would have to look elsewhere for help, and Gus for company.

~

BETH stuck her head in Rob's office Sunday as he was about to leave.

"Hey!"

He jumped, startled.

Beth grinned. She looked to be in a good frame of mind. "I'm starting Labor Day early. I've been fending off journalists for the past hour. Got anything new on the August case, anything I can throw to the slavering dogs?"

"Slavering dogs? Sheriff!"

She gave an elaborate sigh. "I know. God save the First Amendment and so on."

Rob smiled. "How about a forensic tidbit?"

She made a panting noise and dangled her paws like an eager terrier.

"The puddle of water, the one that dried up on the driver's side of the SUV…"

Beth yawned. "Came from the August well?"

Rob smirked. "Nope. It was melted ice of the kind bought in blocks at half the supermarkets and convenience stores in the county."

She came into the room and sat across the desk from him. "That *is* strange. Ice? Somebody spilled a glass of ice water?"

"No." He held up his hands to show the size of the ice block. "Somebody used the weight of an ice block to press the accelerator, stepped out of the vehicle with the engine running, and left it—with the door still ajar—to chug on into the blackberry thicket all by its own self."

She pursed her mouth in a silent whistle. "Clever!"

"Not very. The ice was probably taken from the freezer in the garage. Once I knew the water was melted ice the solution to the puzzle leapt to mind. The car door was open. Nobody bled on those brambles because nobody got out of the SUV in the thicket. Whoever disposed of it that way probably expected it to slide into the Choteau."

"And was frustrated when it didn't? Who?"

Rob hesitated. "Francis, Junior." He tasted the name.

Beth's eyes gleamed. "Excellent."

"Look, Beth—"

"I know. Don't say anything to anybody about young

August. I won't. Yet." Her eyes narrowed. "Go on. He's been your number-one suspect all along, hasn't he?"

"Near the top of the list, at any rate." Rob frowned. "Jane is technically closer to the top now I know about the will, but I don't really buy it."

"Why not? She's too nice?"

He considered. That was only part of the problem. "I'm pretty sure she didn't expect to inherit the whole shooting match. Gus may have."

"And?"

He shrugged. "And she's not in financial trouble, with or without the inheritance."

"Whereas her brother is not just bankrupt, he's looking at fraud charges."

"There you are."

"Motivation, motivation," Beth murmured, licking her lips. "I love it."

"Here's another bit of evidence, though I'm damned if I know what it means. Gus August did not return his rental car the morning his father disappeared, the morning he flew to San Francisco. He made the flight, but he left the car in long-term parking and retrieved it when he returned."

Beth thought about that puzzle and gave her head a shake. "Bizarre. Are you going to take all the evidence to Ellen?" Ellen Koop was the county prosecutor.

Rob grinned. "Can't wait to tell the slavering dogs we have a suspect in custody?"

Beth's returning smile was on the rueful side. "They don't let up."

Rob said, "I'll wait until after the purification to bring August in. I'm waiting because I want to see when, or maybe if, little Frankie will decide to return his car to the airport."

"You just left me behind. Why so?"

"He's supposed to be broke. The family has cars. Why pay rent for the Lexus?"

Beth stared, jaw agape. "As I live and breathe."

Rob laughed. Beth did a great Granny Clampett imitation. "Land sakes. Lawsy me. Cut it out, Sheriff."

She zipped her lip and made a swift exit.

~

AFTER dinner the lot of them went their separate ways, Irma home, Gerd and Gus to the bar by the pool, Jane to her room. When she phoned Russ, the call went to voicemail. Not surprising. She opened her Kindle to the last chapter of the comedy of manners.

She woke abruptly in the middle of the night, conscious that the phone had been ringing for a while. "H'lo." Silence. "Who is it?"

"Russ."

She sat up. "My dear, what happened?"

"Nothing. That is…" He cleared his throat. "Can I come to you?"

Jane shivered. "Yes, yes. Where are you?"

"Leaving Two Falls."

"I'll be at the front door." She struggled into her robe. "Russ?" But he had disconnected. It was three A.M.

She stumbled out to the hallway, scrunched onto a chair near the door, and shivered and waited. Her thoughts bumbled like flies in a bottle. "Nothing" had happened. But it was three in the morning. If Russ was just leaving Two Falls he hadn't been home yet. *Where is the man? It doesn't take ten minutes to drive here. What am I going to say to him?* Jane had no comfortable thoughts to offer. Whatever had happened and to whom, it was not for the better. She thought of Judith's loss of language and started crying. *It isn't fair, not fair, not fucking fair.*

When Russ finally drew up at the door and killed the engine, she blew her nose and stuck her head out the door. He sat still, his head bent to fists clenched on the steering wheel. At last, he stirred. She slid into the passenger seat. He was strapping on the artificial leg. He had been driving without it. He did not look at her.

After a moment she said, "Where's Alice?"

"With Jack and M-maddie. M-maddie said she'll do a p-purification." He gave his head a shake, as if he were clearing his vision in a fog. Maybe he was. He sounded lost. The stammer frightened her.

When he unlatched the door and turned sideways to dismount, Jane slipped out. She ran to the driver's side in time to keep him from falling. She steadied him, making comforting sounds that were not quite words, and they seemed to work. He straightened and leaned on her for balance, but he didn't fall. He also said nothing, explained nothing, just walked, accomplishment enough in the circumstances.

She didn't care. She also didn't care when Libby cracked the door of the master suite and peered out as the two of them approached Jane's room. Her stepmother made a hissing noise, and Russ stumbled. Jane took him into her room. He headed straight to the bathroom and shut the door. She could hear him throwing up. That frightened her as much as the stammer had. He was not drunk. There was no smell of booze.

Purification. What did that mean? Russ had mentioned that he was going to ask his aunt to perform the ceremony. He ought to be glad she was willing, not upset about it. Jane waited, silent and sleepy. At last he came out. He looked green.

"I'm sorry. Lousy day. Hits me in the stomach every time. That stepmother of yours…"

"She's a snake. Is Judith…"

"She's not all right, but she's not worse. It's the VA. They're moving her to a nursing home tomorrow."

"Labor Day?"

"Yeah. For occupational therapy." He made quotation marks with his fingers. "So-called. They'll continue the speech therapy while she's in the skilled care facility but not afterwards."

"They're giving up?"

"Sounds like it. We had a long session with Jack and Maddie, trying to decide what to do."

"I'll say it was long." Jane glanced at her watch.

"I shouldn't have—"

"Cut it out," she said mildly. "I'm glad to see you any time, Russ, and I think I know why you called me now."

"Why?"

She drew a breath. "Because you don't want to be alone in that house." He started to say something about Alice staying in Two Falls again, but Jane touched his lips with her forefinger. "Shall I take your leg off?"

"You can't—"

"Yes, I can. You need to rest now if you have to work in the morning." She pulled his pant leg up and unstrapped the prosthesis with deft fingers. "Off with the clothes. Explanations later."

He slid out of his shirt and pants and fell asleep in his boxers. Jane inched in beside him. She didn't think she'd be able to sleep. It was nearly four, but she had hardly turned her bedside light off when she conked out, too.

~

A moist low-pressure front moved in. By midmorning it was raining, not hard but steadily.

Rob and Meg had gone to bed early. Meg had a Southern California reaction to rain. She wanted to be cuddled and consoled when she heard the musical patter on the windows. Rob was prepared to oblige. Cuddling led to pleasant consequences, including, ultimately, very deep sleep.

They slept late on Labor Day—late for them. The phone rang at seven—Beth McCormick with news of Judith Hough's sad situation. Madeline had already called the sheriff. Meg woke. While she listened to what Beth said to Rob, she began to cry. As he patted her and murmured vague kindnesses, Rob suppressed irritation. Women were so facile. Meg barely knew who Judith was. She ought to be consoling *him*. He didn't want to cry exactly, but sticking his fist through the wall would be an option.

As soon as he decently could, he handed the phone to Meg, and let Beth and Meg cry at each other. He took a shower. When he finally emerged, having run out the hot water, Meg had gone downstairs. He heard her grinding coffee beans. He pulled on his *gi* and waited, head down, centering. No, he would not punch the wall.

He headed to the courthouse annex at eight. A part of him grieved for Judith. The cop part blazed with fury. She would have been his best witness, but she had no language. Did that just mean she had trouble with English or that she was like an infant, her speech patterns blank, waiting to be written on? He felt a stir of hope. If she could understand what *he* said and make some kind of *yes* or *no* signal, he might still have his witness. All he had to do was figure out the right questions.

He spent a couple of hours reviewing what he knew about Judith, trying to generate questions about the August killing— she had clearly considered the burial an invasion of her territory. He wasn't very successful in coming up with good questions. He needed to know if she had seen the SUV, of course, and whether she'd been able to see who had driven it down into the orchard.

Shortly before noon, Russell Hough called him on the office extension. Rob asked after Judith. Hough made polite generalizations—his sister was intermittently conscious, her speech unintelligible. That was what Rob had gathered from Beth's call.

"I'm sorry she can't tell us what she saw." Rob sighed. "But that's less important than her general improvement. I'm glad she recognized you and Alice. Surely it's only a matter of time before she's talking again."

"I suspect her memory of that evening—when she sh-shot herself—is g-gone." Hough broke off and went on with painful clarity, "That's not why I called. It's raining. The fire marshal has lifted the burning ban. Can I burn the slash in the orchard? I had the discarded limbs chipped, so there's not much left to burn."

Rob's impulse was to say *no.*

"I'd like to clear everything away, harrow the orchard, and plant a cover crop before Maddie performs the ceremony."

"I thought that would take place in the house—"

"Some of it will, but the land needs cleansing, too."

That made sense, even though August had not been killed where he was found. Rob reviewed the forensic team's examination of the burial site. They had gone over that part of the orchard teaspoonful by teaspoonful.

"Will your neighbors, er, Jane August, object to the smoke?" There were no other close neighbors.

"No. The forecast calls for wind from the southwest the next few days—should blow most of the smoke past the August house."

"What about the highway?"

Hough didn't think the smoke would cause problems for drivers. Rob wasn't so sure, but he agreed to allow burning if the fire marshal didn't object. They talked for a while about the purification ceremony. It would attract young tribal members, Judith's contemporaries, as well as Bill's. She had been well-liked before her military experiences turned her in on herself, and of course the family was related to the chief by marriage.

"You can burn your slash tomorrow, but not until the morning traffic rush is over," Rob said when Russ had agreed to limit the number of people who would be attending the purification. As for the slash-burning, traffic would be heavy the day after a holiday. "We'll have to close the highway for the cleansing ritual if not for the burning, so let me know as soon as you can what Madeline decides about that. I'll see to it that traffic on Fourteen is diverted at Two Falls the day of the ceremony." To Miller Road, a nice irony. Perhaps Madeline could be persuaded to bless the blackberry thicket. Rob suppressed the thought unspoken. Purification was not a joke.

~

"IT'S not a joke, no. What makes you say that?" Russ set his water glass down. Slow days had passed. He was fasting in anticipation of the purification ceremony the next morning, Sunday, so he hadn't come to dinner and would not stay the night either. *Alas, fasting every which way.*

Saturday evening. It had finally stopped raining. They were out on the deck, all of them, Gerd and Gus working at the scotch and Jane and Libby sipping wine. Undersheriff Neill had approved of Sunday for the ritual because closing the highway then would cause the least inconvenience to passersby.

"I see a certain amount of comedy in drums and dancing." Libby's eyes roamed. She really didn't like to look at Russ. He was wearing shorts. Her mouth curled with distaste.

Russ didn't comment. He kept his face bland and took another judicious sip of water.

"Why don't you go out and play in the mud, Libby?" Jane drew a huge breath. She had about reached her limit with her stepmother. Besides her appalling rudeness, Libby's very presence offended. She had not warned Irma she would show up for dinner, and that had put Irma in a snit.

"I asked an honest question." Libby stirred her wine with her little finger and licked at the residue.

Disgusting, Jane fumed, silent.

"We put up with days of clammy smoke from the farm." Libby gave an ostentatious sniff. "Now we're expected to tolerate hours of primitive caterwauling. I don't mind, I guess. If you think your farm needs 'purifying,' it probably does. I just find it hard to accept that a grown man with a college degree can believe in a bunch of mumbo-jumbo. Purification?" She sniffed again. Maybe she was coming down with a cold.

Gerd said, "People everywhere have customs outsiders find strange. In Spain, the running of the bulls, for instance. Or processions carrying statues of the saints through the streets."

Libby snorted. "That's just Catholics."

Russ said mildly, "My mother's a Catholic."

Oops. Jane kept her eyes on Libby. She had to wonder why Stepmama had chosen to grace them with her presence.

"Well?" Libby took another sip.

Russ wiggled his prosthesis and admired his gleaming ankle. "Well, what?"

"You heard my question."

"Ah, I thought it was a speech." He straightened and looked at her directly. "People will believe anything. If I were malicious I might point out that some people believe Christopher Columbus discovered America."

Libby sneered, but she looked away.

"Speaking as a biologist, I find Christianity odd. Think about the Noah story, for instance. The main god decides to erase the world in a huge flood, but there is one man the god warns. Noah. A faithful man and a clever shipwright. Up in the scrub-covered mountains of Asia Minor, he whips a big boat together to the god's specifications. It doesn't take Noah more than a couple of months to build his ark out of fresh-hewn planks, though he works with stone tools and has nobody to help him but some rather dim sons. He fills the ark with mated pairs of all the animals on earth. That probably takes another month. Then the rains come and drown everyone and everything not on the ark. The salvaged animals on Noah's big boat refrain from eating each other or breeding recklessly or dividing themselves like amoebas. After forty days and nights the rain stops and there's a rainbow. The god promises not to drown the world twice. Next time he says he'll incinerate everything."

"'The fire next time,'" Jane said. *Didn't it rain.*

Russ's mouth quirked in a grin. "A dove is sent out and comes back with, what is it, a leaf in its beak? Noah sends it out again and when it doesn't return, he ties the bobbing boat to a handy pier. The ark sinks into the mud, the animals file out two by two, and Noah instructs them to repopulate the earth. They go forth and multiply on command. Except for one pair of snakes." He looked from Libby to Gus to Gerd and then to Jane.

Jane groaned.

Gerd scowled. "What snakes?"

"Unlike the boa constrictors and cobras on board," Russ said placidly, "those two snakes can't multiply. They're adders."

Gus snorted. After a puzzled moment, light broke across Gerd's face. He giggled and covered his mouth with his napkin. Jane thought "adder" was probably not a pun in German.

"That joke is at least as old as Genesis," she said. "And I think the multiplication directive comes from God not Noah."

"That may be so, but you can see why I have trouble believing such a tall tale. And adders *can* multiply, if they use logs."

Logarithms. Jane covered her laugh with a cough.

Libby shot to her feet, glaring.

Gus sputtered.

"After the flood there weren't any logs around," Russ said sadly. "Not on top of Mount Ararat. Noah must have used all of them to build the ark." Libby stalked from the room. Russ watched her out of sight. He was not smiling.

When the garage door slammed, Jane cocked her head. She listened as Libby's Jeep roared away. "You can stop now."

Gus looked anxious. "You shouldn't provoke Libby, not even joking. She has a real bad temper."

"I believe it. I also believe in Darwin." Russ rose. "If you'll excuse me, I ought to go forth and help Ma tidy the house. She's convinced everyone will diss her housekeeping tomorrow." He smiled at Jane.

She smiled back and saw him to the door. He said he'd take her out to dinner again after all the fuss was over.

She gave him a juicy kiss. She would have volunteered to help with the housekeeping, but she thought mother and son had things to discuss. The move seemed to have set Judith back. At least the VA had chosen a nursing home on the Washington side—near Two Falls.

It was a pity there were so few alternatives for Russ's sister. Jane would have offered to pay for anything up to and including twenty-four-hour nursing, but she knew Russ and his mother would find the offer embarrassing and even intimidating. She was beginning to see how having a lot of money could lead to bullying. It certainly intimidated *her.* Besides, she didn't *have* the money, not yet.

14.

THE DRUMMING started after dawn on the south side of Highway 14. Russ and his uncles and cousins had built a sweat lodge on the Columbia. The purification ceremony would move across to the farmhouse when he was ready to bring the men to the chief and the other dancing women. Jane would hear that when it happened, when the drum took up the burden of the chant on the site of her father's burial.

Jane had slept later than usual with the faint drumbeat pulsing through dreams of Russell, Alice, Judith awake and accusing; Tom Dahl, Gerd, and the *cave*; Libby, Gus, and her father's ghostly killer. She drifted awhile between sleeping and waking, then woke again, dry-mouthed, as the drum, much closer, repeated the established rhythm, cold and clear. It moved to a faster beat.

Russell had invited her to attend the ceremony if she wanted to, but she knew the police had restricted the number of participants, so she'd asked if she could just witness the cleansing of her father's burial site. She could see the spot pretty well from the pool deck and didn't want to intrude. Russ seemed content with that.

He'd thought his aunt would bless the burial site before she purified the house. Jane set the coffee brewing, then showered and dressed hastily. Crumbs on the kitchen counter, juice glass and plate in the sink, suggested that someone had come and gone—Gerd probably. She knew he meant to join the dancing men, but Sunday or no, he would check in at the *cave* first. No one was yet visible below. The garage blocked the area in front of the farmhouse from view. The tension in her shoulders relaxed, and she went back in for a much needed jolt of coffee. To her utter surprise, her brother appeared as she reentered the kitchen.

Gus took a cup from the pot and straggled out to the deck without saying anything. Jane followed. She brought the Thermos with her.

When she thought he had drunk enough coffee to reach the state of articulate speech, she said, "I didn't hear Libby come back last night. Did you?"

He grunted.

"What?"

"No. Wasn't listening for her."

Jane sighed and set her cup down. She went to the rail. The drum—drums, really, there were three—kept up a brisk rhythm. She thought she heard distant chanting in chorus.

"She's right."

Jane turned, blank. "Who?"

"Libby," he said. "The noise is irritating. I wish they'd quit. My head's throbbing."

"Why is that not a surprise?"

"What's it to you?" he snarled.

"You don't really want to know."

He sulked, silent. If she supplied whiskey, she was enabling his hangover. She ought to stop doing that. *Her* head began to ache.

"I'm your sister," she said, "not your mother. I'm not about to enforce Prohibition. I wish you'd moderate your intake, though. I need help."

"*You* need help? What about me?"

"When the estate is settled, I'm thinking of splitting Dad's money. But you're not giving me much reason to want to. I need help," she repeated, "with Libby. I want her to leave."

He watched her with sad puppy eyes. "I don't have any influence on her," he admitted, mouth trembling. "Not anymore."

Jane didn't comment. His eyes fell. At least he was capable of shame.

Below in what had been the orchard, the drumbeat continued, and she could hear a clear soprano voice, probably the chief's, raised in a chant. A murmur of lower voices answered. The beat continued, unbroken. One by one, the three drums were carried up closer to the burial site, which was a featureless dimple in a blank field hazed with green.

Russ had planted his cover crop. Several days back, he'd plowed the former orchard, disked it, and sown alfalfa, a move to enrich the soil. The dancers' feet would wear a pattern in the green, but that didn't matter. Russ would plant his two varieties of berries then crop the alfalfa and plow it under. The burial site would disappear. A good thing.

As they watched Chief Thomas and the dancers come, Gus moved to stand next to Jane. He didn't speak. She thought his color was better. *Wonderful what coffee can do. Or the sound of money.*

She didn't spot Russ in the clump of men. They danced with their backs to her, and all of them wore jeans. Some wore ordinary blue work shirts, others elaborately trimmed dress shirts. Russ had told her that mothers created white story shirts for boys to wear to ceremonies and powwows, ribbons and button trim indicating the young men's accomplishments. The dancers in fancy rig had not yet undergone initiation into manhood.

She squinted and thought she'd spotted Russ among the men in work shirts, but she wasn't sure. There were women dancing, too, some in ornate robes made of elkskin, others in what looked like square-dance dresses though less colorful. The women were probably cousins and friends of Judith's. Russ had said that Alice's role in the tribe was small and passive, but that

Judith had enjoyed the powwows and the company of her cousins. They had showed up for her today.

Watching the dancers, it occurred to Jane that she'd never before seen Russ wearing jeans, if it was Russ she was looking at. He usually wore tan work pants or cargo pants with wider legs. She supposed it might be hard to pull narrow-legged jeans over the prosthesis.

Below in the orchard Madeline Thomas raised a burning feather—it would be a hawk feather, Russ had said, not eagle, not for this kind of purification. Resplendent in headband and beaded robe, the chief moved her arms in blessing, and the smoke sent an indecipherable message. Jane wanted to paint the scene. Her painting gear lay in an alcove off the kitchen where she'd left it last evening. She dashed inside and returned almost at once, but when she got back Gus had gone. His cup sat empty by the Thermos.

Shrugging, she fumbled for her sketchpad. Her camera wasn't in her bag, so she went in again and found her cell phone in its usual place on the kitchen counter. She suppressed the flash and took half a dozen photos from the deck. She made a rough value sketch with notes on colors and shadows. That took awhile.

Chief Thomas moved forward and back. Her burning feather wrote magical words, but for Jane the focus was the array of drums—dark heads bent over them, hands flashing. When she turned west, away from the sun's glare, to check her photos, she thought she caught movement down by the old garage. She raised the phone, took several shots, then looked at them. Libby. What was she doing down there, trespassing? Jane's stepmother walked west behind the garage and south into Russ's "garden." When she took a few steps farther, the garage blocked Jane's view of her. Was anyone there? Tom Dahl rarely worked Sunday mornings. Maybe Libby was meeting Gerd at the *cave*. Why on earth? They could meet any time they wanted to in the guest house, or in the master suite, for that matter.

THUMP, thump, thump, THUMP. Something was happening below in the orchard. Jane turned back to the rail and leaned out. THUMP, *thumpity*, THUMP, *thumpity*. Silence echoed. The clear soprano rose again in what had to be an evocation. A chorus of male voices whispered an answer, then female voices, and finally both together, much louder. The next silence stretched. Jane peered, trying to see Russ. Maybe he wasn't there. Maybe he had decided to stay in the house with Alice. Jane didn't see Gerd either. She hoped he was not one of Libby's coven of warlocks.

She stepped down from the pool deck to the ribbon of mown grass that separated the big house from the top of the bluff. She thought she heard people talking down by the garage, but the drummers started in again and blotted out all extraneous sounds. At the west end of the big house a steep path led downhill to the farmyard. She took it and slid down the last few feet on her butt. She didn't think the noise she made could be heard over the tattoo of drumbeats.

Jane tiptoed through the weed-choked "garden" to the edge of the garage and peered through a crack in the siding, but she could see nothing except undifferentiated black shadow surrounding a rectangular glare of sunlight. The door was wide open. She saw nothing but could hear. Libby must have turned back from garden to garage. She was talking to someone, a man, and she was not pleased.

"I say hit him again."

"No."

"He's coming around."

"So? He can't do anything...for Chrissake, don't light that, Lib. Gas fumes explode."

It couldn't be...

"Let's go," Libby snarled.

"I want to move him first."

"To safety? Are you crazy? He knows about us, and he's sucking up to his sister already."

Jane had heard enough. The man with Libby was Thomas Dahl.

Stunned, Jane tiptoed back to the edge of the bluff, took out her phone, and called 911. She had some trouble explaining what she thought was happening to her brother. Apart from the threat to Gus, a fire in the garage would cause havoc if it spread to the old house, especially with so many people in it. Conveying that involved further explanation. The dispatcher sounded confused.

Finally she assured Jane that help would come quickly—from Two Falls. Jane was told to stay on the line but hung up after listening to nothing for a long, crackling minute. The drumming was softer now, and she heard Madeline Thomas's voice again, rising in exhortation.

Jane's head spun. *Tom Dahl was Libby's collaborator? Or was it Tom and Gus? Surely not Tom, Gus, and Gerd!* Jane closed her eyes and thought hard. *Tom for sure.* She called the bank hotline from her electronic phone book. When the mechanical voice replied, she drew a breath and lied. She reported that she had lost her credit card, the card she and Dahl both held. It was the only access at that moment to her father's wealth. The bank would cancel it at once and replacements would take several days to arrive in the mail.

She could see Libby cajoling Dahl into fleeing with her if they had an ongoing relationship. *And why would they not?* Libby had had no qualms about doing the dirty with both her husband's wine maker and her husband's son. Why not with the man who could withdraw cash or charge expensive items like plane tickets to Brazil? Libby had some money of her own, of course, not to mention the diamonds, but she was used to being paid for. *Rather like a high-ticket call girl.*

As Jane disconnected she watched Libby and Dahl head into the *cave* together. Her stepmother's Jeep was parked in front of the unfinished structure. *Foresight? When had she driven it there? Impossible to tell.* The two conspirators seemed unaware of Jane's presence on the scene. At that point, Jane heard a thump and a groan inside the garage.

Time to rescue her brother. She hoped Libby and Dahl wouldn't spot her as she dashed down the far side of the garage and ducked in the front. She noted in passing that the twenty or so dancers had disappeared, presumably into the house. The drumbeats faded and died. She saw no sign of people. Had they assembled on the front porch?

Neither Russ's Blazer nor the Hough pickup was in the garage, which reeked of gasoline but not of smoke. Jane assumed Russ had parked the vehicles across the highway with all the dancers' cars. The garage had no windows, so it took her a moment to see Gus. He lay on the floor at the very back, bound to a stool that had fallen sideways and taken him down. His cheek pressed hard against the dirt floor. As she squinted, she saw him move and heard a moan. The thump she'd heard must have been the sound he made falling. Perhaps he'd knocked himself out.

"I'm coming, Gus," she said softly, blinking hard as her eyes adjusted. "Be still in case you've broken something." *In case Libby hears us.* A gabble of voices could be heard from inside the farmhouse, but the drums had definitely ceased their masking thumps.

Jane stepped into the pool of darkness her brother lay in. The stench of spilled gas sharpened. A can of the sort used to carry fuel to lawn mowers—or to bone-dry vehicles—lay on its side as if someone had knocked it over. She felt relief. If Libby and Dahl hadn't deliberately slopped gasoline around, perhaps they didn't intend to come back and set fire to the garage.

As she came closer to him, she saw that Gus was trussed with duct tape. A wide slash of it gagged him. She stumbled and nearly fell down, then knelt and ripped the tape from his mouth. "Are you all right?"

He didn't answer. She could hear him breathe in gasps, but his face was slack, his mouth red with blood where the tape had torn him, and his eyes shuttered.

She looked at the interior walls of the garage. Rusty, cobwebbed tools that Russ's father must have hung years before cluttered the dark surfaces. She needed a knife or scissors, neither of which she saw, but she did spot a scythe, if that was the right word. *Scythe? Sickle.* She took it down, and immediately wanted to clean her hands and call for a tetanus shot.

The sickle would have to do. She had to release Gus. Though she'd seen Libby and Tom enter the *cave*, they might return to their prisoner. She pulled the stool away from his jeans-clad legs, tearing the tape that had fastened them to it. Then she began sawing at the tape that kept his hands bound behind him. *Too tight*, she thought. They had swollen and turned purple.

He was groaning now, though he didn't respond to Jane's voice. When she ripped his hands free, his arms relaxed. He rolled to his back.

"Wake up, Gus. We need to get out of here."

He mumbled something.

"They're gone."

"Going...airport." He coughed.

"They're leaving?"

"She is. Flying. He...Tom'll come back to let me out."

"He told you that?"

"Yeah. *She* killed him, killed Dad. Din' meantuh. Ow, hurts." He was rubbing his hands.

"She didn't mean to kill him?"

"'sright. So I helped 'er bury 'm."

How could you? She bit the words back unsaid.

"Hadda help 'er. She said she'd tell..." His words choked, and he threw up, mostly coffee. "Ow. Hands hurt."

"C'mon, Gus. Get up. I can't lift you."

He struggled to sitting position and slumped, head sagging.

She felt like pulling him up by the hair. "Come *on*. I called the police. You have to tell them what you know." She tugged and cajoled. He smelled awful. Finally he staggered to his feet. He leaned on her and almost knocked her down.

So it went. Step by step they waded through the darkness toward the patch of sunlight at the entrance to the garage. Jane could hear a babble of voices from the house but no drumbeats. She supposed the celebrants had reached what Russ called the potlatch stage. In it, the dancers brought gifts for the house. The oldest resident reciprocated. Extravagance was much admired.

Alice had baked up a storm and would be handing out loaves, if not fishes.

"What the hell...?" A man's voice. Dahl.

Jane froze. When she heard no accompanying shriek from Libby, she gambled that her stepmother had already driven off in the Jeep.

Jane pitched her voice slower and lower than normal to simulate calmness. "Ah, Tom. How good of you to come back for Gus. His hands were swelling." As she spoke, she moved directly toward the stocky figure. It was hard to look at Tom in the sun-glare. Gus stumbled beside her.

"Look here..." To her surprise, Dahl sounded confused, even intimidated.

She pressed her advantage. "Has Libby gone off? I suppose you know she killed my father."

"I..."

"She's a fool. If she'd just called the EMTs when Dad died, the worst charge she'd have faced would be manslaughter. More likely assault. She has a clean record. Any judge would have slapped her wrist. Instead she compounded a felony." That sounded impressive, whether or not it was true.

Dahl groaned. So did Gus. Her brother coughed again and vomited coffee almost as an afterthought. At that auspicious moment a patrol car wheeled onto the graveled drive and drew up to the garage. Sgt. Ramos and the young deputy who had come to the house three days after Frank August disappeared got out warily, hands on their weapons. Jane let her breath out in a *whoosh* of relief.

~

MADELINE Thomas's mind drifted down from her first language, her mother tongue, to the second, the language she had learned in kindergarten from her classmates. The purification ceremony always left her feeling empty, but her emptiness was the good kind—like a jar or basket ready to carry a burden. Bitsy Thomas, her cousin, always officiated at the gifting in order to leave Maddie time to reflect.

Most of the dancers knew Judith, and they had brought what they thought she would like, fabric suitable for making quilts, hand-woven cedar baskets, bent-wood boxes. Bill wasn't on their minds. It was almost as if Judith's father had never ruled the farm with an iron hand, never killed himself.

Bill would not have respected the purification rite. Did Alice? Maddie searched her sister-in-law's still features for some clue. Murmurs from the dancers showed their doubt, too. A loaf of bread was a good thing, but it was not a traditional gift and its value fluctuated with circumstances. On the other hand, baking was Alice's art, and Alice, not her children, had inherited the farm. The loaves were a small puzzle inside the large puzzle that was Hawk Farm.

As Maddie resigned herself to unsolved puzzles, Alice raised her hand like a grade school child asking permission to speak. When the murmurs had faded, she said softly, "Thank you all for coming today and dancing for us. I made bread as a token of respect for each of you. However, I have another gift to give, this one to my sister Madeline as principal chief. Last night before they entered the sweat lodge, my son and his uncles..." She used the Klalo word for mother's-brothers. "They came into the house and removed my late husband's gun collection. William was very proud of it, and I believe it is worth a great deal of money, but I also believe it took his life. Russ and my brothers carried it to a place where it can be stored in safety. Insofar as the gun collection is now mine to give, I give it to the Klalo nation. I ask only that it be dealt with piece by piece and not sold as a collection. And I do ask that it be dispersed or destroyed."

The murmurs sharpened almost into words.

Alice raised her hand again. "I'm sure you've noticed that my son Russell is not here. We received word early this morning that Judith has begun to speak in understandable words and phrases."

Something like a murmur of applause passed among the dancers. Maddie spotted the German wine maker standing behind the male dancers. He bowed his head when he caught her eye.

Alice continued, "The undersheriff was anxious to question my daughter. We did not want to cancel the ceremony, but when the drums moved down to the house, I sent Russell off with Robert Neill. Judy needs family with her when she's questioned. Russell was not at the farm when my husband died, so we thought his absence from this part of the ritual would cause no harm." A brief smile touched her mouth. "And besides, he's no great shakes at dancing these days."

The mood lifted. Many of the dancers were smiling, even Bitsy who took purifications very seriously. Madeline was less heartened. As far as she was concerned, receiving the gun collection was like clasping a basket of snakes. She had had no warning. She wondered if Russ had. Or, more to the point, Jack.

"And now," Alice said, "I know you will excuse me if I also go to my daughter. Chief Thomas and Bitsy will stay for the parting. I thank you again." She made her way swiftly out the door, swiftly but with great dignity. Who would drive her?

Madeline spotted her brother-in-law, Leon. He headed for the front door, too, but Madeline caught him in the crowd of departing dancers as the drummers began a soft farewell salute—not a dance. The dancers left one by one. She saw that they clutched their neatly wrapped loaves. The German man, the wine maker, had two. She wondered whether Jane would come down later. Russ had said she didn't want to intrude. Obviously Gerhard Koeppel felt otherwise.

Maddie said, "Where did you take the guns, Leon?"

"Ice cave," her brother-in-law said tersely.

"I hope they're protected from the snow melt."

"Don't fuss, Maddie. We were careful." He sighed. "Bill had some beautiful weapons."

An oxymoron, Maddie thought. *Is that the word?* If she decided to sell those beautiful guns, wouldn't she just pass the poison on with them?

~

"JANE did what?" Meg sat up in bed and punched Rob on his bare shoulder.

"Mmm. Cancelled her credit card." He pulled her down to his side and stroked her silky hair. "The credit card she shared with Tom Dahl. She told the bank she lost it, so they cancelled it."

She burrowed under his arm. "I'm disappointed. She thinks like a banker."

"No. She's just wily. She wanted to stop Dahl in his tracks. If he'd tried to make a run for it, everyone would have hailed her as a genius. As it is, zapping the card just looked silly. At least she called us first."

Meg lay still, considering. "What will happen to her brother?"

"I'm not sure. I wish Judith Hough had seen him more clearly."

"Her family must be glad that her memory's coming back. Her description of the SUV was surely indisputable, taken with Gus August's admissions."

Rob sniffed. "Oh, the defense will dispute everything. I'll find out more now we have Libby August in custody." She had been apprehended approaching the Portland airport in the Jeep with the wind-surfing gear still on the roof of the car. "When I get a chance to interrogate Mrs. August and young Gus again, I'll see what I can uncover."

"I gather the two of them had a brief affair early in the marriage, and they were under the illusion that Frank August didn't know about it."

"Jane believes he must have, and his will bears her out. Mrs. A. bullied Gus into helping her bury her husband. He also disposed of the SUV for her. Either he was still susceptible to her blandishments—"

Meg gave a snort of amusement.

"Hey!" He tweaked her backside. "Have a little respect for my verbalosity, especially at this hour." What with the purification, his questioning of Judith, and the arrests afterwards it had been a long day, long but satisfying.

"Do go on," she said meekly.

"Either he was a pushover, or he was afraid of her."

"Afraid? Of her blackmail?"

Rob said, "Of her vicious temper. She is not a milquetoast maiden, by any means."

"No. On the other hand, she's also not a murderer."

"A killer but not a murderer." They lay silent awhile, considering the distinction.

"Do you think Ellen Koop will settle for a manslaughter charge?"

Rob drowsed as his long day caught up with him. "Mmm. I suppose she ought to be congratulated."

"Who, Ellen?"

"Libby August. Congratulated on her lack of forethought."

He left it at that.

Epilogue

J ANE DECIDED she had to quit her teaching job. The press storm generated by Libby's arrest made it only too probable that reporters would follow Jane around on campus. The dean would like that no better than he'd liked her abrupt resignation. He would not ask her to teach there again.

She didn't mind missing the remaining days of prep and faculty meetings, but classes would begin the next Monday. She was sad when she thought of the students she wouldn't meet and exchange ideas with. She felt increasingly isolated by her hypothetical wealth.

When Russ was with her she was all right. He didn't try to advise her, just listened to her kicking against the prods. She felt safe with him. Not that he wasn't stimulating, no indeed. Given the chance.

Gus spent three nights in the hospital. The medics listened to his lungs, and he stayed reluctantly sober. When her daughter threatened to elope with a Cuban, Irma took the week off. With Libby gone and Tom Dahl, and with Gerd supervising both of the August vineyard crews as well as making wine, Jane and Russ had the huge house to themselves.

After a splendid session exploring the erotic possibilities of the great room, they retreated to the kitchen for a snack to build up their strength. Watching Russ chop peppers for fresh *pico de gallo* to slather on a leftover tamale, Jane made a serious mistake.

"Marry me," she said.

Russ laid the chef's knife down with care and looked at her. He did not smile. "No."

"Russ!" Tears flooded her eyes. She sniffed.

"Not yet, Jane. Not until you've disposed of your father's money."

"You're kidding, right?"

He shook his head. "Not entirely."

Silence separated them. He picked up the knife and finished chopping a pepper.

Jane gulped. "I don't get it. I see the money as a huge complication of my own life. But yours? If we were married…" Her voice faded. What she was saying made no sense even to her.

He cocked an eyebrow at her. "Life would be perfect?"

She grimaced. "Okay, I'll take your word for it. The money would interfere like crazy with *your* life."

"I wouldn't let it interfere." He took a long breath and went on, "That would be a real barrier between us, Jane."

A thoughtful silence ensued.

"What did you mean by 'dispose of' it? Hand the money to Gus?"

Gus was cooperating with the investigators, and Jane was providing him with a lawyer. She hoped he would have cooperated anyway without that bribe, but she wasn't sure of her brother's rectitude, not sure at all. Slowly, feeling her way, she said, "I want to share the estate with Gus, but I won't give him huge, world-damaging amounts of money if I can't trust him."

Russ watched her, eyes intent, but said nothing.

"He did behave badly." She broke off, conscious that she had said something asinine. "He behaved abominably," she amended, "though falling into Libby's clutches when he was twenty-three seems almost predestined."

"Predestined?"

"A sign of hereditary bad taste. But to help Libby bury Dad..." At that she shivered.

Russ looked away.

"Am I wrong in thinking that's a different order of magnitude?"

He met her eyes. "I'd say you're on target, but it's hard to tell about alien relationships."

"Alien?"

"Libby is strictly from outer space."

She found she was smiling. "Not your type?"

"God, I hope she's not a type. One of a kind surely." He gave an exaggerated shiver, picked up the knife again, and cut the tamale into two equal chunks. He arranged the salsa artistically on two small plates and transferred the chunks to the plates.

"Beautiful. Want a beer?"

"Let's split a Dos Equis."

They did. Life and the discussion continued. Slowly, reluctantly, Jane's mind engaged the problem of her father's wealth.

MADELINE Thomas was pleased with the results of the purification ceremony. Judy's progress, in particular, reinforced the chief's feeling that Bill Hough's death-taint no longer darkened house and land. She was less sure about the killing of Francis August, a man whose spirit buzzed like an angry gnat at the edge of perception.

Because of her ceremonial role, Maddie had missed the drama that resulted in Mrs. August's arrest on a charge of second degree murder. Charges against Tom Dahl were dropped when he agreed to testify. Young August was warned but not arrested. Maddie wished that Russell was not involved with Gus August's sister, though she had nothing personal against Jane herself.

Russ had had more than enough to contend with, and now Ms. August did, too. Dealing with the aftermath of the arrest would absorb Jane for some time to come, not to mention the complication of her sudden wealth. Because Maddie had long ago learned to avoid entangling herself in other people's romances, she carefully said nothing to Russ about Jane, but she didn't stop thinking about the two of them.

Alice began to emerge from the spell Bill Hough had cast over her. She actually took—and passed—the driver's test and now drove herself wherever she wanted to go. Even across the river. Definitely to Two Falls. She would bring Judy home soon. And what then?

Then, Jane or no Jane, Russell would want to return to his real job. He would need two things before he could leave: assurance that Judy would be well cared for, and a manager he could trust to run Hawk Farm at a respectable profit using the work crews he had trained. That meant a speaker of Spanish. Maddie decided to put her mind to solutions to both problems.

She must have spoken aloud. Jack looked up from the football game he was watching. She caught herself before she went off half-cocked and blurted something foolish. She smiled at him instead.

"Problems?"

"Not mine. Yours. I was thinking how much I admire your sister's courage."

"She's healing."

"As her daughter heals."

"I hope so." He muted the TV and stood up, stretching. "I wish we could find someone to live with Alice and Judy. That's what Alice needs, not just somebody to help take care of Judy. Alice has never been alone. Gonna need someone to talk to when Russ leaves."

"Did she talk to Bill?"

"Oh, yes, not that it did her any good." He plunked back into the recliner, and they lapsed into silence, both of them thinking hard.

Eventually she said, "We've been looking at Alice's problem. Let's look at Russell's problem—the farm manager. I don't know anybody with the language and the right kind of experience, do you?"

"Horhay," Jack said after a pause in which a football player made an improbably long run. The crowd went silently wild and looked very foolish doing it.

When she had solved the puzzle of Jack's Spanish pronunciation, she ventured a guess. "Jorge Morales?"

"That's the Horhay I had in mind."

"But he's just a kid."

"He's an unemployed kid who's done a lot of farm work. He speaks Spanish. Russ already trained the workers. Now all Russ has to do is train the manager."

Maddie turned that over in her mind. Abby, Jorge's recent bride, was Klalo, a single mother, a bank teller. She had done the exogamous thing and married outside the tribe. Maddie had officiated, without enthusiasm. Jorge was pleasant enough but he needed a job. The newlyweds lived in Two Falls. She thought about what she knew of their situation. "*And* Abby's mother lives with them. I wonder…"

~

"A double play? Is that baseball or basketball?"

"Ignoramus," Rob said affectionately.

Meg strolled over to the kitchen table where he sat absorbing a nice glass of scotch after a long day. When they'd moved into the big house they'd gained a formal dining room, but they still ate in the kitchen.

Meg dropped a kiss on his head, a good gesture but not as satisfying as a kiss elsewhere. She took the cookie plate off to replenish the supply.

"Baseball."

"Okay, so Maddie pulled…projected…caused a double-play."

"*Made* a double play. And I think it was Jack who had the lightbulb moment." Rob took a smug sip.

"Are we dabbling in tropes? Sounds like Jack killed two birds with one stone."

"That's it. He found a manager for the farm, as well as a companion for Alice who just happens to be an LPN."

Meg plunked the plate of cookies in front of him and sat again, took a cookie herself, and nibbled at it.

Rob ate his cookie in two bites. "Yum."

"You didn't even taste it. Tell me, exasperating one, who is this multitalented Spanish-speaking farmer slash nurse?"

"Two people. One man—Jorge; one woman—Jorge's mama-in-law."

"Explain."

So he did.

~

RUSS picked Jane up at the Portland airport when she returned from a two-week learning session in Seattle. It was conducted for her by her father's money men. They didn't like her, and she didn't like them, but they did clarify what she could and could not do with all that wealth, once the will was proven. She took notes. She also read a lot of economic theory in her opulent but lonesome hotel room.

The mere sight of Russ waiting beyond the security apparatus at PDX cheered her, a mood swing that was damped somewhat when he told her he had found a manager for the farm.

"Does that mean you'll be leaving soon?"

He was pulling her suitcase with one hand and hugging her shoulders with the other. He laughed and gave her a squeeze. "As soon as I'm sure he'll work out. Move upriver with me, Jane. I live in a charming single-wide mobile home that used to be the bunkhouse when Hackamore was a ranch."

"What!"

"Rent-free," he added, complacent.

He wasn't kidding.

He went upstream; Jane stayed in Latouche County. It was six months before she got a look at the infamous mobile home though she saw Russ frequently when he came back to check on Hawk Farm and his family. Curiosity finally got the better of her and she drove east.

The manufactured palace turned out to be freshly painted inside and out and comfortably if sparsely furnished. Since she'd never before been inside a mobile home, its singularity charmed her for a good fifteen minutes. Russ's bed looked worth exploring but not yet. He stashed her suitcase in the closet. The other bed-room (the third had been turned into an office) hearkened to the house's previous incarnation. It held four neatly made-up bunk beds and a tall dresser. Jane could envisage four crusty cowboys resorting to it after a long day punching cows. Just.

"You entertain lots of twins?"

Russ grinned. "The bunks are hardly ever used unless one of my friends brings his kids. Parents bed down on the futon in the living room and kids get stashed here these days. My friends from Pullman were younger and less picky when they traveled. I once had three doctoral candidates, a post-graduate spouse, and a labrador retriever parked here for a week while its humans attended a convention at the college."

"Who slept on the futon?"

"Professor Bjornson. He was pushing seventy, so we decided he deserved a little privacy."

"In the living room?"

"That was a minor problem. Come and look at my dissertation."

"Your what?

"My ongoing botanical research." He made a wide gesture toward the north.

"Isn't it a bit cold out there?"

"Alberta Zephyr." Winds from Alberta originated some-where around the North Pole.

It was late February in the high desert, cold and dry. On her drive upriver Jane had felt the push of wind from the north. Her skin crackled just thinking about it. She hoped she hadn't forgotten to bring moisturizer.

Russ ducked out into the back entryway and retrieved their wraps from the hall closet.

Jane pulled her padded jacket on but kept her reservations to herself. The wind hit her in the face when she followed him out the front door—it faced north, away from the approach road. Tears stung her eyes. She took Russ's arm and stumbled beside him across a small concrete patio.

She blinked at the mass of clods and plant-stalks sticking out of half an acre of frigid earth beyond the patio. The cold plot of land was encircled by vineyard. Paths led through the plot but she didn't know what she was seeing, despite Russ's narrative. He kept pointing to frosted clumps of vegetation and saying plant names. Jane grunted a response. Her teeth were chattering too much to speak clearly.

Turning back he caught sight of her face. "Oh, poor honey. You're turning blue."

"Mmmph."

He took her back inside and poured her a cup of very hot coffee. When she thawed, she said, "It looks like your grandmother's garden."

"So it does."

She sipped. "You're studying gardens?"

"The garden is incidental. I'm studying plant communities. Sooner or later we'll have to give up on monoculture."

"Vineyards?" She warmed her hands on the cup.

"Right. And whole counties in Iowa planted in corn. And native forests ripped out in favor of coffee plantations. The shortage of water and the pressure to produce more food at less cost to the soil and the landscape will force agriculture to change."

"Diversify?"

"Right. I have a network of gardens I monitor, here and in Pullman, so these aren't the only plant communities." He smiled, "Hey, lady, I can talk about what I'm doing all day, but I'd rather hear what you've been doing."

She wished he weren't quite so averse to her father's money. She would have been happy to subsidize his gardens.

"What I've been doing," she echoed, setting her cup on the formica-covered bar that separated the kitchen from the living room. "Preparing to get rid of Dad's money so we can hunker down and get married."

His eyes sparkled. "I'm in favor of that. What have you decided to do with it?"

"I intend to found a bank."

She left him speechless.

"A Grameen bank," she added.

At last he said feebly, "And there I was sure you'd establish a foundation, like Bill and Melinda Gates. Or an art museum, like J. Paul Getty."

She grinned. "But no."

"But no." He closed his eyes, frowning, deep in thought. "I'm damned." He opened his eyes wide. "Microcredit?" Russ might be an eccentric one-legged botanist, but dumb he was not. "What's the economist's name? The man from Bangladesh?"

"Muhammad Yunus. He won the Nobel Peace Prize. He also established that low-income people are better than Donald Trump at paying off loans."

He gave her a big hug. "Let me guess. You're going to found your bank and make your brother Gus run it."

"Yes. With a little oversight from my own financial advisors. He does have an MBA. If he loses the money, at least he'll lose it to people who need it."

"Marry me."

"I will, but you'll have to give me the bunk room. I need a place to paint."

ABOUT THE AUTHOR

Sheila Simonson is the author of fifteen novels, nine of them mysteries. She taught English and history at the community college level until she retired to write full-time. Simonson won the Willa Cather award from Women Writing the West for the first in the Latouche County Series.

She is the mother of a grown son and lives with her husband in Vancouver, Washington. She likes to hear from readers, who can visit her website at http://sheila.simonson.googlepages.com.

More Traditional Mysteries from Perseverance Press
For the New Golden Age

K.K. Beck
Tipping the Valet
ISBN 978-1-56474-563-7

Albert A. Bell, Jr.
PLINY THE YOUNGER SERIES
Death in the Ashes
ISBN 978-1-56474-532-3

The Eyes of Aurora
ISBN 978-1-56474-549-1

Fortune's Fool
ISBN 978-1-56474-587-3

The Gods Help Those (forthcoming)
ISBN 978-1-56474-600-9

Taffy Cannon
ROXANNE PRESCOTT SERIES
Guns and Roses
Agatha and Macavity awards nominee, Best Novel
ISBN 978-1-880284-34-6

Blood Matters
ISBN 978-1-880284-86-5

Open Season on Lawyers
ISBN 978-1-880284-51-3

Paradise Lost
ISBN 978-1-880284-80-3

Laura Crum
GAIL MCCARTHY SERIES
Moonblind
ISBN 978-1-880284-90-2

Chasing Cans
ISBN 978-1-880284-94-0

Going, Gone
ISBN 978-1-880284-98-8

Barnstorming
ISBN 978-1-56474-508-8

Jeanne M. Dams
HILDA JOHANSSON SERIES
Crimson Snow
ISBN 978-1-880284-79-7

Indigo Christmas
ISBN 978-1-880284-95-7

Murder in Burnt Orange
ISBN 978-1-56474-503-3

Janet Dawson
JERI HOWARD SERIES
Bit Player
Golden Nugget Award nominee
ISBN 978-1-56474-494-4

Cold Trail
ISBN 978-1-56474-555-2

Water Signs
ISBN 978-1-56474-586-6

What You Wish For
ISBN 978-1-56474-518-7

TRAIN SERIES
Death Rides the Zephyr
ISBN 978-1-56474-530-9

Death Deals a Hand
ISBN 978-1-56474-569-9

*The Ghost in Roomette Four
(forthcoming)*
ISBN 978-1-56474-598-9

Kathy Lynn Emerson
LADY APPLETON SERIES
*Face Down Below the Banqueting
House*
ISBN 978-1-880284-71-1

Face Down Beside St. Anne's Well
ISBN 978-1-880284-82-7

Face Down O'er the Border
ISBN 978-1-880284-91-9

Sara Hoskinson Frommer
JOAN SPENCER SERIES
Her Brother's Keeper
ISBN 978-1-56474-525-5

Margaret Grace
MINIATURE SERIES
Mix-up in Miniature
ISBN 978-1-56474-510-1

Madness in Miniature
ISBN 978-1-56474-543-9

Manhattan in Miniature
ISBN 978-1-56474-562-0

Matrimony in Miniature
ISBN 978-1-56474-575-0

Tony Hays
Shakespeare No More
ISBN 978-1-56474-566-8